£5-50

D1188464

MUSI

ML
60
.T551

C OF THE ANGELS

MUSIC

of the

ANGELS

Essays and Sketchbooks of

Michael Tippett

Selected and Edited by

Meirion Bowen

Eulenburg Books
London

Ernst Eulenburg Ltd
48 Great Marlborough Street
London W1V 1DB

Copyright © 1980 Ernst Eulenburg Ltd, London
First published 1980 by Ernst Eulenburg Ltd

ISBN 0 903873 60 5

Printed and bound in England by
McCorquodale (Newton) Ltd, Newton-le-Willows, Lancashire

'Truth shall shine through me
Once more endue me
Humble yourselves now
I speak as a seer.'

(*Sosostris*)

'Saviour?! Hero?! Me!!
You must be joking.'

(*Astron*)

Contents

Foreword
by
Sir Michael Tippett

While trying to help Meirion Bowen edit this book (in so far as I did anything at all), I had occasion to open my signed copy of T. S. Eliot's *Collected Poems* (fingering the past, as it were, the halcyon time when Eliot was still alive among the currant bushes of a Surrey garden),[1] ostensibly to track down some half-line quotation. Instead, I re-read *The Waste Land*. I was stunned afresh by the power of its verbal magic; astonished, humbled to find how much I had learned, by absorption, from the work — from the drama of that poetry. I feel further that all, but all, I have to dream with now is metaphor and theatre.

Here is another quotation which I first read only recently, in Loren Eiseley's *The Invisible Pyramid*:[2]

> The cosmos gives evidence, on an infinitely greater scale than the stage theatre does, of being just such a trick factory, a set of lights forever changing, and the actors themselves shape shifters, elongated shadows of something above or without. Perhaps in the sense men use the word natural, there is really nothing at all natural in the universe or, at least, that the world is natural only in being unnatural, like some variegated, colour-shifting chameleon.

To quote an hermetic poet of the English Midlands:

> 'I like that,' said Offa, 'sing it again'.[3]

Despite Eiseley's, the new scientist's rhetoric, while music is generally accepted as singularly metaphor, words seem to judder, veering at times towards poetry, more usually towards a supposed objectivity of discourse. All the words printed in this collection of essays, talks etc, are of the latter kind. But they are discoloured by my prejudice and ignorance. So they can be enjoyed, I'm afraid, only by responding to the drama of the prejudice.

---

[1] See below, p. 117
[2] London, 1971, p. 119
[3] See Geoffrey Hill: *Mercian Hymns* (London 1971), I

My editor has understood this. I have been amazed watching him arranging, forcing, shaping the diverse and unequal material into a 'dramatic' unity around a personality.

I tender him my thanks for the effort and exhausting labour involved.

Preface

Music of the Angels began life as a successor to Michael Tippett's *Moving into Aquarius*. But it soon became something different. Like its predecessor, this volume contains reprints of talks broadcast originally on the BBC Third Programme and World Service, some of them being later published in *The Listener*. An initial survey of the material that might be included, however, suggested a book with a wider range of contents and a separate emphasis. It also became clear that Tippett could not himself undertake the tasks of selecting and editing. For his eyesight is rather poor, and now, in his middle seventies, he very sensibly considers his first priority to be composition. If, in editing this book on his behalf, I have allowed him to concentrate his mind on creative work instead, then I think something worthwhile will have been achieved.

In 1959, when *Moving into Aquarius* was first published,[1] the cognoscenti were still inclined to exclude Tippett from the highest ranks of composers. He was an 'instinctive poet of nature and magic' (in the words of one critic); his musical reach invariably exceeded his grasp; his poetic visions were constantly clouded by obscure philosophizing; he was, in short, a composer blessed with prolific imagination, cursed by technical gaucheness: one whose work would never (with the possible exception of *A Child of Our Time*) reach a wider public, and which would continue to baffle even his most faithful admirers. In the last twenty years, all that has changed. All over the world, Tippett is regarded as one of the foremost figures in twentieth-century music, a creative intellectual of tested integrity. It's salutary to recall that when Tippett's first opera, *The Midsummer Marriage,* was rescued from neglect in the 1960s and eventually recorded, the album became a best-seller wherever it was promoted, and especially in the USA. Today's audiences seem no longer to find the work difficult or impenetrable. Its reception at the Henry Wood Promenade Concerts in 1977 and at the Adelaide Festival in 1978 offered ample evidence of the appeal the opera now exerts upon audience and performers alike.

Recognition of Tippett's stature has been so gradual that there

---

[1]Routledge & Kegan Paul (London, 1959); reprinted, with additional material, Paladin Books, 1974

xi

has been a dearth of easily accessible information concerning the composer, his ideas and works — notably, those compositions written since the 1960s. Consequently, Tippett has been more and more besieged by reporters, interviewers, students preparing doctorate research, and so on. They all ask him, for the 5,000th time, 'Why do you write your own opera librettos?'; 'When did you first meet T. S. Eliot?'; 'Do you compose at the piano, or believe in God?' Every month, aspiring interpreters and concert managers write requesting new operas, symphonies, brass quintets, contrabassoon sonatas, and all by next summer. Publishers press upon him ever more favourable contracts to write his autobiography.

Now although Tippett has acquired the knack of interviewing his interviewers (and even psycho-analysing them) and has turned his hand to some entertainingly terse post-cards, in recent years he has come to find it all rather tiring. To relieve him of some of this pressure, in 1978 I set about creating a kind of archive, in written and recorded form, which could be housed at his London publishers, copied for any other library or interested party, and made generally available for consultation by anyone needing to do research, prepare an article or a broadcast on the composer. This book developed partly from my work on the Tippett archive. Although it isn't encyclopaedic, it is intended to some extent as a source-book on the composer, his ideas and the background to many of his major works.

The reader will meet here Tippett the aesthetician, the political revolutionary, the teacher; will observe his dislike for dogma, for religious and political ideology; will note the fervent intellectual pluralism that underlies all his views and attitudes, and which provides a stimulus to remain in close touch with the modern world. Part 1 of the book, *Art, Judgement and Belief,* shows Tippett engaging with many of the major issues affecting creative artists in the twentieth century. It includes some early articles reflecting his involvement in revolutionary politics (he was a Trotskyite, briefly, in the 1930s) and his concern with the relationship between art and life. That he found it necessary—unavoidable, in fact—to follow the most ardent and visionary promptings of his muse, at the possible expense of all other concerns and desires, is emphasized here in the positioning of Part 2 centred on *The Vision of St Augustine.* If Tippett's integrity has ever shown itself, it is in the way he stepped aside from all his worldly involvements to write this extraordinary work. For this reason, I felt that the essay giving the background of thought and feeling behind *The Vision of St Augustine* should also provide the title for this book.

In Part 3 we encounter some of Tippett's idiosyncratic views on other composers and their works. Here, as elsewhere, there is an element of reminiscence which is entirely apposite in a book of this kind. Part 5 also contains some incidental writing on operas other than Tippett's own, as well as a major section on *King Priam*. As his own Foreword indicates, it should throughout be remembered that these are the reflections and opinions of a composer and not a musicologist. They are of genuine interest in that they offer clues and sometimes definite information about Tippett's musical leanings and responses. My task as editor has been often to re-write or re-draft material which was originally delivered impromptu or came out first in interview. I have also added a minimal scholarly apparatus, just to help readers find their way around, and to enable Ph. D. students to trace the sources of Tippett's ideas. Many of the essays that were first published elsewhere contained mis-quotations and proof-reading slips which I have corrected where appropriate — though sometimes I have kept the Tippett version intact.

I hope that I have included here all of the major essays or broadcasts by Tippett which were not featured in *Moving into Aquarius*. It is most unlikely that he will produce further articles or scripted talks, for the urge to compose is now too strong for him to dissipate his energies on literary and other work. There are a few minor articles or interviews that I have discarded: they were either dated or slender in content. Tippett has kindly up-dated one or two that have been included, as well as adding some fresh contributions (e.g. the sixth section, *A Private Mayflower*).

One special feature of the book is the sketchbook material relating to *A Child of Our Time*. Quite understandably, a composer values his preliminary notebooks far less than the final scores. Not until the composer is very well established, indeed, does anyone bother at all about them — even if they are known to exist and to be worthy of attention. I first stumbled across the Tippett sketchbooks when I was staying at his Wiltshire home just after Christmas, 1977. They were piled up in a dark corner of his cloakroom, along with an assortment of coats, bizarre hats, muddy boots and croquet mallets. Reading quickly through them, I noticed that they included the draft scenario for *A Child of Our Time,* which Tippett had himself uncovered some years back (and which he discussed in an article written for an American symposium).[2] There were over thirty

---

[2] See p. 117, note 1 below

sketchbooks in all, and I discerned that about half related to most of his major works. I felt straightaway that here was valuable source-material, possibly of such merit that publication might be worthwhile. But I waited some time before making any decision as to what I might select from them, for the purposes of this book. After all, they were *sketch*-books, and as such, contained drafts and jottings for lectures, broadcasts, letters and so on — much, in fact, that would be of little interest to the musicologist, let alone the general reader: and one could hardly blame the composer for not having ordered his notes more neatly. When, in a hundred year's time, the *urtext* edition of these sketchbooks will have been published, a more complete knowledge of Tippett's mental processes will be possible. It will be observed, for instance, that at the time of the composition of *King Priam,* gardening matters — when to plant the carrots and put in the broccoli, when to move a quantity of dung from one end of the garden to the other — occupied his mind almost as obsessively as did thoughts on the development of Priam's character, or the orchestration of Act II of the opera. The picture that will emerge from the few sketches printed here is one more focused, one primarily concerned with musical affairs.

My final selection from the sketchbooks was easily made. The draft scenario for *A Child of Our Time* has such a fascinating background in Tippett's relations with T. S. Eliot that its publication here could not have been more timely. In order to bring it alive within its context, I persuaded the composer to write a short memoir of his connections with the poet, and I also re-wrote his previous essay on the genesis of the oratorio for the symposium just mentioned. Then comes the scenario itself, in which I have identified (in footnotes), all the quotations and other references on the left-hand pages and supplied (again in footnotes) the final text of the work for comparison with the suggested text on the right-hand pages. This is followed by Tippett's subsequent revaluations of the work in the light of several performances and the response of critics and audiences generally. I have drafted this section from a variety of broadcasts, programme notes etc: I am aware that, in the process, there is some repetition, but I feel that Tippett's commentaries tend to add something extra at each stage; also, if such repetition helps the less scholarly interviewer to absorb the ideas being promulgated, then it will have served a useful purpose.

Acknowledgements

In compiling and editing this book, I have benefited from the help of several individuals and organisations whom I should like to thank here. Tippett's publishers, Schott & Co. Ltd. (London) have assisted in many different ways. I must particularly thank Mr Alan Woolgar for bringing so much published and unpublished material to my attention, and for providing so many other items of essential information. The composer's authorised biographer, Professor Ian Kemp, has also been a major source of facts and obscure material. I hope I have lived up to his high standards of accuracy in the detail of this volume. For other recorded talks and radio interviews, I have to thank the BBC and the British Institute of Recorded Sound.

I owe an enormous debt of gratitude to Miss Gwyn Rhydderch, who initially transcribed the sketchbooks for *The Midsummer Marriage* and typed a major portion of the book in manuscript.

Several individuals have contributed specific information and advice of great value. I am particularly grateful to Mr Eric Walter White for early access to transcripts of the letters written to him by Michael Tippett during the composition of *The Midsummer Marriage* (these are now published in Mr White's study of the four Tippett operas). I must thank Dr Alan Bush for giving me information relevant to the article on the Strasburg Olympiad; Mr Miles Kington, for sending me a copy of an article bearing upon the essay *Some Categories of Judgement*; and Mr John Amis, for permission to reproduce the contents of two interviews with the composer, in addition to an illuminating conversation regarding the early background to *The Midsummer Marriage*. Amongst those who have helped me identify Tippett's many quotations and paraphrases are Mr David Ayerst, Dr Frederick W. Sternfeld, Mr Roger Savage and Mr Symon Clarke.

I am grateful to several publishers for permission to reproduce excerpts as itemised below:

Messrs Collins & Co. (excerpts from Boris Pasternak's *Dr Zhivago* and Alexander Solzhenitsyn's *The First Circle*)

Decca Record Co. (excerpts from the translation of Wagner's *Die Meistersinger*)

CBS Records (excerpts from the sleeve note to a recording of Charles Ives's *Three Places in New England*)

Faber & Faber Ltd. (excerpts from T. S. Eliot's *The Family Reunion* and *Selected Essays*;
excerpts from *The Letters of Bela Bartok*;
excerpts from *Schoenberg's Letters*;
excerpts from Edgar Wind's *Art & Anarchy*)

Friends of Covent Garden (excerpts from David Rudkin's tran lation of Schoenberg's *Moses and Aaron*)

Rupert Hart-Davis (excerpt from Loren Eiseley's *The Invisible Pyramid*)

Methuen & Co. Ltd. (excerpt from Eric Bentley's *The Life of the Drama*).

Finally, I have been greatly encouraged, in this project, by the discerning comments of the General Editor of Eulenburg Books, Sir William Glock.

As to Michael Tippett himself, all I can hope is that this book will help in the deeper and ever more widespread appreciation of the music of an angel.

Meirion Bowen, 1980

1
Art, Judgement and Belief

Towards the Condition of Music[1]

There is a knowledge concerning art, and this knowledge is something quite different from the immediate apprehension of works of art, even from whatever insight we feel we have gained by perceiving and responding to works of art. A simple statement such as: art must be *about* something, is innocent enough till we want to give a name to this something. Then invariably we delude ourselves with words, because with our discursive or descriptive words we cross over into the field of writing or talking *about* art. We have reversed ourselves.

This fundamental difficulty has made all discussion of art, as indeed all discussion of quality, a kind of elaborate metaphor. And since all metaphor is imprecise, the verbal misunderstandings in aesthetics have always been legion. It is only when we remain deliberately in the field of enquiry concerning the facts *surrounding* art, that we amass knowledge of the kind we expect to obtain through such intellectual disciplines as History, Anthropology, Psychology or Philosophy. We can confidently say that we have vastly increased our knowledge concerning art during the last hundred years, chiefly of course the history of art. Anthropology has added further dimensions to our sense of history as a whole, and so to the history of art. Psychology, in my opinion, will eventually make much more precise the terms with which we discuss the processes of artistic creation and enjoyment. Philosophy, in the sense in which we speak of Platonic or Christian Philosophy, has often assigned limits or directions to art considered as a social function. At the present time, when the pretensions of Islam or

---

[1]This is a slightly amended version of a chapter originally contributed to *The Humanist Frame*, ed. Julian Huxley (London, 1961)

Christianity to do this are everywhere receding, only Marxist philosophy and the Communist states make the attempt. The most disturbing feature of Stalinist aesthetic dogma was (in China *is*) the apparent fear of the spontaneous (including the ineffable) element in art, which is gravely endangered by extreme social systematization. Plato, for all his systematizing tendency, accepted this. Socrates says in the *Phaedrus*:

> There is a third form of possession or madness, of which the Muses are the source. This seizes a tender, virgin soul and stimulates it to rapt passionate expression, especially in lyric poetry. But if any man comes to the gates of poetry without the madness of the Muses, persuaded that skill alone will make him a good poet, then shall he and his works of sanity with him be brought to nought by the poetry of madness and see their place is nowhere to be found.[2]

Plato names three other forms of divine madness besides the artistic, viz. the prophetic, the expiatory, and that of the lover. To understand Plato's term 'madness', we must recall the argument of the *Phaedrus* in more detail. Socrates considers first whether what we call madness might not really be of two kinds. One kind is clearly a disease—the rational mind being disordered and unamenable to the will—and even if we picture it as though the sufferer's personality has been possessed by some other and alien personality, yet this possession is unhealthy and often markedly anti-social. But the other kind might be a madness where the invading personality, though unaccountable and irrational, is yet beneficent and creative: possession not by a devil, but by a god.[3] It is this 'divine madness' of Plato's which I call the spontaneous (including the ineffable) element in art, and I think that the intuitions of Plato concerning this spontaneous element are upheld by the findings of psychology, especially depth psychology. From such psychology we have obtained a concept of apparently spontaneous psychic generation; of unconscious psychic drives and inhibitions; of, possibly, an inner psychic collectivity which is boundless and non-discrete. Yet to use the word concept for such notions is, surely, a paradox. In the same way, at the point now at which this discursive essay needs to consider the immediate experience of, and the insight (if that is the right

---

[2] *Plato's Phaedrus*: Transl. with Introduction & Commentary by R. Hackforth, (London, 1952), p.57
[3] Michael Tippett: *Moving into Aquarius* (London, 1959); see esp. the chapter 'The Artist's Mandate' for a fuller discussion of this whole problem

word) obtained from works of art *in themselves*, then, as has been pointed out above, this paradox reappears.

We must begin with the fact of works of art existing objectively and created to be appreciated. And we must accept that even if a state of mind, or an artefact arising from a state of mind, is spontaneously generated and only to be experienced immediately, or even ineffably, it is none the less a natural phenomenon, a fact of human existence. In rare experiences of this sort, such as the states of mysticism, the number of human beings to whom the experiences spontaneously come (or who have desires and techniques to induce them) is, at least in the West, small. Yet the tradition is so constant and the phenomenon so well established that we all have reasonable grounds for accepting them as factual and natural even when we can never ourselves have known them. They can clearly be spiritually refreshing; and may yet turn out to be one of man's hitherto undeveloped social qualities. For if psychosocial survival depends, as it well may do, on correctives to the present overwhelming social valuation given to material welfare, then evolutionary necessities may begin to operate, in an admittedly as yet unimaginable way, on seemingly socially valueless meditative disciplines.

While it would appear that the mystic can only render to society the refreshment received personally from mystic experiences through the quality of his conduct, the creative artist, from whatever source or in whatever medium he receives the spontaneous element, must, by the nature of his mandate, create objective works of art. These works subsist then in society independently of their creator, and many thousands of human beings receive enjoyment, refreshment, enrichment from them. This is a commonplace fact. Perhaps indeed every human being alive has experienced immediately something of this kind. Because the experience is so common and yet capable of being heightened to embody our profoundest apprehensions, it has in every age demanded intellectual understanding of itself. Modern psychology has provided new counters with which to play this age-old game.

If I now proceed to play this game in an up-to-date mode, it must be remembered that all discussion of what art *is*, or what it is *about*, is semantically imprecise. (We are probably on safer ground when we discuss what art *does*.) So it is hardly possible to proceed without the danger of misunderstanding, although our modern counters for discussion are, in my opinion, an improvement on some of those of the past, i.e. are probably semantically less equivocal.

Works of art are images. These images are based on apprehensions of the inner world of feelings.[4] Feelings in this sense contain emotions, intuitions, judgements and values. These feelings are therefore generally supposed to be excluded from scientific enquiry. I make this statement, in so far as it is true, not as an implied judgement, but solely as a fact, in order to emphasize the semantic problems of aesthetic discussion. It is not an easy matter to pass over from language used in the observation of natural objects extended outside us in space and time, to language used to discuss or describe the inner world of feelings, where space and time (at least in certain states of mind) are differently perceived altogether. Even where we succeed in such an attempt the description is always at one remove. The images which are works of art, are our sole means of expressing the inner world of feelings objectively and immediately. If art is a language, it is a language concerned with this inner world alone.

As 'inner' and 'outer' remain philosophically extremely difficult terms, so the dichotomy I have (at least verbally) established between space and time considered outside us and space and time perceived within is certainly not rigid. Hence it often appears as though the raw material of artistic creation was obtained from observation of nature outside us, and that the creative activity resided in the organization and construction which the artist applies to this raw material. The danger of this way of considering the matter is that very quickly we come to talk of works of art as *derived from* nature, which is much too simple. It loses sight of the one absolute idiosyncrasy of art, that works of art are images of *inner* experience, however apparently representational the mode of expression may be.

This difficult matter is best set out by considering first the extreme case of space in painting. (I use the word 'extreme' because the matter is not quite the same in architecture.) And secondly the opposite extreme of time in music.

The vital fact of all pictorial works of art is that the space in the picture is always virtual, not real. The space in the room and of the wall on which the picture hangs is real. Part of the means by which a picture becomes an image of the inner world of feelings is the contrast between the real space of the wall or the room and the virtual space in the picture. Hence it is not of vital concern to the art of painting whether the virtual space is constructed by representational methods or the reverse. We accept this if we are gifted or trained to do so, without demur. We find it difficult if we

---

[4]See Susan Langer: *Feeling and Form* (London, 1953)

consciously or unconsciously believe that art *derives* from experiences of outer nature and not, as is the basic fact, from the inner world of feelings. The representations of outer nature, if present, are always images of the inner experience, which the artist has organized.

At the other pole to painting, music offers images of the inner world of feelings perceived as a flow. As our concept of external time is itself an equivocal one,[5] it is perhaps less easy even than with space in painting, to realise that the time we apprehend in the work of musical art has only a virtual existence in contrast with the time marked by the clock-hands when the work is performed. Works appear short or long from other considerations besides that of performance time, and our sense of performance time will be markedly modified by them.[6]

Because music is concerned not with space but time, this method of artistic creation seems to by-pass the problems of representationalism, present in some degree in all the other arts. Hence the dictum: 'all art constantly aspires towards the condition of music.' This aphorism, wrenched from its original context in an essay of Pater,[7] has nowadays been commonly used in this much looser and wider sense, precisely, in my opinion, to draw attention to this real tendency, For if the matter-of-factness of the outer world gets too much into the foreground of art, then expression of the inner world of feeling is probably correspondingly more difficult. By dispensing *a priori* with all the problems arising from expressing inner feelings through representations of the outer world, music can seem a very favoured art. This is not always a merit. Music's easiness quickly degenerates into escapism; escapism not only because music seems absolutely abstracted from real objects but also because the emotional content of music is both obvious and permitted.

To a certain degree all appreciation of art is escapism—to leave behind the world of matter-of-fact. The important question is always: escape into what? Escape into the true inner world of feelings is one of the most rewarding experiences known to man. When entry into this world is prevented, and still more when it is unsought, a man is certainly to some degree unfulfilled. Yet even escape into the simpler states of appreciation is often self-denied.

[5]cf. Henri Bergson: *Durée et Simultanéité* (Paris, 2nd edn. 1923); also, C.G. Jung, *Synchronicity: An Acausal Connecting Principle* in *The Structure and Dynamics of the Psyche* (Col. Works, transl. R.C.F. Hull, London, 1960)
[6]cf. Stravinsky: *Poétique Musicale* (Cambridge, Mass., 1942)
[7]Walter Pater: *The Renaissance* (London, 1873), essay on Giorgione

Darwin wrote in his *Autobiography*:

> ... now for many years I cannot endure to read a line of poetry ... I have also lost my taste for pictures and music ... My mind seems to have become a kind of machine for grinding general laws out of large collections of facts ... The loss of these tastes is a loss of happiness and may possibly be injurious to the intellect, and more probably to the normal character, by enfeebling the emotional part of our nature.[8]

Darwin puts his finger unerringly on the danger. He uses the word 'machine'. In the vast social apparatus which modern science and technology demand, the person often becomes lost in a 'machine'. Eventually there arises the danger of too great mechanization of the social life in every field.[9] At this point creative artists are sometimes driven to use the shock tactics of a genius like D. H. Lawrence—or in another field, Kokoschka.

As I have already pointed out, within the dazzling achievements of the modern knowledge-explosion we must include the lesser portion of a greatly increased knowledge about art. But the contemporary explosion in the means and methods of art itself over the last hundred years is not of the same kind. The new art is not related to problems of the outer world at all but to apprehensions of the inner world. What can certainly be deduced from the contemporaneity of the two explosions, is that the psychosocial change and consequent adaptation demanded of modern man is without precedent in its totality.

It may in fact be misleading to speak of art as primarily or always responsive to social change — though in many obvious senses this is true. For art is unavoidably and primarily responsive to the inner world of feelings. And this inner world may be spontaneously generative (in the sense I attempted to define the term earlier) independently of, e.g., the social consequences of scientific technology. Or it may be attempting to restore some sort of psychosocial balance. I would say that it is all these things. Yet clearly changes (and these are constantly happening) in our ideas of human personality will be reflected in certain arts, if not necessarily in music. Music may always appear to by-pass such considerations, but literature and the drama in all their forms certainly cannot. It may be that changes in our ideas of human personality reflect changes in the inner world of feelings, and not *vice versa*. We are not

---

[8]See Francis Darwin: *The Life & Letters of Charles Darwin* (London, 1887), Vol. I, Ch. 2 (*Autobiography*), pp. 100–102
[9]cf. Tippett: *Moving into Aquarius* (see note 3 above)

yet able to judge properly what happens in this complex and interrelated field; we cannot yet be certain what is cause and what is effect.

At the present time, for example, we can only see that the knowledge-explosion in all the sciences is a challenge to psychosocial adaptation, while the violent changes in methods in all the arts are symptomatic of deep-seated changes in man's inner world of feelings.

Modern psychology is indeed beginning to produce a kind of relativity of personality, especially in personal relations. This is sufficiently far-advanced in the West (it may be nothing new for the East) for it to be satirized by a cartoonist like Feiffer. Here is a caricatured conversation between a young couple suffering from this relativity of personality — i.e. valid uncertainty as to what is real in their notions of one another and what is projection.

She: You're arguing with me.

He: I'm *not* arguing with you. I'm *trying* to make a point.

She: There is a difference between making a point and embarking on a sadistic attack.

He: If sadism is your equivalent to impartial judgement then I admit to being a sadist.

She: How *easy* to be flip when one precludes responsibility.

He: How irresponsible of one so irresponsible to speak of responsibility.

She: Since you *must* project your own inadequacies into a discussion of the facts I see no point in carrying this further.

He: How like you to use attack as a disguise for retreat.

She: Ah, but if we were not arguing as you so heatedly claim, what is it that I am retreating from?

(silence)

He: I'm getting a stomach-ache.

She: Me too.

He: Let's knock off and go to a movie.

Behind this caricature is something real, to which art cannot be indifferent. The dénouement is also quite serious. We knock off to go to a movie. This is not merely an escape from the currently insoluble problems, it is a therapeutic necessity. We project our problems, whether of dual or multiple relationship, momentarily on to the movie—i.e. on to an objective work of art. Movies are generally works of popular art; and they are socially immensely valuable. For most of us there can be no objective examination of the constant and developing situation such as that caricatured by

Feiffer, except by recourse to the movie or its equivalent: the splendid value of this recourse being that it is mostly un-selfconscious and indeed an enjoyment.

The enjoyment of popular art, in my opinion, is much more often of the same kind as the enjoyment of more serious art (though not of the same quality) than snob circles like to think. There is of course a vast mass of sentimental popular music (to take my own art) which is poor and dispiriting. But there is a great deal indeed of jazz and rock where the dissonances and distortions of the voice or the instruments, the energy and passion and often brilliant timing of the performance, combine to produce an enjoyment which is of better quality, and is also expressive of the tensions produced in man by the inner and outer changes of his life. Carried on the pulse of this music we really do renew in a limited degree our sense of the flow of life, just because this music gives hints of deeper apprehensions through its qualities of style and even form.

As the purely emotional element recedes and the formal element comes forward the music ceases to appeal to vast masses: this is always happening in the world of jazz and rock. When the limitations of popular musical harmonies, rhythms, melodies and forms are left entirely behind, as in music for the concert hall, then the public further diminishes. Yet symphonic music in the hands of great masters truly and fully embodies the otherwise unperceived, unsavoured inner flow of life. In listening to such music we are as though entire again, despite all the insecurity, incoherence, incompleteness and relativity of our everyday life. The miracle is achieved by submitting to the power of its organized flow; a submission which gives us a special pleasure and finally enriches us. The pleasure and the enrichment arise from the fact that the flow is not merely the flow of the music itself, but a significant image of the inner flow of life. Artifice of all kinds is necessary to the musical composition in order that it shall become such an image. Yet when the perfect performance and occasion allows us a truly immediate apprehension of the inner flow 'behind' the music, the artifice is momentarily of no consequence; we are no longer aware of it.

Music of course has a tremendous range of images, from the gay (and, if perhaps rarely, the comic) to the serious and tragic. On the serious side music has always been associated with religious rituals and been a favoured art for expressing certain intuitions of transcendence. That is to say, certain music, to be appreciated as it is, expects a desire and willingness on our part to see reflected in it transcendent elements, unprovable and maybe unknowable analytically, but which infuse the whole work of art. This quality in music has permitted such works as the *St Matthew Passion,* the Ninth Symphony of Beethoven, or *The Ring.*

According to the excellence of the artist, that is to his ability to give formal clarity to these analytically unknowable transcendent intuitions, these works of art endure to enrich later minds when the whole social life from which they sprang has disappeared. Hence the enduring quality of a work such as the Parthenon, even when maimed and uncoloured. And it is these formal considerations alone which enable us to set perhaps the *Matthew Passion* and the 'Ninth Symphony' above *The Ring.* Apparent from all this is the fact that art does not supersede itself in the way science does. Methods and modes may change, and of course, in music, instruments and occasions for making music. These are the things which can make it difficult for us to appreciate, e.g. Pérotin (Perotinus Magnus) now as the great composer his period considered him to be. We may have superseded Pérotin's methods, but we have scarcely superseded his imaginative intuitions. And yet, in another sense, we have. Because the material from the inner world is never quite the same. The extreme changes in the art of the present time are, I am sure, due to more than changes in techniques.

The techniques of music have always changed from time to time with the development of new instruments, e.g. the pianoforte; and even more through the changes of social occasion and means of dissemination, e.g. the invention of the concert hall, or of radio. At the present time there are new electronic methods of producing every imaginable sound known or as yet unknown, and these methods, though they cannot supersede the older ways altogether, will certainly be added to them.

The techniques of musical composition change also. There is a wide-spread preoccupation at present with the methods of serial composition. Changes in composition technique are more the concern of the composer than of the listener, who is usually disconcerted during the period of experimentation, as with serial technique now. The deeper reasons for this constant renewal of artistic techniques are still somewhat mysterious.[10]

The most striking novelty in music was the gradual invention of polyphony in the late middle-ages. All known music up to that time, and right up to our own time in all cultural traditions outside the European and its derivatives, had been, or is still, monodic. This

---

[10] See Anton Ehrenzweig: *The Psycho-Analysis of Artistic Vision and Hearing* (London, 1953)

means that in general the melodic line, endlessly decorated and varied, is the essential (as in India and Asia; until the invention of polyphony, Europe). Or combinations of dynamic or subtle rhythms have been used to build as unending a stream of rhythmical variation as the unending line of monodic invention (Africa, Indonesia). In both these kinds of music, harmony is incidental and secondary. But European polyphony produced the combination of many disparate lines of melody, and such a combination immediately posed problems of harmony new to music. Over the centuries these problems have been resolved in one way or another, and there have been periods of European music when the harmonic element, initially derived from the practice of polyphony, becomes primary, and what polyphony the music contains has become secondary. We are at present in a time when European-derived music has experimented to an unprecedented degree with harmony. This has been pure invention. At the same time discs, tapes and printed collections of folk-songs and dances, and discs and tapes of African, Indonesian, Indian and Chinese music, have stimulated, or been used as basis for a considerable experimentation in rhythm. The melodic element on the other hand (and the formal element in my opinion) has been secondary.

Now European polyphony has proved so powerful an expressive medium that it is mostly sweeping over the whole world and carrying away much of the indigenous traditional music with it. In this way Europe and America appear still as musical initiators for the globe. But this will not last. When the time is ripe the values of the non-European musical traditions, where they have been temporarily lost, will be rediscovered. The speed at which we are having to become industrially and politically one world would seem to be such that the problems of forging a unified expressive medium may be coming upon us faster than the European composers are as yet aware. This question may well, in my opinion, solve itself first through popular music, just because popular music is by definition and purpose music of the people. Popular music is an open music. In order to entertain it will take everything offered, from Bali to New Orleans, and whatever is successful will be amplified round the world. Popular music will become increasingly global rather than local.

In all the manifestations of music the enduring portion is the sense of flow, of the kind I have described above, organized and expressed formally. A wide-ranging Humanism, whether secular or religious, will always seek to extend to more and more people, through education and opportunity, the enrichment of the personality which music gives. In our technological society we should be warned by Darwin:

> The loss of these tastes (for one or more of the arts according to our predilections) is a loss of happiness and may possibly be injurious to the intellect and more probably to the moral character, by enfeebling the emotional part of our nature.

These are wise and serious words. We are morally and emotionally enfeebled if we live our lives without artistic nourishment. Our sense of life is diminished. In music we sense most directly the inner flow which sustains the psyche, or the soul.

Art and Man[1]

Art is concerned with man; man is art's sole measure. By man I mean the passionate curious creature, mixed soul and body with the long, long history, which we all are ourselves. Works of art must exist, of course, as objects in some sense outside us. In fact this is how they subsist for centuries over the generations of mortal humans. But when we respond to a work of art from the past we respond to our own history. Inanimate nature does not produce works of art. Animals do not respond to the art man makes.

What is man doing when he responds to works of art? This is probably an unanswerable question, because all answers seem reductive to something less than the real experience. What is man doing when he falls in love? It is only a reductive answer to say that he is just hoping to reproduce his species. Sex in animals may be thus biological; animals don't fall in love. It is man, not animals, who has made the extraordinary emotion of love the subject of so much art, from Dante's *Divine Comedy* to Shakespeare's Sonnets. I wrote a stanza in the libretto for my first opera *The Midsummer Marriage* which runs:

> *The world is made by our desire.*
> *Its splendour, yes, even its pain*
> *Becomes transfigured in the bright*
> *Furious incandescent light*
> *Of love's perpetually renewed fire.*[2]

That is to state the matter maybe a little pretentiously. It can be quite unpretentious, as the Beatles, who are intelligent young men, show in their record 'All you need is love'.

What is man doing when he composes or performs music? The answers to this question can only be analytical and descriptive. The experience is clearly very old, perhaps as old as man himself. We seem to share the joy (or pain) of singing with the birds. But the making and performing of instruments we do not share. That this activity is, all the same, extremely ancient, is shown by the tiny bone flutes made by our Ice Age ancestors. Music seems to be concerned with Time in a way analogous to painting being concerned with Space. This doesn't tell us very much. But it leads us to the recognition that music deals with the imaginative processes of the

---

[1] This article appeared in the *Christian Science Monitor*, 26 May, 1968, originally as one of a ten contributed by various creative artists
[2] Michael Tippett: *The Midsummer Marriage* (1955), Act III, scene 8

inner world: feelings, qualities, dreams. It hardly deals with the facts of the outside world (as material for its works of art) at all. This is what makes music often seem a much favoured art to painters and poets. Here are some random quotations from articles in the two earlier series in this newspaper. 'As music can be built up from formal elements which in themselves have no descriptive quality, so in this century the idea has developed that painting and sculpture could do likewise' (*Victor Pasmore*).[3] 'Non-objective painting is visual music' (*Jean Xcéron*).[4] 'A poem trembles on the verge of lapsing into music, of breaking into dance; but its virtue lies in resisting the temptation—in remaining language' (*Stanley Kunitz*).[5]

All this straining toward music has sprung from the tremendous need of our time to reach further into the interior world as some balance against our social preoccupation with science and technology. It was predicted by Pater in his famous aphorism 'All art constantly aspires towards the condition of music!'[6]

But music too has been straining towards its own inner world. For, since music uses words for songs and dramatic situations for operas and can itself be used as background to movies and television, it accumulates a kind of impurity of the outer world. Our century has seen a tremendous collective effort to cleanse musical sound of these impurities and to make music absolutely abstract. This cleansing has been positive, exciting and salutary. Unfortunately the negative result has been the appearance of composers who are interested only by abstraction and experimentation. The resulting music leaves too much man out, so it quickly gets boring. I have never been able to forget man in this way. Hermes, in my second opera *King Priam*, speaks for me when he sings

> *O divine music,*
> *O stream of sound*
> *In which the states of soul*
> *Flow, surfacing and drowning,*
> *While we sit watching from the bank*
> *The mirrored world within, for*
> *'Mirror upon mirror mirrored is all the show.'*
> *O divine music,*
> *Melt our hearts,*
> *Renew our love.*[7]

---

[3]*Christian Science Monitor*, 14 December 1965
[4]Ibid., 23 November 1965
[5]Ibid., 26 April 1966
[6]Walter Pater: *The Renaissance* (London, 1873), essay on Giorgione
[7]Michael Tippett: *King Priam* (1962), Act III, interlude between scenes 3 & 4

What does a composer do when he invents music? The answer is, he makes. Our English word poet comes from the old Greek word Πoιετy, to make. The composer is in this sense a poet of tones. He makes structures of tones (and silences) which when performed appear as works of musical art subsisting independently of composer and performer. Plato, through the mouth of Socrates, considered the practice of poetry to be three-fold: one part gift, one part madness, and one part technique. I have found this myself to be about right. In the various works one writes, these three parts all enter but never in the same proportions. Also, you cannot do much about the gift, nor, except at risk, artificially stimulate the madness. But you can polish the technique continually.

I have been composing now for over thirty years. If I compose for another twenty years, say, then I shall have made what we call an *oeuvre* and one in fact of great variety. The better works may survive for a while, the poorer ones will fall away. Those that survive will do so only as part of an imaginative personal world which has explored further fields of man's total inner world. The whole historical process is therefore one of accumulation. Music is imaginatively a very rich art. It goes easily from Intimations of Immortality to dreams of escape. Here is a stanza from my third opera *The Knot Garden* sung by a character who is a musician:

> *O hold our fleeting youth for ever*
> *O stop the world I want to get off*
> *O honey, honey, make love to me*
> *Now (O boy!) now (how play it cool?)*
> *In the fabulous rose-garden.*[8]

---

[8]Michael Tippett: *The Knot Garden* (1970), Act II, scene 9

Music and Life[1]

A Congress with this title was held in London on 28 and 29 May, under the auspices of the London Contemporary Music Centre and in preparation for the I.S.C.M. Festival at the end of June. The Congress discussed both contemporary music and contemporary life. Sometimes one or other of these two notions seemed in danger of being stressed at the expense of its complement, but in general when this happened a passionate demand was made from the floor of the hall for the necessary balance and relationship between the two ideas and for the special need of a re-integration of music and the musician into the dark and stormy flood of contemporary life. The composer's intuitions of the life around him or within him are as varied as the illimitable variations of human personality. In a general discussion at a congress confusion arises when a particular subjective intuition is put forward which is too far removed from the collective ideas, because a general discussion has perforce to generalize. But in reality this limitation is of considerable value, because music in its greater manifestations becomes itself general and social, and a composer whose intuitions are too exclusively subjective — or, shall we say, whose subjectivity is regressive — is destined to a narrow circle of influence and appreciation. It is healthy to bring theories into the light of day and test them in general discussion. This was the vital function of the Congress.

The definitions proposed in answer to the question 'What is contemporary music?' were negative. One speaker suggested that contemporary music was music not built on the tonal or key system and its forms. Another suggested that contemporary art was divorced from the instinctive and sterile, as 'straight' music from jazz, studio painting from the poster, and so on. The first definition provoked a question too late to be discussed. Would someone explain the tenacious emotional satisfaction of the tonal system? Here is the answer. The artistic use of the tonal system is based on the fact that music whose tonal centres are rising in the scale of fifths produces an effect of ascent (struggle, illumination), while tonal centres descending the scale of fifths produce an effect of descent

[1]This article first appeared in *The Monthly Musical Record* (July/August, 1938)

(resignation, despair).[2] Beethoven was the great master of these effects. The first movement of the *Hammerklavier* Sonata is a skilfully continuous use of ascent, while the first movement of the *Appassionata* is an equally continuous descent. The listener is not directly conscious of these effects. His response, I think, is centred in a complementary movement of the stomach muscles. Contemporary life has not given us iron stomachs, very much the contrary. What has happened is that since the nineteenth century composers have ceased to produce the sort of themes that demanded Beethoven's clarity of tonal structure. Wagner's use of rising and falling tonal centres is not conditioned by the theme or the form but by the dramatic situation. This is perfectly legitimate. Debussy went still further and used the tonal effect for impressionist purposes, constructing his forms out of a series of highly differentiated states of feeling. Brahms understood neither Beethoven's nor Wagner's method. The development sections of his sonata forms are often muddled and fail to set up the necessary tension; to borrow the phrase Dr Vaughan Williams used at the Congress, they 'live in sin'.

This is the difficulty. The tonal system related to sonata form is a highly polarized system. Modern people are not polarized, they are split. It may be true, as Dr Egon Wellesz suggested, that we are entering on a period of greater certainty, because of a new integration of our split selves, and it may be that the re-appearance of the tonal forms in modern music is a complementary expression. I am not sure. 'Living in sin' with the tonal system is no better than doing the same with atonality; Mahler, Bruckner, Strauss and the rest are a severe warning against this. The integration of the conflicting parts must be an actual experience, and the musical intuitions must begin to correspond to the collective symbols that have sooner or later to be described and painted and sounded for the mass of humanity who have to come at their redemption in this way.

Meanwhile the nineteenth-century revolt against the classic forms, the experiments in new ranges of expression produced by rapidly

---

[2] See Vincent d'Indy: *Cours de Composition Musicale* (3 vols, Paris, 1903–50); esp. vol. 1, VIII, 'Expression', p. 130

'. . . Toutes les fois qu'une modulation aboutit à une tonalité située, sur le cycle des quintes . . . l'effet expressif est comparable a la montée vers la *lumière,* à l'expansion *lumineuse.*

'Toutes les fois, au contraire, qu'une modulation aboutit à une tonalité située du côré de la *quinte grave* . . . l'effet est comparable à la chûte vers les *ténèbres,* à la concentration dans l'obscurité.'

changing tonalities and their artistic differentiation by the genius of Debussy — in whose music feeling-values practically exclude intellect — has led to the final reaction of Schoenberg and his school, who deliberately put on one side the emotional effect of rising and falling tone-centres as taboo. Their system is based on this precept: no combination or succession of notes may be used that produces the response of a tone-centre. The 'discords' are not just 'wrong notes', they are simply the sounds which our stomachs cannot respond to in a certain traditional manner. No tones, no stomachs; music is to be only in the head. This appears to me to have its compensation in the back-to-the-primitive longing (negroid jazz, Indonesian gong music, etc), whose devotees can pass several hours in one key as long as the rhythm is elemental and the timbre exotic. All this was hinted at in the Congress, and the need for a solution of the conflicts was so imperious that a real breath of the new wind nevertheless blew through our confused utterances.

The Congress constantly came up against the question of music's and the composer's relation to the so-called 'spirit of the age'. Dr Malcolm Sargent frankly expressed an escapist view — he did not want to hear the 'spirit of the age' in music but the solace and comfort of another world. On the whole the Congress rejected this view, though at the same time it endorsed the Unknown Listener's complaint of the 'misery music' which the uncultivated musical public like himself is fobbed off with as the music of liberation and joy. An artist can certainly be in opposition to the external 'spirit of the age' and in tune with some inner need, as, for instance, Blake was. A composer's intuitions of what his age is really searching for may be, and probably will be, not in the least such obvious things as the portrayal of stress and uncertainty by grim and acid harmonies. The important thing, as the Congress showed, is that he should be in some living contact with the age.

International Workers' Music Olympiad [1]

Over the Whitsun week-end an English choir of fifty voices went, under the conductorship of Comrade Alan Bush, to take part in the first international festival for working-class music organisations at Strasburg. The membership was drawn mostly from the London Labour Choral Union and Co-operative choirs (in particular the Federation Operatic at Abbey Wood). There was a competition piece to sing as well as music for the concerts and demonstrations.

There were about ten choirs in our class. The judges (musicians of considerable international standing who are active in the labour movement) awarded a silver trophy. [2]

The most numerous entries to the festival were workers' brass bands. Choral singing has not so strong a tradition in France as wind bands. There were choirs from various parts of France and Switzerland. Russian and Dutch choirs were, unfortunately, refused permits to enter the country by the French Government. The Czecho-Slovakian contingent was unable to come, and all workers' organisations in Germany, Austria, or Italy only carry on illegally underground under the stress of the three forms of fascist terror. [3]

The festival was organised principally by the Strasburg Workers' Music League, with the help of other Alsatian music organisations. [4] These musical and sports unions are very strong in Alsace and Lorraine, in Switzerland and France proper. The membership often runs into thousands. Benefits similar to those of our friendly societies are paid to members, and concerts, practices, and gymnastics are organised. All the unions have a political basis and join together for public demonstrations under the name of the

[1] This article first appeared in the *Comradeship and Wheatsheaf* (a journal of the Royal Arsenal Co-operative Society), August 1935

[2] According to Dr Alan Bush, the judges included the German composer Hanns Eisler and the French composer Charles Koechlin. The London Labour Choral Union shared first prize in the Mixed Choir Section with the Chorale Populaire de Paris. Nine choirs entered this section of the competition, coming from Belgium, Switzerland, France and England. It was not possible for choirs from Germany to participate, owing to the Hitler regime, which was thoroughly established by 1935. The Certificate presented to the LLCU on its success is thought to be in the possession of the Workers' Music Association in London, but it has not come to light: it may contain the names of the other judges.

[3] The three forms of fascist terror were those of Italy, Spain and Germany

[4] No commitment to any political party was demanded of participating choirs (according to Dr Bush), but their members had to proclaim themselves in principle the opponents of (i) fascism, (ii) the exploitation of the working class, (iii) every imperialistic war

United Front against Fascism, which the various socialist and communist parties of France have laboriously built as a weapon in their struggle.

The visit was too short for one to find out how the United Front was forged. But it was pleasing to see the sympathy the English rank and file comrades showed for it, many of the Labour Party members returning the clenched fist communist salute on the march through the streets.

Strasburg is an ideal town for an international festival of this kind. The older men fought in the German army and navy, their sons are conscripted into the French army. The president of the Strasburg Music League fought in the Kiel Mutiny in the German Revolution of 1918. Formerly a communist worker in Germany, he is now a communist worker in France. Working-class international solidarity has been forced on him by blood and war and revolution.

The Rhine, which flows near to the town and is the Franco-German frontier, has been lined by France with underground forts. But these forts were built by Swedish, Italian and *German* workers. So much so that photographs of the fortifications came out in a German newspaper. What are German workers to think of a system which sends them to build entrenchments for the guns which are to blow them to pieces? What is the French worker to think of a system which behind the sham of national patriotism gives the work of national defence to less-paid 'enemy' workers?

To visit Strasburg, to stay with a working-class family, and talk to the men and women once German, now French, is to receive a lesson in international socialism which no books can teach.

I was taken round the town by two boys of eleven and sixteen. They were still at school: nevertheless, they gave me two or three hours of clear-cut teaching in international working-class history. They showed me where the workers had torn up the cobbles to reply to the police rifle-shooting, a bridge where the workers had thrown cyclists into the river, bicycle and all, and a little narrow alley where the workers took their wounded comrades. They told me how the police tried to force an entrance to this alley, and how the workers, from first-floor windows, lifted up the police bodily and threw them out the other side. This occurred two years ago.

There is an international tradition of working-class effort and struggle to get free.

We in England have been in danger of forgetting what our fore-fathers did for us in the Chartist days and what our comrades are doing for us on the Continent. For, let us face the truth, a victory for the working class in France means an enormous moral and material support for our English movement. I felt shamefaced before these youths, who looked to England for resolutions of solidarity: youths who already at fourteen and fifteen had fought for the cause.

At the festival itself one could not help being struck by the delightful air of equality and informality. Everyone was a comrade, whatever language he might speak. It was like a foretaste of a free classless society but for the police ban on street music and the clashes that arose because of it. Over thirty bands marched onto the big festival ground playing 'The International' while thousands of voices sang it in various languages. The children were as free as the grown-ups. They walked onto the microphone platform, they talked to whom they liked. No one was ordered about. Occasionally someone called for space round the microphone so that we might sing there, or a telegram of greetings be read from a sympathetic group of workers.

Finally, we English comrades must not forget that we were practically the guests of Alsatian working-class comrades, whose general standard of living is lower than ours. To them we owe not only thanks, but solidarity. And if, as we hope, there is another Olympiad next year, perhaps the R.A.C.S. choirs will be able to send a genuinely co-operative choir. Personally, I would very much like to see a fund raised to take with us a number of our less fortunate members, to whom, more than others, it would give heart to meet and talk with Continental comrades in such a way.

A great number of the choirs at Strasburg were unemployed organisations from mass unemployment areas. It would be impossible to find money to take a whole unemployed choir, but we might be able to give a holiday to some of our comrades who need it.

Art and Anarchy[1]

When listening to the recent Reith Lectures (before I read any of them) I felt I was continually stimulated by new bits of knowledge — that is, new to me. Thus almost a whole lecture centred on the technique of ascription in cases of unsigned or debatable paintings, and round the extreme forms of connoisseurship to which this problem, or passion, of ascription might lead. This was all so new and interesting to me, as a musician and not a painter, I probably paid more attention to it than to the argument deduced from it: which was that we are in danger of being persuaded by this connoisseurship to overvalue the fragmentary and immediate sketch above the finished and studied painting; and that, as a consequence, we tend to ask only for the fragmentary and immediate in contemporary art: thus reinforcing, as by a kind of concealed patronage, the general marginal condition of art in our time.

When I came later to read this lecture the information about Morelli's methods of ascription was no longer new to me. So it fell into the background and I paid much more attention to the general argument: that art in our time is marginal; and that con-noisseurship is one of the factors that help to make it so. But this special question of connoisseurship now worried me concerning the first of Professor Wind's terms in his general title: 'Art and Anarchy'. Because 'art' is used in English in two rather confusing ways; and Professor Wind's English is so idiomatic he uses the word art in this double way as often as the rest of us.

The point about the word is simple. We traditionally use art to mean specifically the art of painting. We have a Royal College of Art (meaning painting) as we have a Royal College of Music. But we have also come to use art as a direct translation of the German word *Kunst*. Thus we distinguish art from science, and then we mean all the arts and all the sciences.

It is fatally easy to use this double-meaning word with both meanings in the same sentence. I have just done it myself. I spoke of fragmentary and immediate painting; then of the fragmentary in

[1]This was first published, under the title 'Thoughts on Art and Anarchy', in *The Listener,* 2 March, 1961, pp. 383–4. It was one of a series of BBC Third Programme talks commenting on the 1960 Reith Lectures, 'Art and Anarchy', by Edgar Wind. These lectures were first printed in *The Listener,* 17 & 24 November, 1, 8, 15 & 22 December 1960: they later appeared in book form, in a revised and enlarged version (London, 1963).

contemporary art (implying the art of painting); then of the marginal condition of art in our time (implying all the arts). But this disguises the important fact that connoisseurship, in Professor Wind's use of the term for the purpose of his lecture, does not exist in music. There is really no problem of ascription. We do not value the immediate sketch before the finished work (if indeed such sketches exist). So that we are not thereby induced to ask for the immediate and fragmentary in contemporary music. There is a danger nowadays that in the spate of our words about movements of contemporary art in general, and about the place of art in modern society, we are talking without properly defining our terms. In the *Times Literary Supplement* (to give an instance ready to hand), a correspondent writes about the 'cult of dumbness' in the theatre, which, it has been suggested, might lead to drama not in words but in mime. He writes: 'When this new mime is perfected it will be tantamount to the arrival of abstraction in art, or atonalism in music'.[2] Such misleading and misconceived analogies appal me. But they are widespread. It seems to me that if we want to discuss imaginative art in general, or the place of art in society, then we can only make statements of comparable width and generality. There *are* things to be said in this huge field, and many of them were said in the Reith Lectures. But the moment we come to consider each art separately we are involved in their differences. And if we gloss over the differences for the sake of any general argument we are as likely as not falsifying something.

We think of Picasso as one of the great innovators of modern painting. We observe his almost chameleon-like ability to change his style at will. We go to see his film in which he makes and unmakes the immediate and fragmentary pictures before our eyes. If we now try to argue from the particular of this aspect of Picasso to the general, that is to include the other arts, we find ourselves in difficulties. It is just possible to find something of Picasso's change of styles in Stravinsky. But the composer's name more often used to match that of Picasso is Schoenberg. Schoenberg has never practised the immediate, or spontaneous, or fragmentary. Exactly to the contrary — the whole movement of serialism was to produce the greatest possible degree of intellectual coherence. Every single note of the piece of music is to be ordained by its relations within the series.

So that if we want to make out a case that imaginative art in our scientific age is marginal, we must eschew any arguments which

---

[2] Charles Marowitz, Letter to the *Times Literary Supplement*, 6 January, 1961, p. 9

seem to uphold the case, but only in respect of one of the arts. For it is reasonably certain that its contrary will be found in another art.

We must also be wary of large, plausible statements, which may be less precise than we imagine. Professor Wind said in his first lecture:

> Diffusion brings with it a loss of density . . . If a man has the time and the means he can see a comprehensive Picasso show in London one day and the next a comprehensive Poussin exhibition in Paris, and . . . finds himself exhilarated by both. When such large displays of incompatible artists are received with equal interest and appreciation it is clear that those who visit these exhibitions have acquired a strong immunity to them.[3]

This argumentation worried me. If Poussin and Picasso are indeed incompatible, then presumably many other historically separated painters are also incompatible. So that a walk round the Louvre or the National Gallery must be a constant temptation to indifference if we seek to appreciate too many of their varied exhibits. I doubt it. Nor do I think Professor Wind really meant this. I think his argumentation is unclear because his first term, 'diffusion', has not been tested out sufficiently. It needs breaking down statistically. A sentence like: 'More music is offered and heard today than in any age in history',[4] may be much less important than it seems when we have divided 'more' by the vastly increased population.

Summing up the points I have made so far, they are two. First, that in speaking of art generally we must stick firmly to the basic and general, and beware of intellectually attractive analogies between the various arts which are false. For, to make a basic statement myself, art, in the works of the various creative geniuses alive at any one time, is endlessly varied. This is a fact of European history, and is a fact today. It may be an annoying fact when we are trying to uncover the *Zeitgeist,* the general spirit of a time, or of our time. But it is also salutary. It reminds us that though time, or shall we say the climate of opinion, is a reality, the spirit 'moveth where it listeth'. I cannot help remembering in this respect that the Gnostics, who believed the heart of the matter lay in knowledge, held that time, to the creative spirit, is discontinuous. This is a very difficult notion for us to grasp. But it may contain some portion of hidden intuitive truth.

My second point was that even our general terms, like Professor Wind's 'diffusion', or his 'disruption',[5] are dangerously imprecise.

---

[3]'Art and Anarchy' (London, 1963), p. 9
[4]Ibid., p. 8
[5]See p. 40, below

We should be much less confused by our own language if some Confucius would truly 'rectify the names' for us. But, failing a Confucius, we must try our own hand at rectification as we go along. Professor Wind also uses the term 'disruption'. He says:

> If we think, for example, of Manet, Mallarmé, Joyce, or Schoenberg, almost all the artistic triumphs in the last century were triumphs of disruption: the greatness of an artist became manifest in his power to break up our perceptual habits and disclose new ranges of sensibility.[6]

Once again I find myself believing I understand what Wind is really saying, and that what he is saying contains a valuable perception. But all sorts of things worry me in his manner of saying it. Thus, Manet, Mallarmé, Joyce, Schoenberg: but suppose I say, Cézanne, Tolstoy, Yeats, Wagner — have I said any lesser names? Have I moved out of the last century? Do we really think the artistic triumphs of these men, even Wagner, to be triumphs of disruption? Yet Cézanne and Wagner without question had 'power to break up our perceptual habits and disclose new ranges of sensibility'.

I wish Professor Wind had gone much more deeply than he did into the meaning of his term 'anarchy'. He begins by giving it a tremendous sweep, from Plato by way of the Italian Renaissance to Goethe and Baudelaire. He then includes in it the terms 'imagination and disruption'. He says in the first minute of his first lecture:

> Art is . . . an uncomfortable business, and particularly uncomfortable for the artist himself. The forces of the imagination, from which he draws his strength, can be very disruptive.[7]

And, as the final words of his last lecture, he quotes this passage from William James with approval:

> Man's chief difference from the brutes lies in the exuberant excess of his subjective propensities . . . Had his whole life not been a quest for the superfluous, he would never have established himself . . . as he has done in the necessary.[8]

So that when Professor Wind says: 'Almost all the artistic triumphs of the last century were triumphs of disruption'[9] he is

---

[6]Ibid., p. 18; in the revised version, *Stravinsky* is substituted for *Schoenberg*

[7]Ibid., p. 2; in the revised version, the second sentence becomes: 'The forces of the imagination, from which he draws his strength, have a disruptive and capricious power which he must manage with economy.'

[8]Ibid., pp. 101–102

[9]Ibid., p. 18; in the revised version, 'the last century' becomes 'the last hundred years'

really putting the accent on triumph. But at the same time he contrives to make us feel that these nineteenth-century triumphs are in some way slightly perverse, or at least off-centre:

> Art has been displaced from the centre of our life not just by applied science, but above all by its own centrifugal impulse. For more than a century most of Western art has been produced and enjoyed on the assumption that the experience of art will be more intense if it pulls the spectator away from his ordinary habits and preoccupations.[10]

With Sophocles and Euripides dead, I can imagine that sentence spoken by a Greek, 100 years or so after *Oedipus Rex, The Bacchae,* and *Hippolytus.* Perhaps I am distorting Professor Wind's thought. But I do it solely to drive home the fact that in all times, where an artist has experienced the forces of the imagination disruptively, and especially when he has needed to use directly anarchic images, the quality of artistic triumph lies in the power of formal creation. No material is more anarchic than *Oedipus Rex.* No stage play has greater formal clarity and power.

There is, in my opinion, no necessary relationship between the appearance of such an extraordinary masterpiece and the social life around its creator. Because the acts of the creative spirit may be truly anarchic, spontaneous, discontinuous. And yet that is only one side of the coin. We recognise *Oedipus Rex* to be of its time, the more we come to know through classical scholarship what the special quality of the time was. We do not need classical scholarship to make us aware of the special quality of our own time. We feel we know that immediately, because we live in it. We certainly rationalize our experience of it in various ways: and in general we believe our time to be particularly the prey to disruptive forces. We certainly, if naïvely, expect art to be responsive to such social disruption. As Professor Wind said: 'Art just happens to be the most sensitive place in which acute disturbances make themselves felt.'[11] That being so,

---

[10]Ibid., p. 18

[11]the original paragraph (*The Listener,* 22 December, 1960) reads:
'Today the knights of the razor are not a sect, they are the majority; and they are not — in any sense of the word — *raseurs sympathiques.* To them art is a nuisance because it resists automatism. The various forces that have been discussed in these talks can be related to this over-riding impulse: for when things look odd in the artistic life of an age, it is certain that the oddity is not confined to art but pervades the entire mode of living. Art just happens to be the most sensitive place in which acute disturbances make themselves felt. The fear of knowledge, the mechanization of art, the fallacy of pure form, the cult of the fragment for the sake of freshness, are simplifications which spare us the trouble of getting upset, transformed, and Platonically endangered by a passionate participation in art,

we fancy we enjoy barbaric, primitive art more than our forefathers; that we are more attuned than they to the extreme forms of Greek tragedy; even perhaps to the more gruesome of Shakespeare's plays. So that expressionist art can be accounted for, we think, by the general chaos of the time. Yet is our aesthetic pleasure in such art really a reflection of our concern with the disruptive social forces?

Professor Wind puts an apt pin through this fallacious bubble in his account of his own first youthful experience of German expressionist painting. He says:

> In the midst of these pleasures I was struck with a thought which troubled me greatly . . . It occurred to me that if all these intense pictures, one after the other, had been experienced by me with the intensity they demanded, I ought to be out of my mind.[12]

Here we see where our naïvety may get us. To be 'out of one's mind' is to be insane. One is insane because one cannot face up to the terrors of real life. If these expressionist paintings had turned Professor Wind insane, they would not be triumphs at all, but failures. Indeed, I would turn Professor Wind's sentence round and say: 'If all these intense pictures . . . had been experienced by me with the intensity they demanded, I ought to be particularly sane'. One suspects that the problem of how therapeutic we want certain kinds of contemporary art to be (for that is the problem lying behind this argument) is bedevilled in this instance by the general fact that expressionist art is weakest in its formal power. Few of its manifestations, even of a genius like Strindberg, can be equated to *Oedipus Rex*.

Perhaps, after all, it is not the disruptive forces of our time which we hope, or fear, to see reflected in modern art, but the scientific

---

and every device of modern scholarship, from the connoisseur's list to the iconographers label, can be misused, to make art look more manageable than it is.'
cf. the revised version (London, 1963), pp. 99-100:
'Today the knights of the (i.e. Occam's) razor are not a sect, they are the majority; and they are not — in any sense of the word — *raseurs sympathiques*. They prefer not to wrestle with the angel: it takes too long; it is uneconomical; and one is likely to get one's thigh out of joint. The avoidance of risk has become a ruling passion, and many of the forces that have been discussed in these lectures can be related to this over-riding impulse: a desire to spread all manner of art so widely that its effects cancel each other out. Nietzsche saw modern man in his aesthetic Eden "surrounded with the styles and arts of all times so that, like Adam with the beasts he might give them a name". Classification has indeed proved a comfortable way of neutralizing the disturbing effects of art: it spares one the trouble of participation; and above all, it eliminates the will.'
[12]'Art and Anarchy' (London, 1963), p. 27

interests, the passions of order and precision. Abstract painting and functional architecture seem to be excellent examples of such a tendency. Abstract painting at its purest (as with Mondrian or Nicholson) seems to turn its back finally on all the inner and outer disruption; chiefly by a process of exclusion. Contemporary architecture, as Professor Wind rightly points out, at its creative best, accepts the mechanically prefabricated materials as effectively as at another period it used a greater preponderance of craftsmen-shaped stones or beams.

If we do naïvely equate formal and functional elements in modern art with a specifically scientific outlook, then it is time, I think, we took a look at the ambiguities of science itself. This is a point that Professor Wind did not raise in his lectures, though he spoke often of science. It is simply that there has been a 'knowledge-explosion' in all the fields of science, with such consequential technological advances that the social life of the entire world is undergoing continual transformation and adjustment. Viewed from this angle, science, not art, would seem to be the really disruptive force.

But equally we might suppose from the general concern with psychiatric maladjustment that the psyche was the true source of disruption. It is obvious enough that whichever way we look at it our social life is being changed and disrupted by tremendous forces. Is it as obvious that modern art is directly responsive to these forces; whether to express them, tame them, or reject them? I do not think so: I believe, because as a creative artist I feel it, that the inner world of man's psyche is in ferment. And that this ferment is forcing up new, and often unwanted, images. But I am not certain at all that the outer ferment or the inner ferment is a cause or effect of the other. It seems to me equally possible that the simultaneity of these two processes is accidental, although the effects on us of having such a double transformation to accomplish are frightening. I am certainly haunted by the feeling that creative time may really be spontaneous and discontinuous. I cannot easily see how the truly spontaneous can be merely the effect of some cause which we can rationalize.

It is not only that creation forms apparently eternal works of art out of the disruptive, anarchic images from without and within. It is that creative *genius* responds immediately to the spontaneous, timeless spirit. This spirit cannot, I believe, be finally circumscribed by history. So that a crop of geniuses vouchsafed to us in our time would knock all our theories of the marginal nature of modern art out of the ring.

Some Categories
of Judgement in Modern Music[1]

In more stable artistic periods when the dangers of stagnation were so often in evidence, the true innovation had generally to work itself through against a hostile establishment and a hostile criticism. In an extreme innovatory period like our own, innovation *as such* can even become a kind of establishment, and receive a constant critical accolade. The following anecdote sets this out melodramatically but clearly.

After one of the concerts in the BBC's 1969/70 season at the Royal Festival Hall,[2] where three modern Italian works were presented, a young man, declaiming passionately about music, was heard to say: 'The Berio[3] was fine and exciting. The Nono[4] was of course old-fashioned.'

This really is a new category of judgement. Because if the young man is a true lover of music, as we must suppose, he would never make such a judgement about music of the past, say the works of Wagner, Beethoven, Monteverdi, Perotin. Also, if he is intelligent, which we must also suppose, he would know that in another ten years, the Berio would be 'old-fashioned' and the Nono might have dropped right out of the avant-garde stakes, and be therefore ripe for re-consideration as a piece of music in its own right.

Now the music critic of the London *Observer* covered this concert,[5] and wrote of the Berio: 'Apart from Stockhausen's *Gruppen* and Boulez's *Pli selon Pli*, I can think of no other work that expands the range of the symphony orchestra with so impressive a combination of imaginative daring and technical sure-footedness. If this were all, it would still be a remarkable achievement.'

If this had been all the criticism, then it would have been quite within the category of the anecdote. To be fair to the critic, he went on to judge the work within categories more (to use his own word) 'traditional'. But the part of the criticism I have quoted has further

---

[1]This article first appeared in the magazine *Soundings*, University College, Cardiff, Autumn, 1970
[2]18 March, 1970
[3]*Epifanie* (1960; revised 1965)
[4]*Il canto sospeso* (1965)
[5]Peter Heyworth, in the issue dated 22 March, 1970

problems — of nomenclature; e.g. symphony orchestra. One surely needs to ask, *what* symphony orchestra? Or more accurately, *what* orchestra for *what* symphony?

I have dealt with this at length in an essay I contributed to an American symposium.[6] There I quoted Eric Walter White's account of Stravinsky's problems in this field from his book on that master. The gist of the quotations runs as follows:

> ... after *The Nightingale,* he [Stravinsky] became convinced that the normal symphony orchestra [as he received it from his teacher, Rimsky-Korsakov] could not provide him with the type of ensemble he needed for his next full-scale score for the Russian Ballet (*The Wedding*) ...
> ... In arriving at his orchestral specifications he was always prepared to accept conditions dictated by outside circumstances (as in *The Soldier's Tale*) or a series of self-imposed restrictions [examples are then given] ... In fact, every time he wrote a full-scale composition, he deliberately rethought his orchestra.[7]

True to *his* self-imposed restrictions, Eric Walter White states the matter simply as musical history, and leaves all value judgements to be made about each work in its own right, irrespective of the orchestra it was written for; as we do when considering a symphony by Mahler or Mozart. The last sentence quoted above is musically-historically nicely perceptive. As I wrote myself in the symposium referred to, 'I think this is in fact where we have now arrived'.[8] (But like Eric Walter White, I do not award Stravinsky any marks because he arrived there thirty–forty years before Berio, Stockhausen or Boulez. He was born much earlier than any of them.)

A few years ago there was some mild polemic between the jazz critic of *The Times* and a young composer-disciple of Stockhausen. It seems that the disciple had claimed that though Stockhausen eschewed many musical functions that Beethoven used, e.g. harmony, melody, pulse, nevertheless he might, by using some other (analogous) musical functions, yet become the Beethoven of our time. The critic stated bluntly that there are no analogies for the musical functions that Beethoven used, and that without using these in some form, no composer could speak simply of serious things to the 'millions' and the 'world' (of Schiller's *Ode to Joy*) as Beethoven

---

[6]Robert S. Hines (ed.): *The Orchestral Composer's Point of View* (University of Oklahoma, 1970) pp.203–219
[7]Eric Walter White: *Stravinsky, the Composer & his Works* (London, 1966) pp. 515–516.
[8]Hines, op. cit., p.208

had done. The critic expressed the fear that if composers, both jazz and 'straight', went the way of Stockhausen, then the art of music would cease to be a central experience of our culture and would become peripheral. To use his metaphor: 'the gardeners would have withdrawn into the orchid-house.'[9]

So far as Stockhausen is concerned, considering the extreme abstraction into which his music is going, and this abstraction being in no way ameliorated by a certain pretentiousness of public statement and performance, the critic had the right of it. But, of course, if Stockhausen makes no claim himself to work in the humanist tradition Beethoven worked in, but in fact rejects it, then he can hardly be faulted on that score. More substance is to be drawn from a sentence the jazz critic wrote, which I find fruitfully ambivalent. It ran: 'Far from Stockhausen being the Beethoven of our time, Beethoven is.'[10]

It's clear that the critic is referring, first of all, to the fact that at least ninety-per-cent of all music-lovers of *all ages* need the experience which great works of music in this humanistic tradition provide, just as theatre-lovers need Shakespeare. (In my private jargon, I call this the Shakespeare-Beethoven archetype.) And this need goes on continuously, independent of any ten-year movement of avant-garde innovation. The critic implies that it is too rarely satisfied by works of contemporary composers and seems to want to raise this to a category of value-judgement — I mean, as to whether a modern work satisfies the need that Beethoven's music does. The disciple also seems to accept this category of judgement since he is claiming Stockhausen as a prospective Beethoven, suggesting that despite appearances Stockhausen is not in the orchid-house but really out in the main garden. In fact, this category of judgement would only be proper for figures that consciously work in this humanist tradition, and improper for those who deny it. But, of course, the latter may not be speaking to the millions or the world but to the members of a temporary cult or coterie.

---

[9]See Miles Kington, 'The New Wave in Jazz', in *The Times*, Friday 9 February, 1968, p.5; the 'composer-disciple of Stockhausen' referred to is Roger Smalley. Tippett's quotations are, in fact, paraphrases of the original, whose key-sentence reads:
'. . . if Beethoven and his contemporaries were the landscape gardeners of the music of their time, today's composers have shut themselves away in an experimental greenhouse to produce stranger and stranger growths of interest only to a few fascinated fellow-botanists.'
[10]Kington, op. cit: another paraphrase — the original reads: 'Stockhausen is in no sense the Beethoven of our time — if anyone is, it is still Beethoven.'

The recent history of art shows us that there can be temporary confusion of tradition or category with long-lived figures of great creative power who are clearly seen finally to be working within the humanist tradition, but who at a certain time of their career were contingently mixed up with the avant-garde. The sculptor Henry Moore is a good example. Moore has described the tremendous sense of release and development he felt when he cut his first hole through the sculptured body. This procedure was journalistically blown-up into extreme avant-gardism for a while. But Moore himself had no further experience of release or development through later avant-gardisms, such as mass-less sculpture of volume only, or minimal sculpture, or whatever. His own further development went on independent of the run of avant-garde innovation (to which he had been only contingently joined) and the resulting Moore works can only be judged for themselves within the same categories as we use to judge, for example, Michelangelo. Even with an apparently more protean figure like Stravinsky the avant-gardism is ever only contingent, as he himself has many times stated. This experience within a long creative life is not new. Goethe described it in his old age to Eckermann.

What precepts, if any, are there to be drawn for the benefit of composers presently in action?

It is possible that for the very young the most lively way in is still the road of avant-garde innovation: until such time as they know whether this is to be contingent or continuous. But I am quite sure that this, even now, is not the sole road to creative vitality and maturity.

The problem for composers in the middle-age-range is on the other hand much what it always has been: how at all to create enduring works of art. But I think it involves *now* a withdrawal in some degree from the search for innovation *per se*. Innovation will be conditioned solely by the expressive demands of the work which is to endure. Indeed such composers might well hope that they drop journalistically out of the avant-garde stakes as rapidly as possible so that their works cannot be judged any longer by the category of the initial anecdote at the start of this essay. This may make for temporary difficulties as to critical interest and numbers of performances, but it is, I think, the only way out of the cult and the coterie into the real.

As to composers of my generation, it is already too late. The centre of gravity of their *oeuvre* probably lies already in the past. They can only create further within the line or curve *already determined* by the development, if any, of the works *already written*. It is a sobering thought that the middle-group composers will reach this point in about twenty years' time.

What I believe[1]

Although I am going to speak to you now as an individual person hoping to convey to you what *I* believe, and though I must indeed speak with my own particular voice recognisably different from all the other fifty million or so voices of my countrymen; yet it is obvious that I am only a person whose individual characteristics and beliefs are embedded in a tremendous background of given racial and cultural traditions; of special aptitudes and disabilities I share with all the thousands of my musical colleagues; and of particular ways of thinking and feeling forced on me by my psychological type.

I remember remarking, when I first read Evelyn Underhill's celebrated book, *Mysticism*,[2] how the way to the central experiences was inevitably conditioned by the type; whether, for example, the desire was a passion to know or a passion to love. Underhill admits, indeed stresses, the various ways due to differing temperaments (though these are limited and come again and again) to what are probably for all types the same fundamental experiences of the mystic state; but the examples she gives of great mystics are all Christian. She makes no study of Islamic mysticism — to travel a little East from Europe. Because of her eventual full acceptance of Christian dogma, she is unwilling, perhaps even debarred from considering whether the mysticism that can feed Christianity is the same mysticism that can feed other great faiths. And if so, what this may imply.

I know something was made clear for *me* by a statement of T.S. Eliot's where he remarks in a discussion of the necessity for religious faith: '. . . and for us, religion is Christianity.'[3] I know I speak for many beyond myself when I say the question that I at once have to ask is: if religion means for *us* Christianity, who are *they* and what shall be appropriate to *them*? And if the Christian god demands as an article of faith that they and their religion are to be treated to eternity as inferior, without any rational or sympathetic examination, then one can find oneself, as C.G. Jung expresses it, in the intolerable position of being more rational and more humane than one's god.

---

[1]Broadcast on BBC World Service, 2 November, 1956
[2]London, 1911
[3]T. S. Eliot: 'The Humanism of Irving Babbitt', (1928) in *Selected Essays* (London, 3rd edn., 1951), p. 480

Now I believe that this dilemma is deeply significant for the new one world in which London is calling Asia, or Delhi Europe. It is possible that the problem seems simpler to a Hindu because of the traditional tolerance of that religion. But that is deceptive. After all, it is not the humane, tolerant men anywhere that take part in religious riots. Yet the greatest Indian of them all, Gandhi, was a tragic sacrifice to Hindu intolerance and fanaticism. I believe that Gandhi endured, as no one more, in body and spirit, the dilemma of how a religious man shall behave in our modern world. Gandhi is one of the men by whom I have been most deeply influenced.

I don't think the West has produced in this period a religious leader of such power. Our seminal figures are the great scientists, like Einstein or Freud; men who examine sensations, outside and inside, with a discipline of impartiality such as the world has never seen before. These men speak with the tongues of millions, because of the universality of the things they discover in the name of science. Atomic fission is the same process in any continent. So, perhaps, is the Oedipus complex. Freud may appear superficially nihilistic, but there is a creative side to his techniques. He clears away much cant and prejudice to lay bare the essentially human. Aseptic maybe, amoral even, his work is a powerful catalyst in the experience of adjusting to our new world.

For my part I am more moved by Jung than Freud. Without in any way belittling Freud, I know that I cannot abide entirely in his therapeutic examination of the collective primitive in us; I need to balance such a terrifying therapy with an equal examination of the collective non-primitive. All the mass of inherited lore and tradition, of spiritual wisdom and revelatory myth. Jung has found a way to bring this collective non-primitive into relation again with our excessively rationalistic, empirical modern minds. And this way is forced on us by the terrible psychic unbalance caused by our excessive materialism. Not all neuroses will give way to Freudian therapy. Some of us are driven by other agonies to a deeper analysis, until we meet on the labyrinthine paths of the collective unconscious those events, age-old predilections of the mind, which Jung calls the archetypes.

Jung finds that there is in fact a central, or centralizing predilection of the mind, an archetype of integration, of the union of opposites, of deity maybe, that takes often the image of a human figure, the incarnation of a God or a Saviour, of Christ or Buddha. This archetype is endlessly active in the human psyche, even in the periods like the present, when the overt values are entirely those of scientific materialism. So that beyond hope, there is now, I believe, knowledge that our desperate need and longing, as the tension grows greater, will force a re-animation of the archetype of the Saviour.

But Jung is quite clear that the longing for a more spiritually balanced life is still, for the vast mass of our people, pressed down into the unconscious by the dizzying social value given everywhere to the wonders of technics. So that this repressed longing, starved of the life-giving food of our attention and value, breeds violence and discontent. For we are still at the stage when to the individual alone, or shall we say, to certain individuals alone, comes at this time the inescapable duty to make conscious the repressed longing locked up in the inner violence and psychic disarray. But it follows, I am afraid, that any persons driven along the path of integration, will by that in itself, come into a polarity between their new values and the present overt values of our mass societies. Nor can Jung's discoveries escape — that means help *us* to escape, the dilemma I spoke of before as significant for our new one world. Christians have asked Jung if he was prepared to direct his patients to personify the archetype of the Saviour by Christ rather than Buddha. Jung said he could not. For him, as for me and for many many others, the dilemma must be lived with; as a penance or a privilege; with sorrow or with joy. I believe further that this particular dilemma stands as example for many other such problems which we cannot as yet solve but must suffer — and indeed as deeply as we have strength for, if we are to respond to the needs of the time; if we are to be on the side of the angels in the struggle to give aid to what shall be. It is because I know that I am fully committed to these polarities, these dilemmas, these uncertainties, that I cannot find satisfaction in the security of a traditional faith.

I spoke at the start about the special aptitudes and disabilities of being a musician. I am unsure how much these musical charac-teristics colour one's beliefs. Probably very little. But being a composer among musicians is more radical; because one is thereby a member of a further class — one is an artistic creator. I have deliberately said artistic creator rather than 'creative artist' (though that is the more usual) because the English language permits one to throw the accent thus first on one term then on the other — on the artist, or on the creator. If I were wanting you to give your attention more to the artist, then I would be asking you to consider the importance of fantasy and imagination, and the mystery in our sense of the Beautiful. And I know that Plato held our desire to enjoy and possess the Beautiful to be the most immediate proof of a metaphysical reality. But I want you to give your mind rather to the artistic man as creator; to imagine what it feels like to be driven, whether we will or no, to spend one's life fashioning ever new images; to consider how that must colour our beliefs — to have this dominating and imperative faculty within one. The drive to create has been so constant through the ages, and is so intense in its operation, that it is difficult for those submitting to it not to feel it as evidence of things beyond the individually personal. So that maybe Jung is right, when he says that if once the artistic creator, leaving personal idiosyncrasies aside, gives expression to the archetypes of the collective unconscious, then he also speaks with the tongues of millions — as Einstein, or Jung himself, or Gandhi.

I have found this experience, in so far as I have known it, to be the most absolute and positive I know. I have an untarnishable sense of certainty with regard to it. I have faith in its ultimate benevolence, even while I know that the coming to birth of archetypal images is inevitably disquieting and bewildering, before the world achieves a beneficial relation to what is happening. And it is clear that this is something not quite what Plato meant by our desire to enjoy beauty. It is nearer to the creation of the mysterious mythological tragedies, like *Oedipus Rex*. I believe that the faculty the artist may sometimes have to create images through which these mysterious depths of our being speak to us, is a true fundamental. I believe it is part of what we mean by having knowledge of God.

Postscript (1978)

In August this year I took part in the Tanglewood Music Festival. Between rehearsals I was taken to visit the Hancock Shaker Village which is preserved a few miles from Pittsfield, Massachussetts. In a public room of one of the buildings there were three or more pictures, painted by Shaker women, intended originally for private viewing only. One of these pictures I found so striking that I was driven towards reconsideration of a perennial problem — namely, what, if any at all, are to be the religious icons of our period. I made the following notes.

I believe in a reality of the physical world outside, experienced through the senses and formulated generally by the scientific intelligence.

I believe also in a reality of the spiritual world within, experienced, in my own case, by some intuitive, introspective apprehension of a kind which, in the past, was formulated generally by dogmatic, revelatory, received religions.

Since I seem to accept present-day cosmology, geology, biology, etc as scientists propound these matters, and this acceptance is something I share with almost everyone else (other than certain fundamentalists), then the first belief (in an outside reality) seems to join us all together.

The second belief, superficially, is divisive. I suppose I am here using 'believe', already, in a different sense.

I may believe in a spiritual reality, but I don't believe (in the usual sense) that Christ was the son of God, or that Allah dictated the Koran word for word to Mahomet, or that the miraculous life of the Buddha is historical fact. I have always thus to try and disentangle some apprehension of spiritual treasure (which I would want to hold on to) from the elaborate costumes and dogmas associated with 'belief'.

Here it is, surely, that we all join together again. For traditional believers, with various degrees of awareness, are engaged in the same paradox; be they Pope or Dalai Lama. (The fundamentalist is again outside all this.) For it is not possible to believe in a cosmology of incomprehensible, infinite space, of geological time running into billions, and evolutionary time running into millions of years, *and* to believe in the costumes and the dogmas of the great male-dominated authoritarian religions of the past, without a tension in the psyche that is manifest or repressed.

I knew this most vividly in Jerusalem. To enter the breath-takingly beautiful Dome of Rock mosque and peer down at the stone from which Mahomet began the Night Journey to heaven and back; to visit the Church of the Holy Sepulchre and stare at the tomb from which Christ rose from the dead to appear to Mary Magdalene in the garden; to watch Jews of today weeping at the Wailing Wall for the loss of a temple nearly 1400 years ago: for me to do all these things was to find myself temporarily both wonderingly close to the believers around and strikingly apart. On the other hand, to meet Muslim, Christian or Jew in a bar or a coffee-house, later, when we might well have discussed those extraordinary phenomena known in scientific jargon as DNA, black holes, or silicon chips, meant that we could be quite together again. It is not that the 'religious' agnostic is in any better intellectual fettle. He may be more conscious of the general irrelevance, in our time, of the iconographic and ritual aspects of the old faiths. Having no fixed iconographic or ritual reference-point himself, maybe he is equally irrelevant — certainly, he is equally impotent. So then, is nothing to be said or done? Not quite.

To return to the Shaker picture. At my first sight of it, before I had time to rationalize, I thought it might be a Tibetan mandala. I was deeply moved. Here, indeed, there seemed to be an icon of the numinous — sexless, spaceless, timeless. So it seems plausible to imagine a more public iconography from a collection of such pictures: Jung appeared to imply this. It must, however, be an iconography that is detached from established religious ritual: for in effect, it needs a new ritual, in which we are all there, fully defined in terms of sex, space, and time. My intuition is that such a ritual (which might lack a liturgy or dogma) would come, if not *from*, certainly *through* the theatre — using theatre in its widest and most universal sense. For truly, 'the question is no longer one of reconciling Orpheus and Christ, but one of a world vision that makes the sacred possible at all'.[4]

Balzac, in a curious novel, created from his imagination a supernatural figure called Seraphitus-Seraphita: seen as male or female according to the needs of the petitioner or seeker, In *The Ice Break,* I found I had to discard Astron-Astra and be content with an androgynous Astron. Not only because the former seemed so distressingly uncouth a name, but also because only thus can this figure of the 'Chorus-in-imagination' be a legitimately anthropomorphic 'angel' — the messenger not the God. As Astron himself says, somewhat vulgarly (what else?):

> Saviour?! Hero?! Me!!
> You must be joking.[5]

It is left for Yuri, the 'fractured' man, miraculously healed in body, and perhaps temporarily in soul, to say of more mundane but yet more vital matters:

> Chastened, together,
> We try once more.[6]

I wrote these notes before I saw the 1956 talk re-printed above. On re-reading it, I was surprised, reassured, perhaps delighted,

---

[4]Walter A. Strauss: *Descent and Return: the Orphic theme in Modern Literature* (Harvard, 1971), p. 12
[5]Michael Tippett: *The Ice Break,* Act III, Scene 5
[6]Ibid. Act III, Scene 9

even, by the strength of the affirmation contained in the last paragraph.

I should simply like to add now the name of a book which I have come to regard as an essential point of reference in all these fundamental matters of debate: Jacob Bronowski's *The Ascent of Man*.[7] I think it is clear why.

[7]BBC, 1973

2
Music of the Angels

An artist can — maybe sometimes he must — involve himself in the political and social ferment of his time. He can also detach himself completely. There exists a whole genre of twentieth-century creative work (and indeed it is there in all periods and in many cultures) which seems to stand proudly and eloquently alone, independent of external turmoil and internal neurosis, granite-like in its aesthetic objectivity.

I think that, in my own *oeuvre* to date, the most ambitious composition that belongs within this genre is *The Vision of St Augustine* (1963–65). Undoubtedly, it's a work that's difficult to perform, and since its musical language has no direct contact with a vernacular of the present-day, its 'vision' may be difficult to apprehend. The following background ideas may prove useful in stimulating a proper understanding of the piece.

Preface to
The Vision of St Augustine

Augustine (AD 354–430) was born to peasant farmers of North Africa at a time when the Greco-Roman Empire was about to crumble before the Nordic invaders (Rome was sacked by the Goths in AD 410) while Christianity, though already the state religion, was still rent by warring heresies.

His mother, Monica, was a dedicated Christian (his father, Patrick, was not), and in her Augustine found from childhood an ideal of impregnable religious constancy. He himself grew up into a man of intense intuitive belief—that Christianity contained vitally new and revelatory values, as against the crumbling Greco-Roman world and the barbaric tribal civilization of the invading Nordics. He was more concerned, however, with the former.

At great cost to his parents, he was sent to Carthage University, where he graduated in Rhetoric. This meant a sustained study of classical Latin literature, which he loved. (Incidentally, he hated Greek, and it irked him to learn it.) In the Latin authors he found a marvellous world of culture and sensibility, which allied itself to his natural sensuality. But the Bible he found unpalatable (its Latin he thought barbarous), often immoral, and occasionally nonsense. Yet he believed the Bible was the word of God. All his life he battled with this paradox: that this uncultivated, even at times cruel and improbable book, was word for word *God's* word. It is this battle which made him a religious genius, and stamps him for us as a modern. (It has been said that all his great religious intuitions came in fact from mistranslations of the original Hebrew!)

In his twenties, Augustine went first to work in Rome, and then in Milan. Here, he came close to Bishop Ambrose, who influenced him deeply and whose beautiful hymn, *Deus, creator omnium*, he repeated to himself when overwhelmed with grief at his mother's death.

In a garden near Milan, with Alypius, his dearest friend, at thirty-three years of age, Augustine had his first vision (if we may call it that, being only auditory) — of a child singing: *tolle lege* (take up and read). Of course there was no real child, as Augustine realised. Such a vision, whereby something apparently real appears to someone under extreme mental stress, is relatively common. In Augustine's case it led to his final submission to Christianity and to the extreme asceticism that was regarded as necessary in that period.

Some months later he decided to return with his mother to Africa. They travelled overland to Ostia, the port of Rome, and rested there before the sea voyage. Here, five days before Monica's death, Augustine had a second vision, which Monica shared — of Eternity. This experience, known to mystics, is much rarer.

Augustine describes his two visions in the *Confessions*. Vision I concerns the stubbornness of his will, and the dispersal of his emotional energies in dissipation of the senses. Vision II concerns the dispersal of his mind upon the evanescence of things, and came to him through his prolonged inner struggles as to the meaning of Time.

There is no present — because it is instantly past. We cannot in this temporal existence experience a true present. In fact, we only know Time through the mind, which is constantly shifting from the immediacy of sight (*contuitus*) towards the future (*expectatio*) or the past (*memoria*) with such rapidity that the soul is for ever distended (*distentus*) in all directions without centre. To have any inkling of such a centre the contrary is necessary, viz. concentration (*intentio*). (The relevant key passages of St Augustine and Paul appear in the sung text of my composition.)

Vision I, therefore, gives a centre for his affections by submission to his God's will. Vision II gives a centre to his soul. This vision is, however, an act, in Augustine's terminology, of divine grace; and a crowning mercy in his life. For he now knew the reality of this eternal *ante* (before all Time) through experience.

But as a mortal creature within the temporality of our life on earth, he can only experience Eternity momentarily and involuntarily. If — and in Augustine's words this 'if' grows into a tremendous rhetoric — we could prolong this vision (his Vision II) then that, he believes, would be the 'eternal life of the saints' he and Monica discussed as they stood in the window embrasure.

For all his rhetoric, Augustine was a priest, not a poet. He should be compared with Dante, who in *The Divine Comedy* pursues finally the same vision. The composer setting Augustine's text is in this sense a poet. Apart from the music, I have had to amplify the text by other Latin quotations from the *Confessions* and from the Latin Bible. I have also made use of *glossolalia* — an ancient musical tradition, involving an ecstatic melismata of vowel sounds: this appears in various forms, from the traditional *alleluia*, to the set of Greek vowels taken from the *Pistis Sophia*, from a supposed prayer of Christ to his father.

Music of the Angels[1]

The music of the angels, that is, the kind of music the angels sang to the Shepherds at the birth of Christ, focuses attention on the meaning of Time.

Faced with the procession of the seasons within the year, vital to all agrarian societies, peasants and priests alike found religious security in the certainty of recurrence. John Barleycorn had his head cut off in the Summer harvest, but came to life again miraculously in the Spring. Time was but an endless recurrence of seasons. This was obvious enough to a peasant or a Shepherd because it was visible. But this concept of Cyclic Time, as it has been called, is not obvious when extended into past and future, to the recurrence of aeons or world months of 2,000 years; nor when used, as in some Hindu myths, to assume the rise, decay and recurrence of civilizations by immutable law. Such things were unobservable and the so-called immutable laws were of course religious and mythological.

Now although the birth of Christ falls at the winter solstice, when analogically the sun's chariot stands at midpoint in the night-journey under the sea, this is not really of the essence. What is of the essence concerns the matter of eternity in relation to temporality; and the nature of God.

For once we begin to consider Time not as meaningless recurrence, but as development from a beginning to an end, we give meaning at last to history. The development, the acts of history, will appear as progress or degeneration according to the meaning we give. And the meaning depends on the answers to certain questions this new idea of Time inevitably poses. If temporality has a beginning and an end, what was this beginning and what will be the end? And what is before the beginning and after the end? This is as unobservable as the immutable recurrence of aeons, and the answers are as religious and mythological as the immutable laws of Cyclic Time. But the myth is different.

The answer to the beginning was the once and once only creation by God of a temporal universe with an ordained end. The early

[1]First broadcast on BBC Third Programme, 29 September, 1964. It is indebted to: G. B. Chambers, *Folksong-Plainsong: A Study in Origins and Musical Relationships* (London, 1956; esp. Chapters I, II & III); Reinhold Hammerstein, *Die Musik der Engel* (Berne, 1962; esp. ch.II); and a review of Hammerstein. *Op. cit.,* by Frederick W. Sternfeld, published (anonymously) in the *Times Literary Supplement,* 14 June, 1963, p.416

Christian Fathers were then much exercised by the conundrums: 'What did God do before the Creation?' and: 'What is the nature of the eternal life of the saints when, after the resurrection of their bodies, they enter eternity — and all temporality, and the universe with it, ends?' The questions are metaphysical and the answers therefore equally so. But the essence of the myth or belief is a conception of Time as finite — that is with beginning and end, what I have called temporality — and this finite Time is then set against God's eternity. This metaphysical concept enabled the Christian philosophers — I am thinking particularly of Augustine — to see that the question: 'What did God do (with His Time) before the Creation?' was unreal. Time only began with the Creation, and will end with it. God is in Eternity, not Time.[2]

From this duality came the possibility of a relationship, or dialogue, between God and the world, or between Eternity and Time. In a sense the dialogue between God and the world is the dramatization of the metaphysical relation between Eternity and Time. And the music of the angels is part of the expression of this drama — as indeed the angels themselves are important actors in the drama. So that keeping these two aspects of dialogue and relationship in mind we can say that, in the history of God's dealings with man, the next most dramatic moment after the Creation of the universe and Time was the irruption of Eternity into Time through the birth of Christ as God and man. This inexpressible moment of the divine drama — inexpressible by man that is — was actually expressed by the simultaneous appearance of the angels to the shepherds. What the angels then sang was the expression of a minute vision of Eternity — minute in relation to the transcendent magnificence of God the Father. And this vision was a charisma — an act of God's grace — for which the shepherds so far as we know were not specifically prepared but for which they were pre-destined. The seeds of later doctrinal conflicts over pre-destination are all to be found in this apparently simple story.

It is the immediacy and poetry of this story however which kept it alive through so many Christian centuries. It forms one of the most touching scenes of the Medieval Mystery Play cycles. Yet the philosophical concepts are never far away. In the Shepherd's Plays it was a tradition for the shepherds to compare their own rough music with the angels' music which they had just heard. The angelic music is a source of 'Wonder' because it is so much finer. As the *prima*

---

[2]See: *St Augustine's Confessions*, Book XI

pastor of one such play says, the angels' song

> *Was wonder curiose*
> *With small notes emang*

and points out that the melody had 'foure and twenty to a long'.[3] The shepherds 'wonder' at the vocal skill and virtuosity the angels display. The shepherds are no different, except in degree, from Augustine, who 1,000 years before them had pondered on this problem and decided that the music of the angels must in some way be like the music of man but purified. Because only such purified music could express the sense of blessedness which angels enjoy as they sing eternally before the face of God. The shepherds in the Plays also catch a moment of this blessedness. In another Play, after the angelic *Gloria*, the *secundus pastor* says:

> *For never in this world so well I was*

and his friend Garth suggests they sing a jubilation.[4]

Now a *jubilus*, or jubilation, has a long history. St Augustine puts the facts in a nutshell. He is commenting on Psalm 32, whose last verse runs:

> Be glad in the Lord and rejoice,
> ye righteous: and shout for joy,
> all ye that are pure in heart.

His commentary on this verse is as follows:

> Notice the method of singing *and shout for joy* he (i.e. the Psalmist) gives you. Don't look for words that you may be able, as it were, to explain how God is pleased: sing a 'jubilation': What does singing a 'jubilation' mean? It is the realisation that words cannot express the inner music of the heart. For those who sing in the harvest field, or vineyard, or in work deeply occupying the attention, when they are overcome with joy at the words of the song, being filled with such exultation, the words fail to express their emotion, so, leaving the syllables of words, they drop into vowel sounds — the vowel sounds signifying that the heart is yearning to express what the tongue cannot utter.[5]

The principal notion behind this passage is the tradition, common throughout the early Christian centuries and going far back into the pagan past, that ectasy, that is the apprehension of the

---

[3]See: *The Wakefield Prima Pastorum*, vv. 306 & 414, in A. C. Cawley (ed.), *The Wakefield Pageants* (Manchester, 1958), pp.37 & 40

[4]See: *The Chester Shepherds' Play*, v.441, in S. B. Hemingway (ed.), *English Nativity Plays* (New York, 1909) p.56

[5]Adapted from Chambers, op. cit., p.4

transcendent, is too huge to be expressed by words. It can only be expressed by vocalizations, shouts, orgiastic repetitions of vowels. The Greek word for this manifestation was glossolalia. And glossolalia is the central technique, if I may borrow that word, which the angels use in their music.

But angelic glossolalia not only had its origins in Shamanistic ecstasy, it had folk origins as well, as Augustine describes. His father was a wine grower and Augustine in boyhood had regularly heard this North African wordless folk-song which went by the Latin name of 'jubilus'. The peasants sang it to express well-being and joy. It was also used for calling and answering as St Hilary, a century before Augustine, makes clear in his commentary on Psalm 65, where he writes:

> And according to the custom of our language, we name the call of the peasant and agricultural worker a 'jubilus', when in solitary places, either answering or calling, the jubilation of the voice is heard through the emphasis of the long drawn out and expressive rendering.[6]

(This seems incidentally to suggest that the traditional alpine singing we call yodeling is a form of 'jubilus'.)

When the angels sang to the shepherds, before they reached a 'jubilus' of vowels, they sang certain words clearly enough for the shepherds to understand. They sang:

Gloria in excelsis Deo.

> Glory be to God in the highest, and on earth peace and goodwill towards men.

The message of peace and goodwill was the special part of the song — the *Gloria in excelsis Deo* was, if I may put it so, the conventional or usual. For the function of angels, apart from being messengers between heaven and earth, was to enact a perpetual ritual of praise.

This is already present in the famous vision of Isaiah, from which it can be said the whole angelic tradition stems. Isaiah described how:

> In the year King Uzziah died I saw also the Lord sitting upon a throne, high and lifted up, and his train filled the temple. Above it stood the seraphims, each one had six wings; with twain he covered his face, with twain he covered his feet, and with twain he did fly. And one cried unto another, and said, 'Holy, holy, holy, is the Lord of hosts: the whole earth is full of his glory'.[7]

---

[6]Jacques Paul Migne, *Patrologiae cursus completus* (Series Latina, 221 vols., 1844–55), p.1239; see also Chambers, op. cit., p.23
[7]Isaiah 6, vv.1-3

Isaiah's vision is the angels at worship — the covering of face and feet, singing 'Holy, holy, holy' before the transcendent God. The word 'praise' is implicit, not stated. In the shepherd's vision at the birth of Christ, Luke says explicitly: 'And suddenly there was with the angel a multitude of the heavenly host praising God.'[8] But it is Paul who Christianizes the Hebraic tradition finally. In the first chapter of *Hebrews* he tries to place God, man and angel in a new hierarchy. He subsequently accepts the Psalmist's traditional view that man is 'a little lower than the angels',[9] who are of course infinitely lower than God. But Christ, God's son, has altered this older order:

> For verily he took not on him the nature of angels, but he took on him the seed of Abraham.[10]

So that through this divine incarnation the order of man is potentially above that of the angels:

> For unto which of the angels said he at any time, Thou art my Son, This day have I begotten Thee? And again, I will be to him a Father, and he shall be to me a Son?
>
> And again, when he bringeth in the first begotten into the world, he saith, 'And let all the angels of God worship him'.[11]

So the angels do not really enter the scheme of Christian redemption, their function remains what it always was, the everlasting worship and praise of God, not in Time, of course, but in Eternity.

The traditional Hebraic visions of Ezekiel, Isaiah and the Christianizing of Paul receive a tremendous dramatization in the splendid apocalyptic visions which John of Patmos had and which are the substance of *Revelations*. Much of *Revelations* is the description of a heavenly liturgy with direct references to Judaic temple ritual and the slowly forming Christian ritual of the mass: the elders round the throne like the attendant priests around the Bishop's chair; the thrice spoken 'Holy' at the beginning; the opening of the Sacred Book; the praise for the Lamb; the final Amen.

There is however, a verse to be quoted exactly, which runs:

> And the four beasts had each of them six wings about him; and they were full of eyes within: and they rest not day and night, saying, Holy, holy, holy . . .[12]

---

[8]Luke 2, v. 13
[9]Hebrews 2, v. 7; see also Psalm 8, v. 5
[10]Hebrews 2, v. 16
[11]Hebrews 1, v. 5, 6
[12]Revelations 4, v. 8

Three other verses run:

> And I looked, and, lo, a Lamb stood on the mount of Sion, and with him an hundred forty and four thousand, having his Father's name written in their foreheads.
>
> And I heard a voice from Heaven, as the voice of many waters, and as the voice of a great thunder: and I heard the voice of harpers harping with their harps:
>
> And they sung as it were a new song . . .[13]

From these various quotations we can now draw up a list of the most constant characteristics of the music of angels, many of which were directly echoed in Christian Liturgy, and deliberately. For the sacred music of the Church in the world and Time is an imperfect echo of the angelic music in Eternity.

From Isaiah comes the *alter ad alterum*, 'one cried unto another';[14] that is, the two choirs or voices which sing alternate verses one to another. This tradition is still present in the Decani and Cantores of our English Cathedral choirs.

From John of Patmos comes the *sine fine*, 'they have no rest day nor night':[15] that is the idea of a perpetuity of praise. This could only be echoed here on earth by the monks of certain Orders, who divided their members into twelve groups to sing hourly, day and night, in the monastery church. As Hildegard of Bingen put it: 'The members of the Order perform the duties of the angels, in that they offer up hour by hour a singing prayer.'[16]

From John of Patmos comes also the *canticum novum*, 'they sing as it were a new song';[17] which marks the new dispensation of the New Testament. And also the vast numbers 'and with him an hundred forty and four thousand';[18] signifying the gathering in of all creation. And these vast numbers sang *una voce*, as one voice; that is the tremendous tradition of unison singing, the unity of all. In the words of the Apostolic Constitutions:

> This is namely the will of God, that as the heavenly powers praise God with one voice, we men on earth praise the one true God with one mouth and one meaning.[19]

---

[13]Revelations 14, v. 1, 2, 3
[14]Isaiah 6, v. 13
[15]Revelations 14, v. 11
[16]Migne, op. cit. vol. 25, p.515
[17]Revelations 14, v. 3
[18]Ibid.,v. 1
[19]F. Probst, *Liturgiae der drei ersten christlichen Jahrhunderte* (Tübingen, 1870), p.180; quoted (in German) in Hammerstein, op. cit. pp.45-46

Behind it all lay the much stranger tradition of glossolalia — the expression of ecstasy in vowel sounds. This came almost to be standardized in the Alleluia. *Alleluia* was a Hebrew expression meaning *Praise be to Jah* — that is to Jehovah. So that the *allelu* announced the praise, while *ia* was used for the vocalization, the glossolalia. These alleluias were sometimes of enormous length and often extemporized. They form one of the oldest parts of the mass.

Of course the angels also played instruments, but here the problem is too difficult to elucidate. To put it briefly, the harps, trumpets, tubas and cymbals the angels played are not those of any modern orchestra.

Because indeed it is all a metaphor. The music of the angels is the expression of Eternity as against Time. In Christian doctrine it is not possible to know Eternity till after death and resurrection. All that God in His Grace grants us is occasionally a proleptic vision, a minute foretaste of what this might be. Augustine and his mother were granted such a vision. Five days before she died they stood together in a window embrasure of an inn at Ostia on the Tiber, looking into an inner garden. They asked each other that central question: What might the life of the Saints be like in God's Eternity? Augustine describes how they lost the sense of outside things to the degree that they sensed only their souls. But this was not enough. In Augustine's own words:

> We went *beyond* our souls, so that we might touch that region of unending richness, where you feed Israel forever with the food of truth ... And while we were thus talking (of eternal life) and panting for it, we touched it for a moment with the whole effort of our heart[20]

But this moment was wordless, for he continues,

> and we sighed, and left the first fruits of our spirit bound to it, and returned to the sounds of our mouth, where words begin and end.[21]

The central vision, you see, was an experience of ecstasy, which can only be expressed, in echo, by those vowel sounds he commended in his commentary on the Psalms.

I think possibly his most moving sentence is:

> *O felix Alleluia in coelo, ubi templum Dei angeli sunt.*[22]

(O happy Alleluia in Heaven, where the angels are the temple of God.)

[20]op. cit., IX, Chapter 10
[21]cf. 18, above
[22]Migne, op. cit., vol. 38, p.1190

3
Composers
Past and Present

Purcell

(i) *Rediscovery*

Holst and Vaughan Williams, and other composers of their generation, were very drawn towards folksong and the music of the Elizabethans. But it was my generation, including, of course, Britten, that found a new source of inspiration and a fresh example in Purcell.

We were not taught Purcell in the Conservatoire: we discovered him independently for ourselves. When I went to study at the Royal College of Music in London in the early twenties, Purcell's music was much less played than it is these days. It seems to me incomprehensible now that his work was not even recommended in composition lessons as a basic study for the setting of English. I may have been unlucky, but I think the omission was general. However, when I was nineteen, I began to conduct small amateur choirs with the object of studying in action, as it were, the English madrigal school — a repertory equally neglected in my Royal College training. Thus, when much later I found out about Purcell, I already had a good ear for the setting of English by his immediate predecessors. Byrd, Tallis, Gibbons, Dowland were no longer names in a history book, but composers of living music. Through their works, these composers were as alive to me as their great contemporaries, Shakespeare, Marlowe, Spencer and Sidney.

I think it is fairly true to say that the English worship of Handel, and later of Mendelssohn, effectively nullified any possible influence of Purcell. His scores were unavailable, lost from the public gaze, and his music almost unperformed. The Elizabethan composers were also unheard, just as English folksong was unrecorded. But at the turn of the century, Elizabethan madrigals and Tudor church music were rediscovered and printed, the unmatched riches of folksong collected, and the Purcell Society itself was founded, for the publication of that composer's works in *urtext* editions.

The personal discovery of Purcell which Britten and I made later led us not only to initiate performances of as much music as possible, but also to issue performing editions through our respective publishers. Eventually, too, we produced recordings of Purcell's music. Altogether, these have demonstrated that Purcell is a European voice, a master in his own unique right.

(ii) *Purcell, Gibbons and the Verse-anthem*

Henry Purcell was born in 1659, became organist of Westminster Abbey in 1679, and died in 1695. These dates matter because they show that Purcell's professional life coincided with the end of the Puritan era, during which church music had been severely curtailed, and the first flowering of the Restoration period, when music, especially for the theatre, received anew the all-decisive royal patronage.

Through his appointment as organist at Westminster Abbey, Purcell became heir, in the most practical and literal sense, to the great, centuries-old tradition of English church music. This music had itself undergone a change consequent upon the Reformation of the Church in the sixteenth century. Two rules of the reformed church were decisive: (1) that everything must be sung in English, not Latin (except in certain cathedrals and college chapels, where Latin was understood); (2) that for greater clarity of the words, the English language should be set always one syllable to a note.

The English Tudor and Caroline composers, right up to the death of Elizabeth I and after, wrestled with the musical problems consequent on these rules. They succeeded brilliantly: both in composing music sensitive to all the nuances of the English vernacular, and in simplifying the earlier, florid *a cappella* Latin style into something quite new and different. For this purpose, they invented the English verse-anthem, wherein the cathedral choir was broken down into solos and solo ensembles to contrast with the full choir, and accompanied by consorts of stringed instruments, as well as the organ playing from a figured bass.

One might call the Verse Anthem the English Church Cantata. This was the state of English church music when Orlando Gibbons died in 1625 (and I have deliberately omitted the related developments in chamber music of the period — madrigals, string fantasies, keyboard music, etc).

At this point in English history, politics intervened sharply into public music, in that the successful Cromwellian party, in their fanatical asceticism declared illegal the public performance of any church music whatsoever. But when the Stuart court returned from exile in 1660, not only was church music restored, but also the pre-Cromwellian court masques and theatrical pieces, which now required even more elaborate music, and music which could only be successfully composed at that time on Italian models. These models reached England and Purcell, coming more exactly from France and Lully. They were irresistible. I myself realised this when I had to conduct a performance of *Dido and Aeneas* in Italian for Swiss Radio. Purcell sung in English sounds characteristically English; but in Italian it sounds just as natural.

To show both the continuing tradition in church music and the seemingly complete change of temper between Gibbons and Purcell, I'd like to compare two of their verse-anthems: Gibbons's anthem to words from Psalm 30, *Sing unto the Lord,* and Purcell's *My beloved spake,* whose words come from the *Song of Solomon.* Admittedly, by choosing these particular anthems, I've weighted the scales a bit in favour of the difference in temper: for the one is serious, the other gay. It could easily have been the other way round. Nevertheless, in performance, I couldn't, even if I wanted to, make the Purcell sound Elizabethan or the Gibbons Restoration. For they belong to different worlds.

In any case, there are similarities of texture within these anthems that provide some kind of continuity. In each, the verse ensemble (the solo voices chosen to sing the declamatory portion of the anthem) is a quartet: in Gibbons, two counter-tenors and two basses; in Purcell, one counter-tenor, tenor and two basses. Each has a string accompaniment. But there the resemblance ends. Gibbons treats his string parts, when accompanying the verse soloists, just as if they were themselves voices, in imitative polyphony with the solo singers. Purcell uses his strings only for instrumental ritornelli in a much later style of string writing, and accompanies his verse solos with a keyboard instrument and *basso continuo* part for organ for his anthem, thus enabling the verse soloists and string parts to coalesce into a successful ensemble.

Gibbons divides his verse and full sections more consistently than Purcell, because he has a full choral commentary, so to speak, to each verse section. But Purcell treats his verse ensemble as *the* protagonist of the whole piece and only very occasionally resorts to the full choir for emphasis. Purcell also uses his verse ensemble with absolute freedom. Gibbons, here, is almost mathematical: for the first verse is for two basses, the second for two counter-tenors, the third for one counter-tenor and one bass.

In the matter of word-setting they are similar and dissimilar. With both composers we feel that the English words have themselves generated the music to which they are sung. But Gibbons conforms to the rules of the early Anglican reformed church and sets exactly one syllable to a note. By Purcell's time the rule had been allowed to lapse again, as the taste was then for virtuosity in singing, rather than attention to the biblical meaning. So his setting is more florid.

The verse-anthem, as left by Gibbons, is still really within the older polyphonic tradition. The distinctive musical development that occurred between the time of Gibbons and Purcell was the emergence of the continuo accompaniment to a solo voice. In the case of the verse-anthem, this meant that the strings could be removed from their role of accompanying the verse solos, for these solos would be clearer, more obviously in contrast with the full choir, if accompanied only by the string bass and keyboard. And then, too, once the strings *had* been thus separated from the verse solos, they were free to be used as a distinct musical texture of their own — to play a prelude and ritornelli.

In *My beloved spake,* Purcell writes a short string prelude, then lets the four voices begin the first verse. This is commented on, not by the full choir, as in Gibbons, but by the strings. It is the same for the second verse and the full choir first enters at the end of the third verse, and then just for a single phrase; the strings take over the same music, and the solo voices echo it, so leading to the fourth verse. I don't intend to describe the rest in detail, because all I want is to point out how much more flexible in form and techniques the verse-anthem had become by Purcell's time, and especially in his hands.

(iii) *Purcell and the English Language*

In Gibbons's time, the task before the Church composers of making a note-for-note syllable setting of the English liturgy was still a conscious and vital one. Gibbons seems to have set the seal upon it. Purcell inherited a technique that Byrd, Dowland and Gibbons had all worked out, and he marries his music to the English language with no further reference to the long tradition of setting Latin. Byrd sometimes set out an English translation to music which he had previously composed to Latin texts. Gibbons, to my ear, at least, is already purely English. But Purcell's spoken English was, of course quite different from Gibbons's. Really, to explore this fascinating subject fully, we probably need to compare Marlowe, say with Dryden, at the same time as we compare Weelkes or Dowland with Purcell. Even then, we have to remember that the earlier version of the English Bible, which of course persisted, and was set by both Gibbons and Purcell, was already old-fashioned to Ben Jonson.

We can experience the change of tone in a passage from Purcell's *My Beloved Spake* such as — 'flowers appear upon the earth and the time of the singing of birds is come'. The charming musical phrase to the word 'singing' is characteristically Purcell, and it has resonances impossible to find in Gibbons, or in any of the music of his time.

Only Dowland, in my opinion, rivals Purcell in the setting of English. Both had a fine ear for English poetry. Let us consider Purcell's song *Music for a while*. The first word Purcell sets is 'music'. Like thousands of English words this is a trochee — long/short. Purcell sets it as such. In $\frac{4}{4}$ time, the syllable *mu* is a dotted crotchet, the *sic* a quaver. Even when he lengthens the *mu* to a minim, he ties it over to another quaver, making it longer still, so that the *sic* can fill the other side of the short beat.

Heaps of English words are like *music*. Let us take another — *shepherd*: one that is important to Purcell's *Nymphs and Shepherds*. If one compares Purcell's setting of the word *shepherd*, here, with Handel's, in *He shall feed his flock* (from *Messiah*), what do we find? At the end of Handel's lovely phrase, the strong syllable of *shepherd*, the *shep* is on the weaker bit of the bar, and the weak syllable *erd* is on the strong final close. I don't think it's often realised just how much that sort of Handelian usage has harmed our proper sense of the language. We take it for granted because we have heard it from our cradles. I must admit that my own ear, so used now to Dowland and Purcell, receives a jolt, which makes me remember that Handel was an Englishman by adoption, not by birth and tradition. Now Purcell never does the like. However long he may vocalize on the strong vowel of the trochee, he never ends a weak vowel on the strong musical beat, but lets the weak vowel always fall the other side. Listen, for instance, to the word *wondering* in *Music for a While*. What Purcell really does is to end the musical phrase, however long, always in such a way that the word can be spoken at the very end in this natural rhythm.

Returning for a moment to the word *music*, we can observe that it is partly the need to have the fall from strong to weak that brought about the tradition of small nuance crescendo on long whole notes, if set to the long syllable of the trochee. For by this means a high pressure can be made with the voice at the point where the short syllable is ready to fall. This tiny nuance helps, in English especially, to soften the impact of the weak syllable if it has hard consonants in it — like the *ic* of *music*.

In Purcell, we have to differentiate carefully in performance the expressive purposes behind his word-settings. With the two *Hails* at the start of the *St Cecilia Ode* of 1692, for instance, the first is short — a call to the audience — but the second is tied over on to the strong beat, and, to my mind, these demand a different attack. The first should be sung short and strong: and the second begins softer, with the tone growing onto the strong beat, from which can fall the rest of the vocal phrase, *Bright Cecilia.*

Purcell by no means omitted the more naïve forms of word-painting that we find in the vocal music of the Elizabethans, but generally he is after more subtle effects. In the opening chorus of the same *Birthday Ode*, the poem continues, after the opening words, with 'fill every heart with love of thee and thy celestial art'. The word which caught Purcell's imagination in this way was *celestial*. At first he treats it only lightly. But then it is carried up by the voices into the celestial air, and the higher they rise, the softer they should be. In performance, Purcell's vocal music only comes alive when we observe the purpose underlying the treatment of the words. In *Nymphs and Shepherds*, Purcell clearly sets the word *laughs* to get the effect of laughing, and to sing it in a neutral, flat, legato — as often happens—negates its whole point. I think it's important that performing editions (especially those aimed at amateurs) should draw attention to such matters, for it is technically just as important as the bowing-marks in an edition of string music.

Incidentally, I'm not sure whether Purcell was conscious always of which vowels he used for long vocalizations. In the *St Cecilia's Day Ode* (1692), by far the greatest proportion of vocalizations are of the vowel *u* — in words like *flew, true,* and *u* in *music*, and so on. As far as I can remember, there is only one vocalization on the open *a* — that in the word *charms*, which, judging by the way he sets it, Purcell thought to be important.

(iv) *Purcell's Theatre-music and the Purcell Inheritance*

Because of the nature of the Elizabethan theatre and the verse drama which needed very little music, composers like Byrd, Tallis, Gibbons and Dowland wrote little directly for the stage; they wrote for the country house and the church. But already, with the death of Shakespeare, and as Ben Jonson was left supreme, the masque began to supplant the drama; and the masque needed a lot of music. This development was cut short by the Puritan Commonwealth, but taken up again and transformed by the Restoration, with demands for incidental music of all kinds, both vocal and instrumental. Purcell came to maturity in the heyday of this theatre, and had all the gifts and techniques it required. He could pour out overtures, dances, arias, scenas, choruses at need — and his works are the one great compendium of incidental music for the English theatre. Handel became his only rival in this, but he wrote to Italian words for the London season of Italian opera. And after Handel there is no one until our own time.

I have talked of incidental music for the theatre in Purcell's case, rather than of opera, because this is the truth of the matter. Opera is an aesthetic unity of drama and music, in which the music both adds to and eats up the drama. Purcell was asked to provide this special *operatic* unity of music and drama on only one occasion — *Dido and Aeneas*. Apart from that he wrote for theatrical entertainments in which the *spoken* word was more important — what we would call nowadays a musical — like *My Fair Lady*. Nevertheless, the music contained all sorts of things that were to be found, if at all, only in embryo in Elizabethan madrigals or lute airs.

Let us take the sense of situation in drama, or to be exact, the expression in music of the sense of a situation. The madrigal cannot do this, but a song can, and in some of Dowland's monologues we are made aware that the singer is giving a personal expression of an almost dramatic situation. This is already an operatic aria in embryo — of the kind where a character gives a personal reaction to some set of circumstances, while the action is, so to speak, held in suspense. The distinction between the expression of emotion, say grief at love betrayed, in a song and in an aria, is that one is usually more personal and intimate, while the other is more grandiose and public. This is how Dido expresses her emotions at Aeneas's betrayal in the great lament at the end of the opera. There are many other arias of situation in Purcell's incidental music to entertainments like *The Faery Queen* and *The Tempest*. But Dido's lament is such a perfect example that I think it the best piece for me to discuss further.

First of all the situation is quite clear — Aeneas and Dido have been lovers, but Aeneas is called away to found Rome, and not all his eloquence nor appeal to divine commands can persuade Dido that she has not been betrayed. After he has gone, Dido decides to end her life. In this desperate situation she sings the rightly-famed lament. It begins: 'When I am laid in earth' and those opening words we usually catch. After that we are not always sure of every word sung, but it is of no tremendous consequence. Firstly, because the situation, which we appreciate from the drama, is really being expressed in the music: the music is eating up the words. And secondly, because Purcell, in the second half of the aria, places the words 'remember me' in such a vivid light that we hear them as though they summed up everything; as indeed they do. This placing of the key-words is something quite out of the range of the Elizabethans. What is only in embryo in Dowland is now a full-formed creation: an operatic air which is a masterpiece.

Situations occur not only in opera but in oratorios, if they are of the dramatic kind. I like to think I was influenced by Purcellian examples when I needed to express an aria from some of the relatively simple situations of A Child of Our Time. I am thinking particularly of the air for tenor to a tango-like bass — an air which had to express the frustrations of the ordinary man temporarily at odds with life. The things that influence one, in a composition of this kind, are never simple, but always complex. The sense of our time, that is, in this case, of the period between the World Wars, lies musically in the tango, not in any Purcellian turn of phrase. Purcellian is the setting of the scene by a short orchestral introduction; and the manner of repeating a simple, easily understood phrase. Such a phrase is that to the first words the tenor sings — 'I have no money for by bread'.

Returning to Dido's lament. As most of us know, this aria is constructed over a ground-bass many times repeated. I use the word 'constructed' deliberately, because the ground-bass is a constructional device. The repetitions of the ground lay out the ground plan of the piece. To a certain extent Purcell must always have known how may repetitions of the bass there would be before he composed the rest of the music that was to go over the top of it. These constructional devices are one of the mysteries of composition. They are apparently just mathematical (like the present preoccupation with serial devices) yet in the hands of a truly creative composer, like Purcell, they disappear into the *music*, so that we are completely unaware of them. In a case like Dido's Lament the ground-bass itself is immensely expressive in its own right—as are most Bach fugue subjects. We *are* aware, if only subconsciously, of this wealth of expression at the base of Dido's singing. But other ground-basses are much less important in themselves — as might be a more routine fugue subject. The accent is then laid directly onto the music *above*. With Purcell the bass is often immediately forgotten in the wealth of melody he composes above it.

I don't think any of the English composers of any generation who have studied or much performed Purcell's music can fail to have been influenced by the constructional power of Purcell's basses. In the first of the Ritual Dances out of my opera *The Midsummer Marriage,* which represent hunting or chasing in various symbolic forms, I use a long and in itself expressive bass to exemplify the hound that pursues. This bass is first given out on the orchestral cellos and basses with drums and harp. When the bass is to be repeated I have, by rhythmical shortenings, compressed it, so that the tension will be slightly increased. And in a second repetition I compressed it still more. The bass is therefore being used constructionally to repeat the musical motions of the chase and at the same time to force them to be smaller or nearer. Under the direct influence of Purcell (though in quite another style from his) even an expressive bass, like this one, can yet disappear in the general music of what is played *above* it: in this case, music for flute and horn, reinforced later with some brass to accompany the dance movements of the running hare, which is hunted. The constructional device is the ground-bass; but the expressive quality lies in the whole music that proliferates above it.

There is a feature of Purcell's style of a more special kind worth mentioning. It is his ability to create intensity, particularly in poignant moments, by a sort of harmonic polyphony. I want to speak of it because I can't think of any other feature of Purcell's style which has meant so much to me personally. This poignancy is in Dido's lament, especially in the last ritornello after Dido has ceased to sing. But I think an example from the early string fantasies is better, because it is nearer the source. Much of this intensity and poignancy is to be found in the madrigals of Weelkes, and in other Elizabethan music. Purcell did not invent here — he took over a tradition and developed it. The technical means to produce this intense polyphony are chiefly the hanging on to notes in one part so that they make a momentary dissonance with another part before they resolve themselves; and the placing of harmonically unexpected notes at the moments of resolution, so that the music is never quite resolved and still. (It is a method of composing which Wagner used to tremendous effect in *Tristan*.) For instance, the opening of

Purcell's four-part Fantasy for Strings No. 4, shows a polyphony developed out of two contrary-moving themes, heard at once together on viola and cello. It is not so intense and poignant as the end of Dido's lament, but it shows the method in great purity.

Exactly this feature of Purcell's style, developed as it was out of the Elizabethans, has become a feature in its turn of my own musical language: a good example occurs in the slow movement of the String Quartet No. 2, a movement which is also a fugue. Whatever other differences of style there are, the feature of intensity created in the ways I spoke of in relation to Purcell is virtually the same.

Towards the end of his life Purcell became more and more engrossed in his work for the theatre; for civic occasions like the St Cecilia's Day festivals; and for the Court; that is, Welcome Odes to the Royal family, and such like. Not that all this theatrical and civic music of Purcell is full of choruses; it is not. And let's not forget that Purcell's choruses are not Handelian choruses. There has been a tendency, in England at any rate, to consider Purcell as a sort of junior Handel. This is now slowly passing away. Their approach to writing choruses is quite different. Handel's choruses are usually constructed as great vocal fugues. Purcell's choruses are usually enlarged, elaborated madrigals. The fugal chorus is from beginning to end one music, one verse; such as 'He trusted in God that He would deliver him, let Him deliver him, if He believe in him' from *Messiah*. But in the madrigal chorus the music changes with the changing verses; a notable example is the Purcell chorus 'Soul of the World' from the big *St Cecilia's Day Ode*. In the final chorus from this Ode, Purcell seems to be reaching forward to greater splendour and clearer form. The shape of this piece is best described as A-B-C-A. A is exhortatory and uncomplicated. B is elaborate, rich, polyphonic. C is short, highly expressive for solo voices only. Then A comes again. This is still madrigal form — that is, block added to block. But the blocks are so contrasted (and one, of course, is repeated) that we appreciate the simplicity and clarity, as well as the grandeur, of the form.

Benjamin Britten

(i) *First Encounters*

I first met Benjamin Britten during the war, when I was musical director at Morley College. We wanted a tenor soloist for the Gibbons verse-anthem *My Beloved Spake*. Walter Bergmann, who was then chorus master in Morley, suggested Peter Pears, recently returned from America. When Pears came to rehearsal, Britten came with him. I can recall the occasion very clearly.

I had in fact seen Britten before the war at the first public performance of *A Boy was Born* at a Lemare concert in the old Mercury Theatre, Notting Hill.[1] I had no intuition then that the slim figure walking down the gangway to take his bow before the public would become so decisive and beloved a personality in my life. But I have an unusually vivid mental picture of that moment. The aural memory is much vaguer. It is really only of the Brosa Quartet madly counting quavers in the finale of my First Quartet, also a premiere!

Though Britten and I met over one of the Elizabethans, our real musical connection was Purcell. It is a rough generalization, but there is some truth in the contention that while a thirty to forty-year older figure like Vaughan Williams derived special emotional and musical sustenance from the Elizabethans (cf. the *Tallis Fantasia, Sir John in Love*), Britten and I submitted to the influence of Purcell to a degree not seen in English music before. I won't recount what are the points of Purcell we chiefly needed, but certainly we responded to the carry and freedom of his vocal line.

It was also during the war, and not long after I first met Britten, that I was asked by the then Precentor of Canterbury Cathedral to hear one of his lay-clerks sing. This was Alfred Deller. He sang Purcell's *Music for a While*. One outcome of this meeting and of the growing friendship with Peter Pears was the first full-scale performance by Morley College of Purcell's *Ode for St Cecilia's Day, 1692,* with the ravishing duet for counter-tenor and tenor in that work sung by these two incomparable artists accompanied by a bevy of recorders.[2] I don't remember if Britten was present, but I am pretty sure he was.

About this time I wrote my first piece of music for Pears and

---

[1] 17 December, 1934; the first performance had been a BBC broadcast in April the same year
[2] 31 December, 1944 at Friends' House, Euston Road, London

Britten as a duo. Out of the study of Purcell and Monteverdi had come the urge to write a vocal cantata (as opposed to a song cycle). This piece was *Boyhood's End,* and the first performance was given by them in the Holst Room at Morley College.[3]

Ben later asked me what larger works I had written, if any, other than those he knew. I told him of *A Child of Our Time,* of how I had played it to Walter Goehr some time before, who advised me in the circumstances to shut it up in a drawer, which, being rather patient and literal, I did. Ben had the manuscript out of the drawer at once. In looking through the score he noticed how, in one of the Spirituals, the effect could be greatly enhanced by lifting the tenor solo part suddenly an octave higher. This I entirely agreed with and so this minute piece of Britten composition is in the score, He persuaded us to venture on a performance; he was already then close to the Sadler's Wells Opera and talked three of their singers into singing for us: Joan Cross, Peter Pears and Roderick Lloyd. The fourth, Margaret McArthur, came from us at Morley. In the event, through no fault of these artists, it was an imperfect premiere[4] under execrable conditions, but inescapably moving. One year later, Britten's own relations with Sadler's Wells bore fruit, with the premiere of *Peter Grimes.*[5]

Ben and I met first in the war, when we were both conscientious objectors. Here is a small anecdote of those times. It is customary for artists to give concerts free to inmates of H.M.'s prisons. Britten and Pears had already offered to do so before I was sent to a prison myself. They managed to arrange it that they gave a recital in Wormwood Scrubs when I was there.[6] On my side I am ashamed to mention the untruthful wangling by which I convinced the authorities that the recital was impossible unless I turned the pages for the pianist. To the last moment it was touch and go. But finally I stepped out of the ranks and sat down unexpectedly on the platform beside him. A strange moment for us both. He remembers, I am sure, that 'primitive responsive audience' of gaol-birds. It is exactly twenty years ago. But these twenty years have piled up the works in that catalogue right up to the *War Requiem* where his pacifism, as much else, has found decisive utterance.

---

[3] 5 June, 1943
[4] 19 March, 1944 at the Adelphi Theatre
[5] 7 June, 1945
[6] 11 July, 1943

(ii) *Britten at fifty*[7]

I will begin with an objective fact. Britten's publishers[8] are producing a catalogue of all his work to date — to his fiftieth year that is. There are ninety-nine published works as separate items in this catalogue. Ten of these are operas; seven of them are major vocal works for the concert hall; four are large-scale orchestral works; there are three canticles, two string quartets, not to speak of works for small choirs (a favourite of mine is the *Hymn to St Cecilia*), small groups of all kinds, music for all occasions.

Considering the artistically chaotic period in which we live, without an agreed musical style, so that composers must wrestle with their own language in a manner unknown, say, to Mozart and considering the tremendous range of subjects, in the widest sense of the word, which Britten has involved himself in, then the sheer scale of his accomplishment is staggering. Here is the first of the facets of his genius. Phenomenal productivity arising from the combination of great gifts with continuous hard work.

Britten's technical mastery is often treated as part of the musical gifts which Mother Nature undoubtedly showered on him. But this mastery is not a gift at all (like the ability in childhood to win chess tournaments from older masters). It is the result of sheer hard work. If anyone can be said to have been initially responsible for this temper in the critical early years, then it was Frank Bridge. But once that has been said it still needs to be realised that the hard work is done year in year out by Britten himself. By hard work I am not thinking so much of the hours of intense activity, but rather of the prolonged struggle, even agony, which composition is for Britten. In a letter to me he writes, 'I am having a ferocious time between these public functions and my own work (more and more difficult!) but that's our old problem, isn't it?'. By 'our', he meant that I (who better being so close a colleague?) would immediately understand this problem of creative work as against public presentation. But he also meant by 'problem' the unending struggle within the work of composition itself. And 'more and more difficult!' means just what it says. The older we grow in art and the profounder our sensibilities, the more we find creation — despite all the mastery of experience — difficult.

We can uncover now a further facet of his genius. For if we consider the difficulties, not of the future for him, but simply of the

---

[7]First published in *The Observer*, 17 November, 1963
[8]Boosey & Hawkes Ltd

past, we can see that Britten by his very gifts had his full share of the problems bequeathed to us all in this period. There being no single tradition now, each artist forges his links (or blows up his bridges) according solely to temperament and his individual *kairos*. Britten's *kairos* has never been, even in extreme youth (nor will be in the future) to make his music out of destruction. (I use the word destruction in its healthy affirmative sense.) It is interesting that Britten said of his youthful admiration for Auden, 'Auden was a powerful revolutionary figure. He was very much anti-bourgeois and that appealed'. Yet there is no early Britten work to match Auden's *The Orators* for example. Britten must make his music out of his own creative gifts in relation *always* to the music of our forebears. So that he is inescapably involved in a fiendish problem of choice. That is, for each work he has to choose (in his finest works only after agonizing struggles) the style and substance afresh and in relation to some tradition. For the purposes of his own music, in nearly every work, his intuitions in this manner have been infallible.

As a third facet of his genius I treasure his lucidity. As Britten said to Murray Schafer 'Music for me is clarification; I try to clarify, to refine, to sensitize. Stravinsky once said that one must work perpetually at one's technique. But what is technique? Schoenberg's technique is often a tremendous elaboration. My technique is to tear all the waste away; to achieve perfect clarity of expression, that is my aim'.[9] Britten does not misunderstand Stravinsky, nor does he criticize Schoenberg. He points a finger to himself, because *that* is what he has to be.

Turning now to his productions there is nothing useful in parading here my likes or dislikes. Nor shall I make any judgement of quality with regard to his works. I am a composer and a deeply attached friend, not a critic. There is also a further reason, which I will discuss in a moment. What I have to say concerns style and individual voice. Britten, as everyone knows who listens much to his music, has a marked style of his own. We can always immediately recognize any 'piece of music' by him, and can trace imitations of this style in younger admirers. But every composer with enough personality to possess an individual voice writes works which go further. Of these works we tend to say, not merely that this is by so-and-so, but that this is such-and-such a work. (Think of *Tristan and Isolde*—then think of *Meistersinger*.) So, however much Britten grew beyond *Peter Grimes,* there are tones, procedures, orchestral and

[9]Murray Schafer: *British Composers in Interview* (London, 1963), p. 118

vocal colours which are more than just Britten in his general style, for they have such a 'Grimes'-ness about them, they are that opera and none other.

For me, though this has not been recognized so generally, the style of the *Spring Symphony* has also this quality. A gaiety and exuberance unique and inimitable. Between these poles of dark and light (*Grimes* and the *Spring Symphony*) is the style of the *Canticles;* flower of his natural piety. We are both of us religious composers, i.e. bound, *religati*, to a sense of the numinous, but Britten is more properly Christian.

To attempt an account of Britten's place in contemporary music is to enter on a vexed question, bedevilled by the inability of so many music critics and others to distinguish between the facts of public acclaim and the pretentions (and maybe necessity) of value judgements. To deal with the facts first. When his own generation comes into the title, that is, when the substantial figures of Stravinsky and Hindemith reside in the memory, then Britten will share the top of the world's acclaim solely with Shostakovich. This is an honour for England (and of course for Russia) and we may 'shine forth' through Britten as a country of no mean musical worth. We want more of this not less. That is, the world audience for music, and the huge audiences that are to come, can explore and enjoy more such figures. To assess Britten's music in a judgement of value is to my mind pretention not fact. It will only be a fact when his works are *all* there (we have as yet not the half) and he too must reside in the memory. Yet I am in no way suggesting that critics should not make value judgements of new music, Britten's or anyone's. That is the burden of their job. We need, I think, more judgements, illuminatory assessments of the general stage of musical affairs; especially, one would think, of the state of the emperor's clothes. But not on the other hand a manic hunt for masterpieces and the one true way announced of God. This is stultifying, especially to the younger English composers struggling to find their individual song. (I make this plea within the birthday tribute to an older figure, because Britten himself would so signally approve my doing so.)

Great disservice has been done to Britten by the indiscriminate coupling of his name with great figures of the past. It cannot be too clearly stated that this can never have emanated from the composer himself. He does not ask himself, 'Am I the xxxxxxxx of my time?' But: 'How can I hammer out these objective works of art which are the proper and full fruits of my gifts in relation to this period?'

(iii) *Obituary*[10]

The news of Benjamin Britten's death brought a sense of loss to every musical person of the whole world. To those like myself who knew him closely, the sense of loss is probably no greater. I have memories that go back for a very long period. But I think of him now, in 1945, just after the war, when he had come back from America to England, and I remember walking into the darkened auditorium of Sadler's Wells Opera Theatre, and there was a high sound of violins — in fact, the very opening of the first interlude of *Peter Grimes* — and, with his back to me, this shadowy figure in the orchestral pit, rehearsing the orchestra. And I remember remarking to myself at that time — how fantastically professional this young man was who had not only composed this work, but was performing it there with all the authority of a top-ranking conductor. It is difficult for us now, after so many years, to realise what this event, in every sense, meant, not only to us in England but to, I think, the musical world in general. Because, though it did, in fact, happen first in England, the resonances were, in the end, and very quickly indeed, international. But in England itself, the sense of excitement was probably due to the feeling that here, at last, after the very first performance on the stage, was an opera whose professionalism, whose quality, in the best sense of the word, was something which had not been seen in England since the single completed opera, *Dido and Aeneas,* of Henry Purcell, centuries before.

For Britten himself, this triumph meant something more than the immediacy of being an internationally recognized composer. It meant for him that he was now willing in himself, and, indeed, determined to be, within the twentieth century, a professional opera composer. That in itself is an extraordinarily difficult thing to do, and one of the achievements for which he will always be remembered in musical history books, is that, in fact, he actually *did* it. For himself, this meant that he had to consider very seriously the question of the economics of opera in modern society, or rather the society of that time, 1945, just after the war, when as far as England was concerned, it was a period of impoverishment. He considered the matter in great detail and at great length with Peter Pears, the singer, and between them they decided that it was possible to have operas of quality and power, using a very much smaller number of players in the orchestral pit.

---

[10]Published in *The Listener,* 16 December, 1976

In order to do this, the two of them decided they should found the English Opera Group, a small group of professional singers who were, in general, to be accompanied by a brilliant group of up to twelve instrumental players. In order that the English Opera Group should have a permanent place where it could perform the operas written for it, Peter Pears and Benjamin Britten decided that they would begin a festival in Aldeburgh where they lived, and, though the conditions seemed improbable, it is true that within a very tiny building in that old town, this whole series of Britten works was conceived and produced. Indeed, this series contained, for me at least, one masterpiece that equals *Grimes* in the larger opera house, and that is *The Turn of the Screw*, to the libretto out of Henry James.

Nearly as fascinating as the whole series of operas, to my mind, is the whole series of song cycles. These were written, generally, for Peter Pears, and one must realise that this close and intimate relationship produced from Britten some of the most tender, beautiful music that he ever wrote. I first heard them together during the war at a very early, if not the first, performance of the *Michelangelo Sonnets*. I can remember again, as a composer, being struck by this extraordinary musicality in both composition and performance: with an additional sense of surprise, indeed, almost bewilderment, that these songs were written to Italian words, with a fantastic sense, so far as I could hear, of the relation of the music to the Italian. So it is really no surprise that within this series of works for voice and piano, or voice and small numbers of instruments, also, Britten wrote music not only for English, but for French, German, and even Russian texts.

I would also say that this seems to me the way in which we should appreciate this composer, as being a figure who lived all his life totally within his native country, but who always had a professional and international attitude to the music of his time. And surely we can see that his pacifism and his feelings about international war sprang from something of the same source, and that, sooner or later, this passion concerning the things that human beings did to each other during the two great wars that he had lived through would issue in some profound work of art. I am referring, of course, to the *War Requiem* which he meditated on many years before it was actually performed.

I want to say, here and now, that Britten has been for me the most purely musical person I have ever met and I have ever known. It always seemed to me that music sprang out of his fingers when he played the piano, as it did out of his mind when he composed. I am sure that the core and centre of his great achievement lies in the works for voices and instruments.

Through his extraordinary musicality and fantastic technical equipment, Britten was probably one of the finest accompanists on the piano of anyone of his generation. Anybody who heard Pears and Britten, year after year, do their annual recital at the Aldeburgh Festival or, luckily, heard them during the great tours they took right round the world, has a memory which, I feel, is ineffaceable. But I think that all of us who were close to Ben had for him something dangerously near to love. And it gave us, perhaps, an almost anguished concern for what might happen to this figure.

It seems to me that certain obsessions belonged naturally to the works of art which he produced. I don't think it matters at all that they may not in any way have belonged to his personality. I refer to a deep sense of cruelty upon people, cruelty as a suffering. A sense, I think, also of the fragility of all existence, leading him to a sense of death. He had a special sensitivity, I am sure, for the works of Henry James, and the whole period running from 1890 to 1920, during which a figure like Thomas Mann was writing. The penultimate opera, *Owen Wingrave*, had been in Britten's mind as an intended opera years and years ago, probably even before he returned to England from America. In *Wingrave*, the artistic obsession with cruelty and death is clear for us to see, but a sense of death was sharper still in *Death in Venice*, the last of all the operas. Here is a work of extraordinary tenderness, and I think all the love which he had for his singer flowed out into this work. But there was a sense, with those of us outside the immediate circle, of apprehension: an apprehension which was deepened as we knew of his illness. The apprehension is totally fulfilled, and we are left with a sense of sorrow and loss.

Stravinsky and *Les Noces*[1]

Stravinsky's life-span has covered a quite unprecedented period of change and upheaval. So our first duty, always, is to try to imagine what it was like to grow up in Czarist Russia before 1900 — or rather, because that is more important in this talk, what it meant to be thirty years old, a composer in Paris, in 1912.

Secondly, when we come to consider a work like *Les Noces*, we must first remember that it is dedicated to Diaghilev: and it simply isn't possible to understand how *Les Noces* came to be written at all, without some account of that extraordinary man; how he revolutionized ballet and the musical theatre, and how he set the young Stravinsky on a royal road.

Thirdly, Stravinsky wrote the words of *Les Noces* himself. They are based on his long study of Russian folk poetry. *Les Noces* is simply, in English, *The Wedding*. In Germany it is known as 'Russian Peasant's Wedding', and the published score has a sub-title, *Russian Choreographic Scenes*. Stravinsky cannot be critically understood unless we attempt to evaluate the struggle between his innate Russian-ness, and his life-long intellectual fascination for West European classical forms. After *Les Noces* the Russian element weakens.

Fourthly, *Les Noces* is scored for four pianos and percussion, as an accompaniment to singing that is absolutely continuous. This unusual orchestration is anything but an accident. It sums up many of the most decisive musical interests and influences in Stravinsky's life at that time — and indeed later. There is a lot to be said about it.

These four aspects — Stravinsky in relation to his, and our, time; Stravinsky in relation to Diaghilev and the musical theatre; in relation to Russia and the countries of his exile; in relation to a certain kind of verbal and musical sound — these are essential preliminaries to any account of the scenario of *Les Noces*.

Stravinsky was born in 1882. From about that date to the end of the century the temper of all the arts in Europe became tinged with a kind of malaise, engendered by an irrational self-consciousness concerning the approaching new century. The term *fin de siècle* was coined to describe this malaise. The weaker characters gave way to

---

[1] First broadcast on the BBC Third Programme, in 1947, in connection with a radio broadcast of *Les Noces*, performed by Morley College forces under the direction of Walter Goehr; the performance was repeated in a Morley College concert not long afterwards.

pessimism and decadence. The stronger and more flamboyant were revolutionary and shocking. They set out quite deliberately to shock, because they could see no other way of shaking the complacent respectability of the bourgeois society whose values were still unquestioned, and whose art seemed, to the younger men, so tame and stuffy, so sentimental and idealistic — and never at all tough and realistic, or even experimental. There is no better example of the new shocking, vigorous realism than the plays of Bernard Shaw. Shocking in a different way, but equally typical of the time, was Oscar Wilde's *Salomé* — which he wrote in French. Later, Shaw's musical hero — not his friend, Elgar, but his other hero, Richard Strauss—made *Salomé* into a truly extreme and gruesome opera.

Now, seeing we live in a scientific age, it is natural enough that we take scientific innovations in our stride. All the vast mass of experiment and invention, which dates back to the turn of the century, and which has issued eventually in nuclear fission, was accepted and gloried in — until latterly, when a dreadful question-mark seems to hang over all humanity. Already, however, innovation in a scientific discipline like psycho-therapy caused a violent shock. Freud, by his birth date, is also a *fin de siècle* figure, and the shock of his discoveries is still reverberating round the world. But the uproar caused by the *fin de siècle* poets, painters and musicians was far more immediate and violent, totally out of proportion to the small and restricted occasions of their display. The artists themselves did of course set out to shock; but the responsible ones certainly felt they were also renewing the language of their respective arts — as indeed they were. The art establishments and the public, however, were offended and embittered. The new art became at once the expression of and the scapegoat for the underlying and general malaise. Although the subsequent horrors and catastrophes of our own period have shaken bourgeois complacency, one would have thought, to its foundations, the art establishments and the public, and the new state bureaucracies, still prefer a mediocre, sentimental or idealistic art, and if no longer so bitterly hostile to great figures like Picasso and Stravinsky, still commission the conventional and the second rate where they can.

Born into this *fin de siècle* period, Stravinsky, as a student in Moscow, caused no such scandal as, say, the young Kokoshka in Vienna. He belonged indeed to those circles in Russia that were interested in new music: but his sudden, wonderful maturity and development came only from his meeting with Diaghilev. Diaghilev was a unique and quite extraordinary figure. His enormous value, I think, lay in his power to stimulate the general condition of the arts as a whole. He first picked out Stravinsky through his music at a new music concert. He had hoped to become a composer himself. Failing in that, he organized a remarkable Moscow Exhibition of new painting. But, naturally enough, he turned eventually and finally to the theatre, where many arts could be combined. And his outstanding and incredible artistic success with his first seasons of Russian ballet in Paris before the first world war, was due not only to the quality of the dancers he assembled, but equally to his inflexible determination to have the same quality in all the arts involved. Diaghilev never made the movements of the dancers an end in themselves. It was not dancing to music; but it was music danced. In the same way the scenery was not just painted wings and backcloths, it was an imagined stage space, wherein the dancers could move, and by which they were also conditioned within the scope of the collaborate enterprise. For what came out of all this, was the clear necessity of early conference and collaboration between choreographer, designer and musician. (This notion is not quite the same as Wagner's, though it might appear so, if for the simple reason that Wagner did not, or could not, collaborate with anybody.) It was the genius of Diaghilev to bring extraordinary ever-fresh individual talents into collaboration. The kind of work which resulted was summed up in an aphorism of Cocteau: 'a work of art must be inspired by all nine muses.'

Stravinsky entered absolutely into this exciting Diaghilevian world. We must always remember that artists like Stravinsky can never be fettered in one art alone, even when the one art is their craft and profession. They inhabit naturally a whole world of sensibility that has as many intellectual and aesthetic forms as there are human tastes and characteristics. I find myself in immediate sympathy with this attitude. Judging by all that Stravinsky has written about his artistic life and his aesthetic views, I am certain I am nearer to him in presenting his work within the widest cultural context rather than just as important modern music. For despite the fact that *Les Noces* was not, in fact, a product of Diaghilevian collaboration (it was all Stravinsky's), yet it conforms to the general aesthetic attitude that Diaghilev stood for and that Cocteau expressed with his dictum: that a work of art should be inspired by all nine muses.

Now Diaghilev was too shrewd a showman not to see the publicity value of shocking the bourgeois art world, and the conservative public. As I have pointed out, the general malaise at the time made it extremely easy to do so. We simply cannot imagine happening nowadays the sort of riot that accompanied the first performance of *Le Sacre du Printemps*. Although Stravinsky's name (as a wild revolutionary, of course) became overnight a world name from this event, it is certain that Stravinsky did not intend it that way. He had merely, but unswervingly, gone the way he had to go in order to do his part in the collaboration that eventually produced the stage performance. But the general inclination of the period to be shocked and scandalized by artistic novelties could hardly be gainsaid. Whatever Stravinsky thought about himself, the public put him in the same boat as Picasso, or James Joyce. In his Harvard lectures of 1939, *Poétique Musicale*,[2] Stravinsky denies that he was ever a revolutionary — even in *Le Sacre*. He says:

> In truth, I should be hard pressed to cite for you a single fact in the history of art that might be qualified as revolutionary. Art is by essence constructive. Revolution implies a disruption of equilibrium. To speak of revolution is to speak of a temporary chaos. Now art is the contrary of chaos. It never gives itself up to chaos without immediately finding its living works, its very existence, threatened.[3]

In order to understand how Stravinsky, the composer of *Le Sacre du Printemps,* can yet present himself, as he tries to do, as a traditionalist, we must bear in mind that he, like the rest of us in this time, is a double man. His great quality lies in the strength of passion of the two sides of his nature. He had on the one hand the gift of immediately arresting and dynamic invention — on the other he had an equally extreme intellectual passion for order. When he writes about aesthetics he tends to write solely from the intellectual, ordering side of his nature. Yet in the Harvard lectures he does say that 'we shall always find at the origin of invention an irrational element on which the spirit of submission has no hold and that escapes all constraint'.[4] Nevertheless, he concludes by saying: 'what is important for the lucid ordering of the work — for its crystallization — is that all the Dionysian elements which set the imagination of the artist in motion and make the life-sap rise must be properly subjugated before they intoxicate us, and must finally be made to submit to the law: Apollo demands it.'[5]

[2]'Poétique musicale': *Sous forme de Six Leçons.* The Charles Eliot Norton Lectures for 1939–40. (Cambridge, Mass. 1942; English transl., Cambridge, Mass. & London, 1947)
[3]Ibid., transl. Arthur Knodel & Ingolf Dahl, ch. 1
[4]Ibid., ch.4
[5]Ibid., ch.4

In the series of theatrical works, *Petrouchka*, *Le Sacre du Printemps* and *Les Noces*, Stravinsky's Dionysian tendencies were at their apogee. After *Les Noces* Stravinsky made an apparently final and quite voluntary sacrifice to Apollo. The Dionysian elements never return in the same force. Instead we get the fullest possible development of Stravinsky's passion for classical order, clarity of texture and precision of technique. That is why *Les Noces* is both a summation and a turning point.

After the production of *Le Sacre du Printemps* in 1913, Stravinsky settled with his family in Switzerland. In June 1914 he made his first visit to England, in order to attend performances of *Le Rossignol*.[6] In London he had the first embryonic conception of the work which nine years later would be completed as *Les Noces*. He imagined, so he writes in *Chronicle of My Life* 'a grand divertissement, or rather a cantata, depicting peasant nuptials'.[7] After this visit to London he made a short trip to Russia — partly in order to secure material for the new composition. To quote from Eric Walter White's *Stravinsky*:

> At Kiev he picked up a copy of the volume in Peter Kirjeievsky's *Collection of Popular Poems* devoted to marriage songs; and he arranged for various books, including Sukharov's *Collection* and *Dal's Dictionary of Russian Phrases,* to be sent to him from his father's library. A fortnight after his return to Switzerland via Warsaw, Berlin and Basle, war broke out. Thenceforward, he and his family were to live in exile, completely cut off from their native country.[8]

It is ironical that having mentioned exile I now discuss Stravinsky's Russian-ness. It is usual to equate the Dionysian element in Stravinsky's early music with his Russian birth, and the Apollonian element of his later music to western influences. In a rough and tumble way this is probably correct. The point I want to make is that Stravinsky had a natural sympathy for both the religious mysticism of the Russian soul, and the sceptical pessimism. In *Petrouchka* the pessimism is at its strongest. *Le Sacre du Printemps,* on the other hand, is a drama of renewal. But it is a renewal only at the cost of sacrificing a virgin girl. Life is only renewed by death. Yet life is renewed — if only by an ecstatic religious rite. *Les Noces* is also a drama of renewal, through marriage and the begetting of children — but where *Le Sacre du Printemps* is deadly serious, *Les Noces* is

---

[6]Given at Drury Lane Theatre, with Emile Cooper conducting, in June, 1914

[7]*Chroniques de ma vie* (Paris, 1935); English translation, *Chronicle of My Life* (London 1936), p.90

[8]*Stravinsky: A Critical Survey* (London, 1947), p.54

fundamentally comic (in the high sense), though the same ingredients of religious feeling and sceptical pessimism are in the theatrical mixture. The more primitive pagan men and women of *Le Sacre* have changed, in *Les Noces,* to hard-headed, warm-hearted, naïvely religious Russian peasants. And though in a sense peasants are the same the world over, these peasants are, I should have thought, unmistakably Russian. He says:

> According to my idea, the spectacle should have been a divertissement, and that is what I wanted to call it. It was not my intention to reproduce the ritual of peasant weddings; and I paid little heed to ethnographic considerations. My idea was to compose a sort of scenic ceremony, using as I liked those ritualistic elements so abundantly provided by village customs which had been established for centuries in the celebration of Russian marriages. I took my inspiration from those customs, but reserved to myself the right to use them with absolute freedom.[9]

This was written to explain his disagreements with Diaghilev over the eventual choreography to the first performance in 1923. I think Stravinsky had to pay the price that time for not having had earlier conference and consultation with the choreographer. The real point is, I think, that already in *Les Noces* we have that scaling down of orchestral apparatus, which is so colossal in *Le Sacre,* and which he seemed to need then to express the violence of the ritualistic dynamism, towards the tiny scale of *Histoire du Soldat,* the Wind Octet and later works. It was all part of the sacrifice to Apollo. And what was sacrificed (and perhaps had to be sacrificed because of exile) was inspiration from Russian customs, and the divisions of the Russian soul. One should think, for a moment, of the nostalgia of another and contemporary Russian composer, Rachmaninov. Stravinsky can give expression to a fundamental pessimism, but not to nostalgia. This sceptical pessimism (and the religious element) is still there in a later stage-work like *The Rake's Progress,* quite translated from Russian peasants into English eighteenth-century dandyism. But I doubt if the essentials have really changed.

During the first world war years Stravinsky lived in Switzerland and worked slowly on the vocal piano score of *Les Noces,* along with some lesser works. He became great friends with the Swiss writer Ramuz. Ramuz has described in his *Souvenirs sur Igor Stravinsky* what an intriguing figure Stravinsky was to the village women of Morges,

---

[9]*Chronicle of My Life*, pp. 174–75

during the composition of *Les Noces*. How the women sat knitting in the little square onto which Stravinsky's upper apartment window looked, and how, when a particularly violent sound of the piano issued from the work room in the ground floor they would look up and say: 'C'est le Monsieur Russe.'[10]

Ramuz agreed to do the translations of Stravinsky's Russian texts into French. He gives a fascinating account of how they tackled the problem. Stravinsky explained first of all that his verbal accents in Russian sometimes did and sometimes did not coincide with the musical accents. Because he felt that there would be monotony if either coincidence or non-coincidence were made a rule. But in general the accents do in fact coincide; and Stravinsky demanded from Ramuz that the French text had as exact a correspondence. Stravinsky gave Ramuz a word for word translation of the Russian and made him write down into a notebook the number of syllables in each word, the verbal accents, and then a metrical scheme of each voice part. Ramuz tells how he went home each evening on the last train his head full of $\frac{3}{8}$s and $\frac{5}{8}$s and every kind of 4×8. Because *Les Noces* has as one of its main musical features the uninterrupted flow of additive rhythm — that is, a never ending series of longs and shorts, $\frac{2}{8}$ or $\frac{3}{8}$ (counted 1, 2 or 1, 2, 3,) combined into various larger groups, but always variable and free. During the morning Ramuz found, if he could, the best French text that would do what the composer demanded, and in the evening, in Stravinsky's home, it went on again. Slowly enough the whole work was translated. When I quote the words to *Les Noces,* I shall use Ramuz's text, because it is in essentials also Stravinsky's.

Stravinsky sometimes repeats monosyllabic words arbitrarily to fit the music — or even syllables within a word. Thus the whole work opens with a sentence about combing Nastasia's hair, which runs grammatically:

Ma tresse à moi, elle l'avait peignée avec un peigne d'argent.

The line of the music has to give an effect of bells — marriage bells presumably — and to fit the music the sentence actually runs:

Tresse, Tresse, ma tresse à moi, ma tresse à moi,
Tresse, elle l'avait peignée etc

Now although the music to *Les Noces* was finished by 1918, Stravinsky could not find the right orchestration. He began first of all with a few pages of scoring for the kind of orchestra one might

---

[10]C. F. Ramuz: *Souvenirs sur Igor Stravinsky* (Lausanne, 1929), p.76

have expected from the composer of *Le Sacre*. It needed perhaps 150 players and was therefore abandoned. Besides, Stravinsky began to see that his continuously singing voices were the real instrumentalists, so to speak, that they did what in *Le Sacre* the strings and wind did. So he decided to accompany the voices by only instruments of percussion. And he naturally thought of those that were most novel to him at the time. The first of these was the mechanical piano, the pianola. He was fascinated by this novelty of that time and so his new scoring began with an electrically driven pianola.

Next, he was exceedingly taken with the Hungarian gypsy instrument, the cimbalom: and partly because in playing it the strings are struck by the player, with his two mallets, openly, for all to see. He was captivated by the virtuosity of the Hungarian player Aladar Rácz, who was in Switzerland at that time. (I myself had the good fortune to hear Rácz as an older man play privately at Budapest, in 1948. It was extremely exciting.) Anyhow, Stravinsky had managed to acquire a cimbalom and had even taught himself to play it. So the new scoring had two cimbaloms — to which, with the pianola, he added a harmonium and normal percussion. He scored two tableaux in this second version, before he decided that the problem of synchronizing the electronic pianola with the rest was insoluble. Five years later he found what he really wanted. He chose an orchestra of four (non-mechanical) pianos, xylophone, timpani, two crotales and a bell (which are all instruments of percussion with a definite pitch) and added to that two side drums (with and without snares), two larger drums (with and without snares), tambourine, bass drum and triangle. (These instruments have of course no definite pitch.)

Stravinsky has always liked the piano. He likes its percussive possibilities, and the feel of his own hands playing. I'd even say that Stravinsky's music is often curiously tactile. He composes at the piano partly because he believes the fingers themselves can invent sometimes directly from some inner source. This is similar to some kinds of modern painting. But the chief thing about the final orchestration to *Les Noces* is the great step forward in clarity, mechanical precision, and hardness. The hardness is very hard indeed, but perfectly suits the unwavering linear counterpoint of the voices. There the lines are in themselves relatively simple and occasionally even soft, but they are made to overlap in ways that produce violent clashes. And these clashes the percussive orchestra deliberately makes absolutely certain and unmistakable.

Then the never-ending additive rhythms have in themselves

something quite mechanical. And again the orchestration aids and abets this mechanical effect, until it becomes in fact the chief effect. So that though *Les Noces* took Stravinsky longer to finish than any other piece of comparable length, it has an extraordinary unity. The notion of unity is one of the key notions in Stravinskian aesthetics.

The scenario of *Les Noces*, and the musical sequences that derive from the scenario, are basically very simple. There are four tableaux. In the first we see the bride being got ready by the act of combing her hair. In the second it is the bridegroom's hair that is being brushed. In the third the bride leaves her parents' house for that of the bridegroom. In the fourth the whole village partakes of a feast, and the bride and bridegroom are then put to bed, and the four parents settle down to wait outside the bedroom door.

Each tableau is stuffed out to the requisite length by small details of possible action, and by the endless repetition of small sections of text. Thus the first tableau, at the bride's house, begins immediately with the combing of the hair. There is a kind of dialogue set up between the bride's complaints about the combing and her girl friends' comments. Thus the bride says:

Pauvre, pauvre d'moi, encore une fois!

and the other girls reply in chorus:

Console toi, console toi, petit oiseau.

(It needs to be realised that the chorus who sing are not the dancers who are on stage. The singers are not always even of the same sex as the appropriate stage-figures, and they have to be imagined in the orchestral pit.) The theme of the tress of hair goes on a longish time and as a kind of rondo.

Then the bride's parents begin to sing of the nightingale in the bridegroom's garden, how it sings really for the bride:

C'est pour toi Nastasie Timofeevna,
C'est pour toi qu'il chante, qu'il chantera.

Finally we come to the religious note, the simple request to the Mother of God to come into the cottage and help arrange the hair:

Daigne, daigne très aimable mère
Entrer dans notre chaumière.

always with the burden of the girls' chorus, which comes over and over again.

In the second tableau all is male, except for the bridegroom's mother. The music quite suddenly switches to the men's voices — and yet by using the same words and the same sentiments,

Stravinsky underlines the unity in multiplicity. For the groom's men friends ask the Mother of God to *his* cottage to help with his hair.

> *Daigne, aimable mère, daigne entrer dans la chaumière,*
> *daigne nous aider les boucles à defaire, les boucles du marié.*

It is very masculine and compelling.

In the men's tableau, Stravinsky gets an effect of mundane simplicity by embedding in the ever-running music bits of text that are quite concrete, for example, where to buy the hair oil for the groom.

> *Vite, amis, jetons nous dans les trois marchés de la ville;*
> *Et là-bas, là-bas une bouteille d'huile on aura.*

and always, as with the girls', the men's chorus repeats afterwards their motto theme.

The parents of the groom now sing in turn of how their son's hair, and his person, belong now to the bride. The section begins quite gently, on a kind of variation of the bride's opening bell-theme. We eventually reach perhaps the highest point of the whole work: the family blessing. First the parents are asked to bless.

> *Et vous père et mère bénissez votre enfant.*

then all outcasts and good for nothings:

> *Rodeurs de route, traineurs de pieds et vous tous les pas grand chose,*
> *frères, arrivez,*
> *Bénissez tous le jeune prince qui va se marier.*

Then God himself and the saints.

> *Seigneur Dieu, bénis nous tous du plus grand au plus petit*

and

> *Viens avec nous! Saint Luc également.*

—altogether a wonderful build-up of ritual.

In the third tableau we return to the bride, and to the lamentation of the parents at losing their daughter. Stravinsky uses a bit of text from a fairy story: the princess happy in the parental palace.

> *Comme on voit dedans le ciel la blanche lune et le soleil*
> *Ainsi vivait dans le palais auprès de son vieux père la princesse*
> *Et elle était heureuse près de son père et de sa mère.*

But the reality is harder to bear; for the princess must go away.

> *Bénis moi, mon père, je m'en vais et plus jamais je ne reviendrai.*

And like the first two tableaux, the third also ends with a prayer — to the apostles and to Christ, to keep the wedding pair united. The music carries the voices away as the bride and her friends leave the parental house for ever.

In the fourth and last tableau, the sexes and two choruses are joined. It is to be thought of, according to Ramuz, as a room with a huge round table, where the guests eat and drink, and through doors at the back one can see the marriage bed. The jollification begins by likening the couple to two flowers:

> *La deux fleurs sur la branche, une rouge une blanche.*

But words are often now given over to just cries. There is a delightful section about a goose.

> *Qui est arrivée, arrivée? L'oie est arrivée, arrivée?*

The bride is now given to the groom with suitable advice. This section is very charming. He must sow linseed; she must wash his shirts and so on and so forth.

In all the continuous percussive sound Stravinsky must have felt the need for some lyricism. The section about the nightingale in tableau one, is matched by the more extended section here about the swan and the sea. It begins like another fairy story:

> *J'étais loin sur la mer, j'étais loin sur la mer immense.*

The orchestration is correspondingly more gentle and provides some relief.

Now a married couple are chosen to go in and warm the bed. This little section should remind us that despite the tones of resignation and even melancholy, the whole work is really gay and comic. The text is all broken up:

> *J'y va. Prends moi. Le lit est étroit. On s'arrangera.*

and so on: it is very amusing.

So we come to the last section, where the bride and bridegroom are led in to bed. The doors are closed on them; and the parents settle down with their backs to the bedroom door, and the guests facing them. The bridegroom is heard singing from within of his love. The work ends in a kind of timeless magic.

By the time *Les Noces* was all scored, Stravinsky had become friends again with Diaghilev after a temporary estrangement. Diaghilev confided the choreography of *Les Noces* to Nijinsky's sister, Nijinska. It was first performed in Paris in June, 1923, with Ansermet conducting. Stravinsky describes the staging thus:

> The framework of the decor was composed exclusively of backcloths, with just a few details of a Russian peasant cottage interior . . . the costumes [also were] very ingeniously simplified

and made uniform.[11]

Unfortunately when the ballet went to London a month later, *Les Noces* was howled down by the English critics.[12] More shame to them: for the music has outlived them.

[11]*Chronicle of My Life,* p.176
[12]See Eric Walter White: *Stravinsky: A Critical Survey*, pp.75-6

Schoenberg

(i) *Schoenberg in his letters*[1]

Schoenberg's letters are endlessly fascinating. They offer a great deal of insight into his character, and into the circumstances that led him to produce his famous method of composition with twelve notes. We ought first to remember that Schoenberg was deeply traditional in his relations to European music, especially to German music. I nearly wrote *exclusively* to German music, because in a sense I feel this to have been true. He was certainly moulded once and for all by a German musical training. This training saw harmony as the basis of all music. No student could study composition before completing a preliminary year or more investigating harmony in its own right.

It is no accident that Schoenberg's first major theoretical work was the *Harmonielehre,* of 1911, and his last, the *Structural Functions of Harmony,* of 1948. (Were I to compare all this with my own training in England, we should find it beginning, certainly, with an examination of the basis of non-metrical polyphony, as exemplified in the three-part fantasies of Orlando Gibbons, and in English music before and after Gibbons.) Only when we realise the paramount value Schoenberg attached to harmony can we see why the crisis, or (as some felt) the total breakdown of the tonal system affected him as a kind of historically inevitable end-point; why he regarded it as his task to discover *the* inevitable solution. I myself have never felt like this about the so-called breakdown of the tonal system. For I do not feel, as the Germans do, that for the purposes of my composition harmony is basic to *all* music.)

Schoenberg wrote to a fellow composer Josef Matthias Hauer:

And I meant to say also: 'Let us show the world that *music,*[2] if nothing else, would not have advanced if it had not been for the Austrians, and that *we* know what the next step must be!'[3]

This step had to be the freeing of the twelve semitones of the tempered scale from the functional harmonic relations of the tonal system, and then the replacement of the coherence (Schoenberg's cherished word) of this system by a new but analogous coherence.

[1]This is a re-drafted version of a review of 'Schoenberg's Letters', ed. Erwin Stein (London, 1964), first published in *Composer* magazine, No. 15, April 1965, pp. 2–3.
[2]Italics original
[3]'Schoenberg's Letters' op. cit., p. 104, Letter 78 (December, 1923)

As he writes from America to G. F. Stegmann (a South African music-lover who had asked Schoenberg for enlightenment regarding contemporary musical trends):

> This seems to me the most attractive feature of the method of composing with twelve tones: that, from the very beginning, to a certain degree, coherence is assured. In no other method such an advantage is offered. The kind of tonality which is preferred today, which uses all kinds of incoherent dissonances and returns without any reasons to a major triad or a minor triad, and rests there for a time and considers this the tonality of the piece, seems to me doomed.[4]

Within his own premises Schoenberg is very logical (another of his favourite words).

Dissonances are incoherent (to him) unless clearly accounted for within the systematic apprehensions of consonances and dissonances of the tonal system. As soon as these apprehensions become unsystematic they are incoherent. The twelve-tone method 'emancipated the dissonance' by reducing consonance and dissonance to non-existence within a plurality of non-tonal semi-tones. It then replaced the coherence of the old by the analogous coherence of the new system.

Another German figure, Hindemith, thought along such fundamentally harmonic lines. But his theoretical effort was directed towards demonstrating that the so-called breakdown of the tonal system was in no way total or historically inevitable. I must admit I have found, for reasons hinted at above, his *Unterweisung Im Tonsatz*[5] as unrewarding as Schoenberg's theoretical works. I cannot breathe for long in this exclusively harmonic atmosphere.

Bartok also was trained the German way. But he forged for himself a curious twelve-tone tonal system built on the cycle of fifths.[6] This harmonic system seems completely personal. Furthermore, Bartok's discovery within the heartlands of south-eastern Europe of pentatonic melodies with tremendous seminal power has proved an historically necessary step within the world-wide musical revolution in progress. Likewise with Stravinsky: in *Les Noces* we have not only additive rhythm (that breaks with the Teutonic metric system absolutely) but the use of this material to build a tremendous

---

[4] op. cit., p. 267, Letter 233 (26 January, 1949)
[5] 3 vols, Mainz, 1937, 1938 and 1970
[6] cf. Serge Moreux: *Bela Bartok, sa vie, ses oeuvres, son langage* (Paris, 1949), pp. 112–116

additive *structure* where *rhythm* is the functional force not harmony at all.[7]

Earlier still there was Debussy. His reaction to Wagnerian chromaticism, which was so widely thought to have sounded the death-knell of the tonal system, was to compose music from within different sensibilities altogether. The raw material of sound itself seems to have mattered more to Debussy than any preconceived notions about technique as such: hence his openness to influence from non-Western musics (especially the Javanese gamelan), which has been as much a watershed in twentieth-century composition as any of the accomplishments of Schoenberg and his disciples. I know it is heretical, but maybe Debussy will be eventually regarded as even more crucial to contemporary music than Schoenberg. We shall see!

Schoenberg's exile in America was in a curious way paradoxical. He found there Stravinsky and Bartok, whom he valued if not loved, but also the revered teacher Nadia Boulanger, whom, it is clear from his letters, he intensely despised: Writing to G. F. Stegmann he says:

> One of the influences which is a great obstacle to richer development is the models they (American composers) imitate. It would not be so bad to imitate Stravinsky, Bartok or Hindemith, but worse is that they have been taught by a woman of Russian-French descent, who is a reactionary, and has had much influence on many composers.[8]

Writing also to the violinist Rudolf Kolisch he says:

> . . . there is great activity on the part of American composers, la Boulanger's pupils, the imitators of Stravinsky, Hindemith and now Bartok as well. These people regard musical life as a market they mean to conquer, and they are sure they will do it with ease in the colony that Europe amounts to for them.[9]

I think it is easy to see why Schoenberg was so discomfited. Bartok, Stravinsky, Debussy are all part of the modern revolution, with often greater public acclaim than Schoenberg, and this left Schoenberg puzzled and hurt. He did not conceive how their music was anything but finally illogical and incoherent: while the indigenous popular music of America, the blues and jazz, music that was to go right around the world, was for him no possible material for music at all.

---

[7] See pp. 85–96 above
[8] op. cit., p. 267, Letter 233 (26 January, 1949)
[9] op. cit., p. 270, Letter 237 (12 April, 1949)

(ii) *Schoenberg's* Moses and Aaron[10]

Schoenberg's *Moses and Aaron* is neo-romanticism, just as Stravinsky's *The Rake's Progress* is neo-classicism. That is a melodramatic way of stating their difference, but often these over-sharp contrasts help us to find our way around and to know what we are looking at. Romanticism and classicism are enduring attitudes as well as ways of depicting periods of history. They have never absolutely excluded each other. This is why I think neo-romanticism and neo-classicism have appeared in modern music simultaneously. Neo-romanticism tends towards expressionism while neo-classicism tends towards abstraction.

There is a third modernistic tendency in opposition to both, which is anti-art or Dada, but both Schoenberg and Stravinsky have been too positive in their traditional allegiances ever to dabble with Dada. Both these tremendous figures were revolutionaries once, but are known now to be part of the unbroken continuity we call a tradition. T. S. Eliot, writing of tradition, said:

> The existing monuments [of art] form an ideal order among themselves, which is modified by the introduction of the new, the really new work of art among them. The existing order is complete before the new work arrives. For order to persist out of the supervention of novelty, the whole existing order must be, if ever so slightly, altered.[11]

Eliot's point is that the new and the old, the revolutionary and the traditional, is a two-way traffic. The old affects the new; that is obvious. But Eliot believed that what he calls the really new affects the old. If this is so, and leaving anti-art and Dada aside, then the really new works of art are only those by which our view of the whole pre-existing order of works of art is ever so slightly altered. The greatest works of Schoenberg and Stravinsky are in this category.

Traditions within which these composers have worked can still be different in locality and temper. Schoenberg was rootedly Germanic in his music. Stravinsky begins by writing music out of the Russian tradition, and it is only after what has been called the 'Sacrifice to Apollo' that his music entered into his neo-classic period. Once his

[10]This is an amended version of a BBC Third Programme talk, first published in *The Listener*, 29 July, 1965; it was prepared in relation to the Covent Garden production of *Moses and Aaron* that year

[11]T. S. Eliot: 'Tradition and the Individual Talent' (London, 1917); see *Selected Essays* (3rd edition, London, 1951), p.15

neo-classicism becomes a confirmed temper of mind, it is hardly surprising when his one full-length opera, *The Rake's Progress*, reaches back to the techniques of the eighteenth century: recitatives, arias, set ensembles. In the same way operatic neo-romanticism as in *Moses and Aaron* reaches back to the techniques of nineteenth-century German leitmotivs, transpositions of unchanging themes. Finally, Stravinsky and all his librettists are Catholic Christians, so behind Tom Rakewell stands Don Giovanni. Schoenberg's own librettist was a Jew, and his opera is deeply Judaic. There stands no direct Judaic hero behind Moses, but there seems to me to be the Nordic, non-Christian figure of Wotan. Tom Rakewell and Don Giovanni are utterly human, transcendents or gods act on them as it were from the outside. Moses and Wotan are non-human, and the problems of transcendence are inside them. Most of the theatrical time of *The Rake's Progress* and *Don Giovanni* is a presentation of their heroes' escapades, and only the final scene hints at or exemplifies a divine retribution. All the theatrical time of *Moses and Aaron* or *The Ring* is about transcendence of the Divine in contradiction with itself. Wotan's withdrawal into burning Valhalla at the end of *Götterdämmerung* is curiously similar in feeling to Moses's abdication for Aaron at the end of Act II. Perhaps that is a hint as to one of the many reasons why Act III of *Moses and Aaron* was never composed.

I think, therefore, it is worthwhile when considering the story of the opera, to examine why Schoenberg turned, for Judaic, not Christian, reasons, to the Bible.

Schoenberg was born a Jew racially. His family did not practise the cult: they were agnostic, humanist, even perhaps vaguely Christian; but anti-Semitism, especially after the Great War in Germany, affected Schoenberg deeply. He wrote to Kandinsky in April 1923:

> . . . I have at last learned the lesson that has been forced upon me during this year, and I shall not ever forget it. It is that I am not a German, not a European, indeed perhaps scarcely even a human being (at least the Europeans prefer the worst of their race to me), but I am a Jew.[12]

In 1933 he was forced to leave Germany, and as a kind of protest he formally rejoined the Jewish community which he had left as a young man. He wrote to Alban Berg about this ceremony, which took place in Paris:

> As you've doubtless realised, my return to the Jewish religion

---

[12]Letters, ed. Stein, p.88 (Letter 63)

took place long ago, and is indeed demonstrated in some of my published work . . . and in *Moses and Aaron*, which you have known since 1928, but which dates from at least five years earlier; but especially in my drama, *The Biblical Way*, which was also conceived in 1922 or 1923.[13]

Schoenberg does not bother to mention the unfinished oratorio *Jacob's Ladder* which Berg knew all about; the point for us is that *Moses and Aaron* had two forerunners, and is the artistic culmination of Schoenberg's Jewishness but not at all of Jewish racialism: solely of the Judaic sense of God, and of the impossibility of communication with the utterly transcendent. As the psalmist expressed it: 'Even the heavens are not clean in Thy sight.'

In another letter of 1933 to the author Walter Eidlitz, who had sent him his book written also about Moses,[14] Schoenberg wrote:

The elements in this tremendous subject that I myself have placed in the foreground are: the idea of the inconceivable God, of the Chosen People, and of the leader of the people. My Aaron rather more resembles your Moses, although I have not portrayed him in so many aspects or shown him in terms of his human limitations, as you have. My Moses more resembles of course only in outward aspects Michelangelo's. He is not human at all.[15]

If Schoenberg says his hero is not human, then what is he? There is no clear answer. I think this contradiction in the character is why Moses is both remote and fascinating.

Wotan is a God, reaching out through the moral contradictions of omnipotence towards the richer world of humanity. Moses, despite Schoenberg's statement, is a man reaching out towards the purity of the inconceivably omnipotent Godhead. Both fail tragically. But a work of art, as in all true tragedy, in the demonstration of their struggle enhances us.

Of Schoenberg's three elements which he placed in the foreground — the inconceivable God, the Chosen People, the people's leader — the first is the most difficult. If God is inconceivable, it is virtually impossible to represent him. In fact, as we all know from the second Commandment, representations of God in any form are Judaically taboo. Schoenberg solves this problem just as the Bible did, by allowing God to speak. In the opera this Voice is represented by a six-voice invisible choir. The Chosen People are the easiest. They are represented in the

[13]Ibid., p.184 (Letter 156)
[14]*Der Berg in der Wüste* ('The Mountain in the Wilderness'; 1923)
[15]op. cit., p.172, (Letter 151)

traditional way by the visible operatic chorus. The people's leader is difficult again, but for a different reason, and this difficulty is the essence of the drama. For Moses and Aaron are both leaders of the people but they have different views on what the nature and quality of this leadership is. This difference is set out for us in the first scene.

When the curtain rises, on Moses beside the burning bush, he is praying aloud to the

> Only God, infinite, dwelling in every thing
> Whom none can see, no mind imagine: oh God![16]

This God, then, is Judaic, not Christian. There is here no Trinity of Three in One, no Virgin Mary, Mother of God's Son. This inconceivable God speaks to Moses out of the burning bush, calling to him to be a prophet. Moses wrestles with his God in his unwillingness, springing from his humility, to take up the burden of prophecy. He only agrees because God assigns Aaron, his brother, to be Moses's voice. A hierarchy is proposed. God speaks to Moses, who speaks to Aaron, who speaks to the people. This hierarchy contains all the metaphysical problems concerning communication between the incommensurable Transcendence and the finite creature. For the purpose of poetry, a parable; for operatic representation, a bush burns which is unconsumed, and a Voice speaks from the bush. But Moses, I am sure, was really like Blake, who could perceive the infinite despite all appearances, however common, including bushes which do not burn and are silent. And Aaron also half intuits Moses's thoughts by a kind of spiritual telepathy. All this is made clear by the Voice from the burning bush:

> Just as from this thornbush,
> sombre, till the light of
> truth shone, burning through,
> so you'll hear My voice speak to you,
> through anything.[17]

With this covenant agreed, Moses accepts his calling.

In the second scene of Act I, Moses and Aaron meet and argue. Already from what I have said, you can see why Schoenberg makes Moses use only speech-song, while Aaron alone sings. It is an operatic symbol of the Moses and Aaron part of the covenant; also, why their conversation goes on simultaneously. For this simultaneity is a musical symbol of the telepathy which unites their minds

---

[16]Libretto transl. David Rudkin (London 1965), p.11
[17]Ibid., p.12

directly. But their argument is both about the problem of the covenant with God, and about the problem of the Chosen People: it is Aaron singing alone who eventually states this new matter unequivocally. Only an Almighty God could choose out so weak and downtrodden a people, to show His might and His miracles to them, to teach them to believe only in Him. But while Aaron delights in such miracles to convince the impious masses of God's power, Moses in his inner soul abhors them, so the leader of the people is fatally split in two.

Schoenberg now presents us with his third character: the Chosen People. Their disputes and arguments fill out the third scene, which then leads directly to the fourth, in which the Chosen People meet their Leader, fatally split as we have seen into two, and this Leader brings them a Covenant with a new God. This new God is, according to Moses, inconceivable, invisible, a God of pure Spirit. This new God, according to Aaron, is omnipotent, even a God of wrath and vengeance, and will show forth His power before His Chosen People by a miracle. This is just what the people want. And the new God in Aaron's view prevails. As Moses describes it, in prayer to the God of his vision:

> Almighty God, all my power has gone from me
> and my vision is helpless in Aaron's word.[18]

For within the hierarchy of the covenant, Moses's thought can only be expressed by Aaron's intuition of it.

The libretto's consequent stage-direction makes the dramatic meaning clear. It reads: 'Aaron begins to dominate the scene.'[19] So, with Moses more and more in the background, Aaron snatches Moses's staff, much as Siegfried takes Wotan's spear, and himself performs the biblical miracles of a staff turned into a snake, Moses's hand made leprous, the Nile water turned into blood. This completes Act I: it makes a splendid procession of scenes, from the calling of Moses to the co-option of Aaron to the decision of the Chosen People to flee from Pharaoh and take to the desert, with no more tangible goal than a Promised Land, far in the future.

Before Act II is a choral interlude. Once in the desert Aaron is even more in the foreground and Moses withdrawn even more into the background, until he once more reaches his own solitary vision of God. The Chosen People sense this withdrawal as a loss. 'Where is Moses?' they whisper. 'Where is this Almighty God?'[20] So that

---

[18]Ibid., p.19
[19]Ibid., p.19
[20]Ibid., p.25

when Act II begins, the stage is set for open revolt against a leader who had vanished for forty days already to the mountain-top, and against a God whose transcendence is too remote from human conditions to be communicated with. And this leads in the second scene to the idolatrous worship of the Golden Calf, an act of total and horrible impiety from Moses's point of view, of natural religious abandon from Aaron's. Certainly Schoenberg was not all on Moses's side. In the letter to Walter Eidlitz from which I have already quoted, he says:

> . . . What is interesting is that we come fairly close to each other in the introduction, formal presentation, and even in the evaluation of the scene of the Golden Calf. For me, too, this signifies a sacrifice made by the masses, trying to break loose from a 'soulless' belief. In the treatment of this scene, which actually represents the very core of my thought, I went pretty much to the limit, and this too is probably where my piece is most *operatic*.[21]

What Schoenberg means by 'most operatic' and 'pretty much to the limit' is operatic stage-spectacle. Speaking entirely for myself, I find this stage spectacle old-fashioned even although it deals with what Schoenberg calls the very core of his thought. I would have welcomed something more abstract, but I do not suppose this fantastic scene, the dances round the Golden Calf, strikes anyone else that way. The dances move from religious exaltation to bestiality, human sacrifice. Exhaustion follows satiety, then Moses returns from the Mountain, with the tablets of the Ten Commandments. To the Golden Calf he cries: 'Away! Vile Image of impotence that would bind the Boundless on a bounded image.'[22] And so the Calf vanishes. The Chosen People cry:

> *The gleam of the gold is no more.*
> *Now our god is out of sight again*
> *All our joy, all our rapture, all we'd hoped for*
> *. . . is gone*
> *All again is dark and lightless.*
> *We must run away from this Power.*[23]

This final scene of the act is a tremendous dispute between the brothers. The quick-tongued Aaron wins the day. He argues that even the Tables of the Law are some kind of graven image. In

---

[21]Letters ed. Stein, p.172
[22]op. cit., p.32
[23]op. cit., p.32

despair, Moses breaks them. Aaron then shows Moses how through him, Aaron, the Chosen People are led by the pillar of fire at night and the pillar of smoke by day. To Moses this is still idolatry. So, left alone, he sinks in despair to the ground:

> *So I am defeated.*
> *That was all delusion, then, I*
> *Believed before,*
> *None can, none may give Him utterance.*
> *Oh Word, Word, Word, that I lack!*[24]

Schoenberg finished the music to the end of Act II, but he never wrote the music to Act III. The libretto which he did write has one long scene of further dispute between the brothers. Aaron is somehow in chains, and Moses in the ascendant. Nothing in the finished two earlier acts hints at how or why this reversal is obtained. Moses finally releases Aaron for him to live as he can, but Aaron at once falls dead. There is no biblical authority for this scene; Aaron in fact outlived Moses, and there is no dramatic inevitability. I am certain Schoenberg sensed this. I am even more certain that Covent Garden was right to produce the opera in two acts, and not to have the libretto of the third act either read or spoken over a repetition of some music in the first act. This second attempted solution, which was used in the Berlin performance which I saw, is particularly unpleasant and stupid. If *Moses and Aaron* is a torso, it is a torso of immense satisfaction and significance. Fate somehow intervened for it to be left to posterity in this form. It must be accepted as it is, and rejoiced in.

When we come to consider the music there are problems: but not of the music itself; in my opinion, only, of the intellectual and emotional attitudes that bedevil us all from the outside. These attitudes — pros and cons — are so embedded that they will not be changed by anything I say here. So I am going to cut through the crust of this attitudinizing to the music itself. For the music is indeed intellectually and emotionally ordered, and this order can be tolerably discussed pragmatically without descent into mere grammatical parsing.

I have said that *Moses and Aaron* is in the tradition of neo-romanticism. Its forebears are the operas of Wagner, not Verdi. Essential to this tradition is the notion of the opera being musically through-composed; it is all in one piece: not so much by the proportion of the individual numbers, as all Verdi is, but by the

---

[24]op. cit., p.35

endless variation of a limited set of procedures — particularly chosen for the opera in mind. These procedures can be of many kinds, but their signal character is to be germinatory.

The simplest example is that of the musical procedure which opens *Tristan and Isolde*, because we all now accept the extraordinary fact that the whole of that enormous opera proceeds somehow from the opening harmonic and melodic sequence. I put harmonic before melodic deliberately; without the underpinning harmony, the melodic movement is merely banal. I believe Schoenberg to be in this respect — that is, in regard to the contrast between melody as a self-generating totality of line, and melody as conditioned by the underpinning harmony — entirely German. This is the tradition in which *Moses and Aaron* has been composed, and if you can appreciate it in Wagner you will appreciate it in Schoenberg. *Moses and Aaron* begins, like *Tristan*, with just such a German harmonic procedure.

Just as the *Tristan* motto carries us immediately to the heart of the matter, the romantic love, so the *Moses and Aaron* motto carries us immediately into the heart of Schoenberg's matter: the representation, the symbolization, of pure spirit, of the single, eternal omnipresent, invisible and inconceivable God. The sound that we hear is a six-voice choir. There are no words to this, true to the music of the angels, only a single vowel 'O'.

The musical procedure is simply a set of four three-part chords which resolve or move in such a way that they form a kind of internal symmetry — intellectually and emotionally complete. They never return in this pristine purity, but they return in variations, endlessly and inexhaustibly. Their first appearance occupies three bars; at bar twelve comes a six-note theme which also returns in variations endlessly and inexhaustibly. As much as *Tristan* is derived from the initial bars, so the whole of *Moses and Aaron* can be shown to derive from these chords and this theme. This is of no intrinsic importance, but we should be conscious of it. I speak of it because this is to help place the opera for us in the unbroken history. I must dramatize this point all over again. Stravinsky's *The Rake's Progress* lies within the tradition of neo-classicism. It was preceded in the composer's *The Poetics of Music* by an acclamation to Bellini and the power of line.[25] *Moses and Aaron* lies within the tradition of neo-romanticism, or, if you prefer, expressionism. *Moses and Aaron* therefore is musically extremely close-knit; it is a pattern of sound symbols and reaches back to many such tremendous patterns of

---

[25]Stravinsky: op. cit., lecture 2

sound symbols. The final disposition of these musical symbols, when Moses falls in his despair to the ground at the very end, has a mastery that is deeply, tragically moving, a frightening but glorious moment of the theatre.

Kodaly, Bartok and Nationalism[1]

(i)

Vaughan Williams, when he first heard *Bushes and Briars* sung to him by an elderly Essex labourer, thought that he had encountered the natural soul of the nation.[2] At about the same time — that is, when he and Cecil Sharp began collecting English folk-songs — Kodaly and Bartok were engaged in similar work in Hungary: and they too felt drawn to make folk-music the basis of their individual musical idioms. Kodaly writes thus of the expanding horizons produced by such nationalist enthusiasm:

> . . . nearly all the peoples in Europe begin to speak their own language. Even America is still seeking for the musical expression of her own spirit. All of them had to start with the surface, the most accessible layer. As the miner penetrates gradually deeper, so the musicians can reach deeper and deeper into the strata of the inscrutable national soul.[3]

Kodaly's rhetoric is too imprecise. The history of nationalism in this century has been much more curious. I don't think Kodaly understood the matter of America — either Scott Joplin in Louisiana, or Charles Ives in Connecticut, both his contemporaries. With Ives, we have a kind of primitive frontier mentality that seized upon anything sung or played in the streets, the front parlour or the church: this was then combined, with complete sophistication (the non-primitive mentality), into an elaborate web of sounds whose strands need to be 'referred back' for its total effect to be understood.

With all these figures, the nationalist impulse was part and parcel of an attempt to come free of teutonic musical and sometimes, also, political domination. Kodaly, indeed, was not alone in turning to Debussy and French music generally as an alternative source of ideas about compositional technique.

However, the movements that began as nationalist became by the middle of the century markedly internationalist. The natural course of most popular music since then has been towards the cultivation of an international audience, and even an international 'style'. Jazz

---

[1]Based on a BBC radio interview with John Amis, 10 October, 1967
[2]cf. Ursula Vaughan Williams: *RVW—A Biography of Ralph Vaughan Williams* (London, 1964), p. 66
[3]Percy Young: *Zoltan Kodaly* (London, 1964), Foreword by the composer, pp. vii-viii

seeping under the Iron Curtain; the Beatles going to India; Henry Cow playing 'progressive' rock in communist-run Italian towns; Balinese gamelan orchestras coming to Sadler's Wells: they all sound the death-knell for older forms of nationalism in music. Whether current ethnomusicology (which, I was told by a lady in Texas, a few years back, would soon be 'taking over' the university music departments!) can match its conservationist impulse with equally strong creative stimulus remains to be seen. Certainly, the nationalism of the future looks like being a very hybrid kind.

In all this, a figure like Kodaly tends to lose out. For a start, he concentrated so much effort into choral music, which evidently meant a lot to him:

> All my activity, musical or other, was devoted entirely to my country. It was for me an unexpected pleasure and satisfaction, that my work found so many friends abroad, especially in English speaking countries.

> Does this mean, perhaps, some mental affinity? We discussed that several times with the late Professor Edward Dent; both peoples are fond of singing, assert justice and exercise humanity.[4]

Kodaly seems here to draw a veil over the lack of justice and humanity that have often prevailed in his native country: but leaving that aside, the sheer language problem has prevented his many settings of Hungarian texts from gaining him wider recognition. There are some notable exceptions, of course, such as the *Psalmus Hungaricus* (which stands up well in Dent's translation) and the *Missa Brevis* (sung in Latin). But the element in Hungarian music that is probably best disseminated *to the wider world* is that which is not so tied to the inflexions of language. (If Kodaly had been English, he would undoubtedly have had a better deal: for English has become more and more indispensable as an international tongue). Bartok, concentrating his attention on instrumental music, soon (if only posthumously) inherited the world-wide audience for the classics of the concert repertoire. Even Carl Orff has made more impact, through his interest in *instrumental* innovation for the classroom. Kodaly, far more absorbed in educational work than either Bartok or Vaughan Williams, dissipated too much of his creative vitality. By the end, he was indeed beloved of his countrymen for giving such genuine attention to their musical well-being. But he paid the price for all this as a composer.

---

[4]Ibid., p.viii

(ii) *Bartok in his Letters*[5]

I am no Bartok scholar, but I feel a particular sensibility to his genius and to what I imagine to have been his temperament. I never met him and saw him only once. He came with his second wife, Ditta, to England just before the last war and played with her the Sonata for two Pianos and Percussion.[6] After the concert he was dawdling by the piano and our eyes accidentally met as I watched him from among the seats. I remember the sense of being for a second the object of an acute spiritual vision, which seemed to look at once right inside me from right inside himself. I am certain he had no consciousness of the extreme subjective impression this moment made on me, and which I can recall to this day with eidetic accuracy. But I am also certain I saw something of the real Bartok, if only by intimation.

Sometime after the war, in a radio talk at Schoenberg's death, I spoke of Bartok when discussing the relation of creative artists to movements and cliques. I said: 'So universal in our time seems this experience of collectivities, parties, groups, that the really strange figures are those who do the dedicated, difficult work, who face the crises alone, Bartok, for example. He had as tough a struggle in Budapest as Schoenberg in Vienna. What gave him the strength to stand so alone? and is that strength a value of his music? Personally, I believe so.'[7] And of course I still believe so. Bartok's letters cannot truly confirm this judgement, but they make it credible. In an early letter to his mother, he writes:

> . . . yet there are times when I suddenly become aware of the fact that I am absolutely alone. And I prophesy, I have a foreknowledge, that this spiritual loneliness is to be my destiny.[8]

Admittedly this may have been 'prophecy' out of a momentary mood, but one suspects it rings deeper.

Bartok did not enjoy writing letters. He cries:

> But letter writing is my weak point; it is such a torture to me that as long as possible I go on putting it off from one day to the next.[9]

This means that to a large extent only those letters which *had* to be

---

[5]From the Preface to *Bela Bartok: Letters,* edited & annotated by Janos Demeny (London, 1971), pp. 9–10
[6]ISCM Festival concert, June, 1938
[7]Michael Tippett: *Moving into Aquarius,* (1958, pp.34–35; 2nd edn., 1974, p.38)
[8]op. cit. Letter 27, p. 53
[9]Ibid., Letter 201, p.256

written got written. Adding to this the natural hazards of just which letters were preserved, it is clear that the collection only mirrors Bartok's life accidentally. There are, for example, many more and quite lengthy letters about folk-song collecting than about composition. But all the same he *was* a composer first and foremost, although the work in folk-song was passionate and dedicated. To get the relation between composition and folk-song right would mean a prolonged study from other sources. It is the tiny hints, by occasional remarks in the letters, about what things meant to Bartok that are so rewarding. Thus in one of the letters to Delius he writes:

> I think the language of these piano pieces is less deliberate and strained than that of the Suite. Since writing them, I have regained some inner 'harmony', so that, today, I am not in need of the contradictory . . . dissonances which express that particular mood. This may be the consequence of allowing myself to become more and more influenced by folk music.[10]

Bartok uses the word 'dissonances' in other letters, also, and in much the same sense: a mixture of the musically objective and the subjective expressive, i.e., having regained some inner (subjective) 'harmony', he does not need so much 'contradictory musical dissonance', an interesting polarity.

The final letters, from America, are of course clouded by the gradual accession of the leukaemia which killed him. As I know from other personal sources, he was desperately, sometimes almost pathologically, troubled also in mind (when he felt driven to leave as the Nazis overran Europe). These tensions of mind and body could not predicate a new life in a New Found Land. But nevertheless he is a true part of that artistic emigration to America as European culture went foul in the concentration camps. Out of the values for which he fought—nationalism and internationalism, those of his own folk, those of the world—maybe some rebirth of those cultures that went foul must one day come.

---

[10]Ibid., Letter 73, p.105

The Noise in the Pool at Noon: the Music of Charles Ives[1]

In this country, as yet, we know the music of Ives chiefly through records and the BBC's transmission of them. Most of his work has been recorded now in America and most of these discs are commercially available here. The sleeve-notes of some are good, concise and informative. I am referring not so much to the circumstances of Ives's life (which are by now pretty well-known in the relevant circles in Britain) as to the proper place of his music in the formation of an American tradition, if such a national tradition is thought to be at all possible or viable in our age. I certainly think it is for an area of social experience as huge as North America. (The problems of an English, or British, national musical tradition in relation to a comparable area to the west, and to the much smaller, but more intensive, area of Europe to the east are different and for the moment much less clear-cut).

On the assumption that we can speak of a potential national experience in the United States which might be reflected in literature and music, I shall quote from the sleeve-note to the Ormandy recording of *Three Places in New England,* possibly Ives's best single work. (It is lamentable that this is not yet in the regular repertoire of any first-class English orchestra). The note, by James Goodfriend, discusses Copland and Ives as representative *American* composers:

> There is no false magic in this. It rests on the fact that there are certain things today common to virtually all of us (Americans), not ethnic or racial qualities, but the stuff of everyday experience, of growing up in some part of this country. Just about every American, at some point in his life, will have eaten a hot dog and Southern-fried chicken and Thanksgiving dinner, heard the music of a Broadway show, a Negro spiritual, a hymn, a mountain tune, a square dance and a cowboy song, watched a parade, seen a Western movie, chewed on a straw or a pine needle, read or heard a bit of Emerson or Thoreau, drunk a malted milk, sung 'My country, 'tis of thee', and had a thousand and one other experiences that together make up life at this time and this place. Both Ives and Copland dipped their hands into this enormous stock of American sound and experience, and each made a personable and viable music of it.[2]

[1]First published in *The Listener,* 5 June 1969
[2]CBS record

If we add Gershwin to this list of names we do indeed come close to the real popular (in the sociological sense) basis of American music. Because Gershwin equally dipped his hand into the 'enormous stock of American sound' and equally made a 'personal and viable music of it'. (A notable omission from Goodfriend's list of American sounds is jazz).

Now, because of the spoken language and the early development of literature in the colonial period, American writing has always had English literature as its earlier tradition. But the universities in America are chiefly German in tradition, not English. And the music schools have been entirely German. This is part of the reason why Schoenberg and Hindemith fitted into America so easily, and perhaps one reason why Bartok didn't. The only other great academic musical figure has been Nadia Boulanger. Nobody English at all, apart from Holst, whose stay at Harvard University lasted only six months because of illness (amongst his pupils was Elliott Carter).

Ives lived and worked right outside this American-German musical world; and, quite apart from his experimental methods, this, as well as his own 'Sunday-composer' attitude, made his music difficult at first for his countrymen. It still makes his music unacceptable to those — and they are many — who remain hung up in the narrow world of Schoenberg and Webern and their present-day epigones. It would not be proper for me as an Englishman to give advice to Americans as to where their true traditions lie. After all, with the great immigrations from Europe of the nineteenth century, America has many more ethnic groups than Wasp and Negro.

German music might literally transplant to the United States along with the Germans. But, though the ethnic groups — like the New York Jews, for example — are far bigger, longer-lived and tougher than the melting-pot theory would take account of in the short run, I have the feeling that, in the long run, Goodfriend's description of American life as presenting an enormous stock of common sounds and experience as 'stuff' for the composer is the right one. Ives, Gershwin, Copland have all responded to it in their varying ways.

Ives was a New Englander, and has been called 'pragmatic, level-headed'. He was an insurance executive. 'I have experienced a great fullness of life in business,' he wrote. 'You cannot set an art off in the corner and hope for it to have vitality, reality and substance.' And again: 'My work in music helped my business, and my work in business helped my music.' But if Ives found a complementary relationship between his business and his art, there is also, I think, a complementary relationship, within the music itself, between the externally derived sounds and experiences (brass bands, hymn tunes, Fourth of July jollifications, historic occasions of the War of Independence etc) and the inner sensibilities, intimations of the spirit, in the tradition of the literary Flowering of New England before the Civil War. This dichotomy between inner tenderness and outer toughness runs through all American experience — there is, for instance, a longing for primal innocence even within the violence of the frontier. I find this tradition fascinating, though often alien. (At the risk of its being merely a play on words, I hazard the remark that perhaps the true English tradition is opposite — outer tenderness and inner toughness.)

Like all such dichotomies within the psyche, individual or collective, the American dichotomy can generate enormous forces, destructive or creative. Thus Black Power, and the literature that expresses it, are absolutely caught up in this ambivalence. But with Ives the ambivalence is not so extreme or so violent. For all that he belongs within the total American experience, he is also bound within the limitations (if that is the right word) of his New England heritage and his period. His apprehensions should be set beside the extraordinary remark of Emily Dickinson:

'. . . and the noise in the pool at noon excels my piano.'[3]

This half-sentence might be an exact description of the tiny moment of visionary, almost silent sound which comes at the end of Ives's *Fourth of July* after the *fff*'s of the multiple brass bands. These often minute visionary moments are difficult to bring off in performance just because they are so intense, so short and yet so inwardly tender.

In practice we usually try first to find our way to Ives by thinking of him as an American experimenter before his time. We wonder at his collages of sound, his complexes of cross-rhythms, his dissonances, his transcendental difficulties of performance (as with the *Concord Sonata*). But the 'noise in the pool at noon' is what all the noise of the collages, and the cross-rhythms, and the dissonances, are to uncover. I do not think any American music does this with the power and vision of American literature. The literary tradition is, of course, much older. Ives is already two generations beyond the

---

[3]Emily Dickinson, Letter to Thomas Higginson, 25 April, 1862: 'They are better than Beings — because — they know — but do not tell — and the noise in the Pool, at Noon — excels my piano.'

Flowering of New England. So he is a pioneer (in American music), not a late cultivator. His experiments can become uncouth, his philosophical transcendentalism can overwhelm his art. (This is nearly the case in *The Unanswered Question.*)

In the *Three Harvest Home Chorales* Ives is trying to break up the rigidities and banalities of New England church music by means of tonal and rhythmical experiment. They are set for choir, organ and brass. The original manuscript was lost early in this century and it is not known how much Ives rewrote them in his later revision. *General William Booth enters into Heaven* is a setting of Vachel Lindsay's poem, which Ives first composed as a solo song and later arranged, with the collaboration of John Becker, as a piece for solo voice and small orchestra (with choir voices occasionally used as a kind of off-stage chorus). This second version is the better. Ives's purpose here is to lift the usual, obvious and even sentimental music of Salvationists ('Are you washed in the blood of the Lamb?') by dramatic force to a true visionary level. It is thus, in small, an epitome of everything that Ives was aiming at: to accept the local, the contemporary, the immediate, and so transform it, or contrast against it, that we obtain glimpses of a visionary, even transcendental reality.

4
A Child of our Time

T. S. Eliot and *A Child of Our Time*[1]

It was quite by accident that I came into contact with T. S. Eliot. Yet soon he was to turn into a sort of artistic mentor. I met him through Frank Morley, an American colleague of Eliot's. Morley was seconded from Harcourt Brace, the New York publishers, to Faber & Faber in London, where Eliot worked in the afternoons. Morley's younger son, Oliver, then about six, while musically very gifted, was virtually inarticulate verbally. If he spoke at all he would make remarks like: 'That dog barks in B flat.' This was a real headache for the family. Morley asked W. H. Auden for advice. Auden recommended me, as someone musically well versed and interested in psychology. Thus it came about that Morley visited me at my tiny cottage (two up, two down) in Limpsfield, Surrey, on his way home to Crowhurst, further south down the road. The notion was that I should 'teach' Oliver at the piano about his obsessively beloved music, in order to tempt him to speak. Terms were discussed and agreed: and all the time I could see through the window, mooching about the minute grass frontage, the famous figure in the clerical hat — Eliot himself.

Through Oliver, I got to know the Morley family. On summer weekends, I bicycled over to enjoy some vicarious family life — only to find that Eliot, who had rented rooms nearby (they were soon known as Uncle Tom's Cabin), also turned up at the house proper. On such occasions, he divested himself of his poet's mantle and helped Morley's wife in her domestic duties, both in the kitchen and in the garden (where once I found him studiously picking blackcurrants). After supper in the evenings we all played monopoly. Eliot was, in fact, quite good at monopoly. The problem was always Oliver. If Oliver ever lost, it was simply calamitous. Eliot bore with it all, good-humouredly. (Oliver, I ought to mention, had

[1] A newly extended version of an essay first published in *The Composer's Point of View*, ed. Robert S. Hines (University of Oklahoma, 1963), pp. 111–122

an amusing side to his nature. He loved to show off — most of all, by standing on his head. Once I took him to hear Schnabel play a recital of late Beethoven piano sonatas. In the interval, Oliver did a head-stand in the foyer!).

Although we had no professional involvement, I managed to talk to Eliot extensively then about the nature of poetry and drama: matters which were deeply occupying his own mind at that time (i.e. 1936–8). Our talks took place later in his room at Faber & Faber's. I would indicate that I'd like to see him and he would generally invite me to tea. At these tea-time conversations he (above all others) helped me clarify my notions of the aesthetics of theatre and opera. Unwittingly, he became my spiritual father. Sometimes he even guided my reading. For instance, it was through Eliot, later, that I came to read and identify closely with Yeats. Gradually, after the War, I saw less of him, for one reason or another. I remember one late encounter at a lunch-party given by the Sitwells (one of several which I attended, where a surprisingly tolerant attitude was taken to my irreverent leftist views). Eliot had just returned from Sweden where he had been awarded the Nobel Prize. Drily, he told of his discomfiture when, just before dinner with the King, he had received back his only spare underwear from the laundry, in an impossibly shrunken state. On his return to England he had to buy replacements and parted with an appalling number of clothing coupons!

My last meeting with Eliot was in Edinburgh, at one of the performances of the first production of *The Elder Statesman,* in 1958. I found myself sitting beside him. Both of us were unaccompanied, so we were able to talk freely. I chided him gently, I recall, for going so far away from the poetic language of *The Family Reunion* to the near-prose of the subsequent plays. Would he move back once more towards poetry? He said it was possible. If that was truly in his mind, it was not in his fate.

In the early days, before the war, I must have known Eliot better than I can now recall, for when I came to write *A Child of Our Time,* I plucked up courage to ask him if he would provide a text. This he agreed to do, as long as I gave him a precise scheme of musical numbers, and an exact indication of the number and kinds of words I considered necessary for each musical section. I returned home to do just this for him, because I saw at once what he meant. In oratorio or opera, the musical schemes must be paramount, if the work is to live. I had not read Susanne K. Langer at that time, but taught, in part, by Eliot, I instinctively appreciated her dictum:

'Every work of art has its being in only one order of art; compositions of different orders are not simply conjoined, but all except one will cease to appear as what they are.'[2] So that, while drama eats up all incidental music and painted stage sets, 'music,' in Miss Langer's words, 'ordinarily swallows words and action creating (thereby) opera, oratorio, or song'.[3]

This then was the reason Eliot demanded that I, as the musician, prepare a musical scheme, before he as a poet did anything whatsoever. Also, since he knew as well as I did that narrative recitative needs many words, while a vocal fugue may use next to none, he asked for precise directions concerning the numbers and kinds of words. As he expressed it: 'I need my homework set for me.'

I put down on paper for Eliot what has been recently unearthed under the title, *Sketch for a Modern Oratorio*[4] (the final title for the piece had not then appeared). Eliot considered this *Sketch* for some weeks and then gave me the surprising advice to write all the words myself. He felt the *Sketch* was already a text in embryo (as, in fact, it was), and whatever words he, Eliot, wrote would be of such greater *poetic* quality they would 'stick out a mile'. While remaining true to his belief in the primacy of the *musical* imagination in opera and oratorio, he considered the *poetically* imaginative words of a real poet to be often unnecessary.

Thus it was that I began the somewhat unusual task for a composer: to invent or find the necessary words for my own musical scheme.

Set down coldly like this, it might almost appear as though the musical scheme which the composer needs is to be sought for or conceived as absolutely independent of his dramatic or other verbal material. But the issue is only one of *primacy*. In the case of *A Child of Our Time* the inner feelings, which could only be expressed in some artistic image, were finally given objective substance in the musical scheme of an oratorio. But the dramatic and even philosophic material which the music had to 'swallow' was entirely embedded in the gradually forming musical apprehensions from the very start. A great deal of this fusion of words and music is of necessity traditional. Or rather, there are certain constructive or functional practices which are basic and unchangeable. If the dramatic material

---

[2] Suzanne Langer: *Problems of Art* (London, 1957), p. 85
[3] Ibid., p. 85
[4] See pp. 127–187 below

requires narrative, then this part of the musical scheme will be fundamentally different from the musical correlative to the contemplation or expression of a single situation or emotion. The one is recitative and the other aria; and if they are to play their proper functional or constructive parts in the scheme, they will be, at any rate, analytically recognizable as such.

Narrative or contemplation, recitative or aria, whether for solo voice or for a chorus, these then are the basic functions in any and every scheme of oratorio. Being quite clear on the matter, I found it easier, when I came to prepare this homework for Eliot, to sketch out an embryo text, where of course my proposed words were already at one with my musical scheme.

But from music of the past, I also knew of two local traditions of arrangements which had always fascinated me. The scheme of Handel's *Messiah* and the scheme of the Lutheran *Passions*. The shape of *Messiah* is tripartite. The first part is all prophecy and preparation. The second part is epic: from the birth of Christ to the second coming, judgement, millennium and world's end. The third part is meditative: chiefly, the words of St Paul. Incomplete performances grievously impair this wonderful shape. But I have always observed and admired it. I decided to accept this format for *A Child of Our Time,* by keeping a first part entirely general, restricting the epic material to a second part, and using a third part for consequential comment.

The scheme of the Lutheran *Passions* is of course more unitary, based as it must be on the liturgical gospel set for Passion Sunday. Within that unitary scheme the traditional musico-verbal functions can always be distinguished: narrational recitative, descriptive chorus, contemplative aria, and finally the special Protestant constituent of the congregational hymn. I wanted to use *all* these functional practices within the tripartite shape borrowed from *Messiah.*

The obvious difficulty lay over the congregational hymn. A modern oratorio based on sensibilities of emotion expressive of inner and outer events in Europe and America between the world wars, and destined for the concert hall, not the church, cannot merely use the metaphorical language of liturgical Christianity. Christian hymns could not speak to agnostics or Jews; Jewish hymns could speak to the general concert-hall public even less. For to 'speak' in this sense is to do the operation which much-loved hymns do to the appropriate congregation of the faithful. But in what sense at all are listeners in a concert hall congregation of the faithful?

For some time I was at a loss. Then one never-to-be-forgotten

Sunday, I heard a singer on the radio sing the Negro spiritual, *Steal Away*. At the phrase, *The trumpet sounds within-a my soul*, I was blessed with an immediate intuition: that I was being moved by this phrase in some way beyond what the musical phrase in itself warranted. I realised that in England or America everyone would be moved in this way, forcing me to see that the unique verbal and musical metaphor for this particular function in this particular oratorio had been found. But it was not until after the world war which soon supervened that I could test in performance the fact that the Negro spiritual presented no expressional barriers anywhere in Europe. Nor maybe anywhere in the world.

I sent to America for a collection of spirituals,[5] and when these came, I had an experience possibly similar to those of the Lutheran composers. I opened the collection and found that it contained words and tunes for every dramatic or religious situation that could be imagined. I chose five spirituals, therefore, for their tunes and words, which provided the exact 'congregational' metaphor for five calculated situations in my scheme.

The next question, that of presentation, meant a further purchase from America: this time recordings of *a cappella* performances of spirituals by the relatively conventional Hal Johnson Choir (whom I remembered from the soundtrack of the film *Green Pastures*),[6] and by the 'hot' vocal group called the Mitchell Christian Singers. These latter went in for cross-rhythmical counterpoint by the spoken voice, as well as a great deal of blues-provoked ambiguity of pitch. Fascinating though this disc was, I had to forego such extreme methods of presentation, if only for the sake of the normal European concert-hall choir. I also realised that I would have to purify the harmonies and clarify the contrapuntal texture.

I did not need to use Negro material for its own characteristic flamboyance, its nostalgia or its rhythmic exhilaration (all of which are elements Gershwin uses powerfully in *Porgy and Bess*, for instance). I had to elevate this musical vernacular to take charge of feelings of a rather higher order without at all losing its immediacy of impact and appeal. This did not just mean purging the conventional harmonies of sentimentality: but rather in apparently excluding all harmonies whatsoever. I accepted the underlying conventional chord of the added seventh particular to each spiritual, and often sought variety only through rhythmic counterpoint and

[5] See p. 143, note 16 below
[6] See p. 142, note 15 below

by playing tonal masses of choral sound off against solo-voiced leaders. The harmonically static choruses, thus, at the five critical points, provided a peculiar contrast to the much more harmonically ambiguous music of the other numbers. They became periods of rest.

Having got so far, I had to accept also that this virtue of emotional release supplied by the spirituals had to be paid for by allowing the popular words and music to affect the *general* style, within which the 'sophisticated' parts of the oratorio had to be written. I used the interval of a minor third, produced so characteristically in the melodies of the spirituals when moving from the fifth of the tonic to the flat seventh, as a basic interval of the whole work — sometimes on its own, sometimes superimposed upon the open fifth below the note. These intervals (minor third, fifth, and flat seventh) could lead on the one hand to a kind of sliding chromatic fugue (cf. No.5, *Chorus of the Oppressed*); and on the other, to a Kurt Weill-like tango (cf. No.6, Tenor solo, *I have no money for my bread*); or even to a dance-like accompaniment (cf. No.27, Alto solo, *The soul of man*). Initially, there was a good deal of press criticism concerning the propriety of turning the popular into something sophisticated in this way. Subsequently, however, the spirituals have been seen as an integral and essential part of the work, and the transitions to them are regarded as effective.

When I took the *Sketch* to Eliot, I had already decided upon the five spirituals and observed their brand of folk-poetry. There were first and foremost specific references to the Bible:

> Go down Moses,
> Way down in Egypt land;

echoes of the Apocalypse:

> The trumpet sounds within-a my soul;

homely phrases such as

> Nobody knows the trouble I see

and

> I'm goin' to lay down my heavy load;

and wonderful, poetically fresh metaphors like the line from *Deep River*,

> I want to cross over into camp-ground,

which particularly stirred me. As with the Negro melodies, therefore, when I came to take stock of how I could best indicate to Eliot the kind of words I imagined suitable, I turned first to the verses of the spirituals, and noted the various metaphors I have listed above.

The taking stock was actually more elaborate. I tried to set in order all the considerations of musical and dramatic shape (*Messiah* and the *Passions*) and all the considerations which I had so long pondered concerning the dramatic and philosophic material itself. After such prolonged deliberation, I was now ready to lay down a viable scheme of numbers with their lengths and kinds, ready even to indicate by actual words what I meant. Since I was always expecting that Eliot's words would replace mine, I wrote my words on every right-hand page of the manuscript book and wrote an explanation of what I was intending on every left-hand page.

Comparing the *Sketch* with the published work, it is clear that I was able to set down straightaway a musico-dramatic scheme (of three parts, each containing several numbers) which could remain unchanged. I prefaced each part (but especially Part I) with a chorus which I considered functionally as a kind of *Prologue in Heaven* on the lines of Goethe's *Faust*: i.e. everything seen in the most general terms in relation to the cosmos. I then proceeded inward from that point. In the overall tripartite scheme, the same inward movement takes place from the general to the individual, from Part I to Part II (and then out again in Part III) as happens within Part I itself. In tabular form, it looks like this:

I   The overall pattern.

      Part I   The 'situation' in general terms: from cosmic to human.

      Part II   The effects of the 'situation' on an individual human being.

      Part III   Meditations on this drama; moving outward again toward the generally human.

II   The outward-inward-outward movement of the scheme of Part I, which was to echo the same rhythm as between the three parts:

    1 Choral overture: the 'cosmological' position.

    2 Alto solo: a generalized argument; with Alto considered as personification of the soul, whether of the world or of man.

    3 A scene of question and answer between Chorus and Alto concerning the Argument. (This and the two numbers above made up my idea of a *Prologue in Heaven*.)

    4 Bass solo: narration of the general human situation in our

     time; the Bass considered (to quote the *Sketch*) 'as a father-God figure'.

5 Choral fugue: for which I first wrote no words, simply writing, *Chorus of the Oppressed*; the Chorus personifying the generally human.

6 Tenor solo: statement of the ordinary man within this general mass; i.e. (in terms of my theme) his cry of anguish.

7 Soprano solo: statement of the ordinary woman; her cry of anguish.

8 A spiritual: the first hint of comfort, at least in simple generalized terms.

If we look back for a moment, first, at the overall pattern, we can see that if each part began with a prologue-chorus, then the choruses would be in relation to each other as well as in relation to the coming part each prefaced. Using the final text, this is how they read:

Part I   The world turns on its dark side. It is winter.

Part II   A star rises in mid-winter. Behold the man! The scapegoat! The child of our time.

Part III   The cold deepens. The world descends into the icy waters. Where lies the jewel of great price.

From the above finished example, the problems of writing or constructing one's own text to one's own musico-dramatic scheme can be seen quite easily. Thus, having decided on the function of the choral overtures and having decided that musically each was 'to be a short constructed chorus on a "text" or two "texts", to last about a minute or more' (to quote from the instruction to Eliot for Chorus 1),[7] the verbal problem reduced itself from the nebulous to the particular — to that of style and metaphor.

Eschewing the poetic, which seemed to be inappropriate to the theme, I wanted a style of short statements, whether of story or comment. I called this style to myself 'lapidaric'. Remembering the poet Wilfred Owen, killed in World War I, who had always seemed close to me in Spirit, I thought of two lines from one of his prophetic poems:

---

[7] See p. 128 below

> *War broke. And now the winter of the world*
> *With perishing great darkness closes in.*[8]

I joined this notion of seasons in history with personal experience concerning the 'dark' and the 'shadow' in C. G. Jung's terminology, and then wrote for Eliot the two texts of Chorus 1 in my own oversimple words:

> *The world turns on its dark side.*
> *It is winter.*[9]

On the opposite left-hand page, I explained discursively for Eliot what I needed, and quoted the lines from Wilfred Owen. I proceeded in this way for every number. I considered carefully the function of the proposed number, its duration, etc; invented or borrowed words that could stand as example; and wrote an explanation. Where I could think of no example, I wrote only the explanation and left the right-hand page free.

Now once Eliot had persuaded me that the *Sketch* had a viable shape, in his opinion, and that I myself had already done much of the strictly verbal work, I had to get down to filling up the gaps and the words. Not being a poet but a composer, I took endless advice, whether for whole phrases or simple words. I also hunted around in literature. Thus, for the short text needed for the choral fugue, *Chorus of the Oppressed*, I eventually twisted a sentence from Isaiah to read:

> *When shall the usurer's city cease?*[10]

And I was excited, I remember, when I made use of an anonymous 'folk' expression in a later declamatory chorus, *Let them starve in No-Man's-Land! No-Man's Land* had a fine ring to it, expressed exactly what I wanted, and joined itself admirably to the Negro metaphors, such as, I want to cross over into camp-ground, Lord. Much less successful, in my opinion, were the occasional indigestible psychological metaphors which produced phrases like

> *I am caught between my desires*
> *and their frustration*
> *as between the hammer and the anvil.*[11]

But the psychological jargon gave one tremendous phrase which is the motto for the whole work:

---

[8] See p. 128, note 2 below
[9] See p. 129, note 3 below
[10] See p. 137, note 11 below
[11] See p. 139 below

> *I would know my shadow and my light,*
> *so shall I at last be whole.* [12]

The seasonal metaphor supplies the final words (before the last spiritual):

It is Spring. [13]

Summing up, regarding this matter of shape and text, it seems to me that the composer works with himself as librettist in much the same way as he would work with a poet. However, unless he is willing to give over the whole conception of shape to the poet, he *must* prepare the poet's homework, in something like the manner of my *Sketch* for Eliot.

[12] See p. 185, note 56 below
[13] See p. 185 below

Sketch
for a
Modern Oratorio[1]

---

[1] See pp.xiv–xv above

PART I

1.

This is to be a short constructed Chorus on a 'text', or two 'texts'. To last about a minute or more. Enough to set the mood of descent. The metaphor of winter and spring is perhaps a necessary one, as will be seen later.

> ('War broke. And now the winter of the world
> With perishing great darkness closes in.')[2]

---

[2]Wilfred Owen, *The Seed;* see note 5 below

PART I

1.

CHORUS:

The world turns on its dark side. It is winter.[3]

---

[3]Final layout: *The world turns on its dark side.*
        It is winter.

2.

This solo is 'rhythmic translation', either a sort of recitative, or sung speech, rising to specific points of expression by the slight use of purely musical means. The alto voice is conceived as a personification of the soul, the anima, descended into the deeps of chaos, whence she has drawn the gods after her. The great price paid for the necessary advance in empirical science is the severance of the spiritual union with the anima. Hence the accumulation of unconscious, dark, destructive powers that burst up in man as disease, war, revolution and so forth. Man, by bringing the gods down from heaven, has brought them into his own passions and body. As yet he does not comprehend this, and so the 'Living God' is a gnawing pain in the vitals. This section is as yet simply a statement of the position; the prologue in heaven.

(The time is 2 or 3 minutes)

2.

ALTO SOLO:

The Promethean intellect has measured the heavens with a
telescope and driven the gods from their empty thrones.
But the soul, from the depths of chaos, watches the gods
return to man as vultures feeding on the liver. The living
God consumes within and turns the flesh to cancer.[4]

---

[4]*Man has measured the heavens with a telescope, driven the Gods from their thrones. But the
soul, watching the chaotic mirror, knows that the Gods return. Truly, the living God consumes
within and turns the flesh to cancer.*

See notes 46 & 48 below: cf. Jung: 'Our intellect has achieved the most tremendous
things, but in the meantime our spiritual dwelling has fallen into disrepair. We are
absolutely convinced that even with the aid of the latest and largest reflecting
telescope, now being built in America, men will discover behind the farthest
nebulae no fiery empyrean; and we know that our eyes will wander despairingly
through the dead emptiness of interstellar space. Nor is it any better when
mathematical physics reveals to us the world of the infinitely small. In the end we
dig up the wisdom of all ages and peoples, only to find that everything most dear
and precious to us has already been said in the most superb language . . .' (*Collected
Works*, transl. R. F. C. Hull, Vol. 9, Part 1, London, 1959, p.16).

3.

This dialogue is all 'rhythmic translation'. The chorus is conceived of here as mankind in general. The alto is still the world soul. The paradoxes are beyond the mass of men, so they feel a sense of powerlessness before the events (the Sept. crisis, etc) — they feel the spiritual impulses in an untempered form, out of all control, as seeds before the wind. The association to the war and the general upheaval is in Wilfred Owen's lines:

> *But now the exigent winter, and the need*
> *Of sowings for new spring, and flesh for seed.*[5]

(Time: 1 to 2 minutes.)

This more or less ends the feeling of 'the prologue in heaven', and may need an instrumental interlude[6] before the next singing.

---

[5]*The Seed:* in the second draft of this poem, entitled *1914,* these lines became:
> But now, for us, wild Winter, and the need
> Of sowings for new Spring, and blood for seed.

The Seed was published in *The Poems of Wilfred Owen,* Edited with a memoir and notes by Edmund Blunden (London, 1931); the later version, *1914,* appears in *The Collected Poems of Wilfred Owen.* Edited with an introduction and notes by C. Day Lewis (London, 1963)

[6]See note 7 below

3.

CHORUS SCENA WITH ALTO:[7]

CHORUS: Is evil then good?
                Is reason untrue?

ALTO: Reason is true to itself;
                But pity breaks open the heart.

CHORUS:[8]   We are lost.
                We are as seed before the wind.
                We are led to a great slaughter.[9]

---

[7] Linked to the previous number by an instrumental interludium
[8] Linked to the previous section by an instrumental interludium
[9] This line became: *We are carried to a great slaughter.*

4.

This is 'rhythmic translation', probably recitative like the Narrator in the Bach passions. (Time is about 1 minute.)

The Bass solo is a father-God figure, appearing as the narrator in the first part, and as the boy's uncle in the second part.

The Alto solo, in the same way, will appear as the boy's aunt in the middle part.

The Bass describes the division in the commonwealth that corresponds to the division in the individual and general psyche.

4.

BASS SOLO: THE NARRATOR.

Now in each nation there were some cast out by authority and tormented. — a human symbol of the vile thing.

Purges in the east, lynching in the west, Europe with a cancerous growth in the vitals.

And a great cry went up from the people.[10]

---

[10]*Now in each nation there were some cast out by authority and tormented; made to suffer for the general wrong. Pogroms in the east, lynching in the west; Europe brooding on a war of starvation. And a great cry went up from the people.*

5.

This should be a constructed chorus on an appropriate text, (in the manner of the populace at the foot of the cross, in Handel's *Messiah,* who sing a terrific fugue to the words: 'He trusted in God that He would deliver him, let Him deliver him if we delight in Him.') The bitterness of the oppressed will be expressed in the musical construction, as long as the text itself contains also some verbal expression of the cry.

(Time: 2 or 3 minutes, enough to stabilize the musical movement in counter poise to the realistic descriptive solos, etc)

5.

CHORUS:

(Chorus of the oppressed.)[11]

---

[11]**Chorus of the Oppressed**
When shall the usurers' city cease,
And famine depart from the fruitful land?

6.

This is 'rhythmic translation' again.

The Tenor and Soprano soloists are conceived of here as the personification, humanisation of the common man and woman (young). The metaphor should be homely, proletarian, warm and human — as a foil to the abstractions of the soul and the Father-God. The man tells of his psychological split self which appears to him, and actually is on a certain plane the frustrations of his condition in the commonwealth. He has lost the relation to his soul, to the impersonal things, hence the feminine, the women have demonic power (or he has an infantile fixation, etc.). He projects the anima on his women-folk, with devastating personal misunderstandings and complexes. But the imagery used should be entirely personal, practical and homely, so that the ordinary man listening, still embedded in concretisations, can feel himself truly expressed and understood. Without this coming down to earth, the oratorio would fail of its purpose.

(Time: 1 to 2 minutes.)

6.

TENOR SOLO:[12]

'Starvation of body and mind is eating into my spirit.

I am caught between my desires and their frustration as between the hammer and the anvil.

Women have hold on my entrails,
how can I grow to a man's stature?'[13]

---

[12]This has an extended instrumental introduction and postlude.

[13]*I have no money for my bread;*
I have no gift for my love.
I am caught between my desires
and their frustration
as between the hammer and the anvil.
How can I grow to a man's stature?

7.

('Rhythmic translation')

The Soprano voice is the young mother comforting her children; her doubts and fears. She experiences the same false dichotomy between instinct and the oppressed circumstances. Her sense of it is practical — wages, war. The imagery again must be homely, simple and warm, so that the clear young voice sings free and high; a sort of inverted cradle-song, that is also a personal expression of fear and uncertainty.

(Time: 1 to 2 minutes.)

7.

SOPRANO SOLO:

'How can I cherish my man in such days, or become a mother in a world of destruction?

How shall I feed my children on so little wages?

How can I comfort them when I am dead?'[14]

---

[14]*How can I cherish my man in such days,*
 Or become a mother in a world of destruction?
 How shall I feed my children on so small a wage?
 How can I comfort them when I am dead?

8.

Here the oratorio reaches the modern universal musical symbol. The setting will be in the style of the singing to 'Green Pastures',[15] e.g. a strong line of the spiritual and a choral descant at the back using probably the solo voices as well.

[15]Film (Warner Bros, 1936) based on *The Green Pastures — A Fable in dramatic form* by Marcus C. Connelly (London, 1930)

8.

CHORUS & SOLOISTS: A Spiritual.[16]

1.   'Steal away, steal away, steal away to Jesus!
     Steal away, steal away home—
     I ain't got long to stay here.[17]

     My Lord, he calls me, he calls me by the thunder.[18]
     The trumpet sounds within-a my soul,
     I ain't got long to stay here.

2.   Steal away, steal away, steal away to Jesus!
     Steal away, steal away home—
     I ain't got long to stay here.

     Green trees a-bending, po' sinner stand a -trembling,[19]
     The trumpet sounds within-a my soul,
     I ain't got long to stay here.'

---

[16]Taken from *The Book of American Negro Spirituals*, ed. James Weldon Johnson (New York, 1925; London, 1926)
[17]*ain't* becomes *han't* throughout the Spiritual
[18]*he* becomes *He* in this line
[19]*po'* becomes *poor*

PART II

9.

This is a short constructed chorus as at the start of Part I. In Handel's *Messiah* the second part, which follows on the joyful prophecies, starts with a grave and solemn chorus on a text which begins: 'Behold the Lamb of God . . . etc.' Something of the same feeling is wanted here. After the argument the drama begins.

A Child of our Time is the title of a story by a young German writer, (Von Horvath, d. 1936) on an allied subject, and is the sort of title needed for this oratorio.[20]

(Time: $\frac{1}{2}$ to 1 minute.)

---

[20]Odön von Horvath (b. 1901, d. 1938, *not* 1936): *Ein Kind unserer Zeit* (1938)

PART II

9.

CHORUS:

The action unfolds.

Behold the man! the scapegoat, the child of our time.[21]

---

[21]*A star rises in mid-winter.*
  Behold the man! The scapegoat!
  The child of our time.

10.

This is 'rhythmic translation' — like No. 2.

The Narrator becomes in Part II closer to earth, less distant and 'god-like'.

(Time: $\frac{1}{2}$ minute.)

10.

BASS SOLO: THE NARRATOR.

And a time came when amid the universal tyrannies and oppression one race became the symbol of persecution.[22]

---

[22] *And a time came when in the continual persecution one race stood for all.*

11.

This is a dramatic chorus such as Bach used in the Passion music for similar exclamatory choruses. It tends to 'rhythmic translation' rather than repetition of the words. It is short. The desperate questions of the persecuted will be interjected into the violence of the incitations of the persecutors.

(Time: 1 minute.)

11.

DOUBLE CHORUS OF PERSECUTORS AND PERSECUTED.

'Away with them!
Curse them! Kill them!
They infect the State.'

'Where? How? Why?
We have no sanctuary.'[23]

---

[23]Chorus 1: *Away with them!*
Curse them! Kill them!
They infect the state.

Chorus II *Where? Why? How?*
We have no refuge.

12.

This is 'recitative' again, as in No. 10

(Time: $\frac{3}{4}$ minute.)

12.

BASS SOLO: THE NARRATOR.

Where they could, they fled from the terror.

And among them a young lad escaped secretly, and was kept in hiding in a great city by his uncle and aunt.[24]

---

[24] *Where they could, they fled from the terror.*
And among them a boy escaped secretly,
and was kept in hiding in a great city.

13.

This is a declamatory chorus, like choral recitative, possibly in unison singing. It is the point at which the oratorio gets nearest to the danger zone of political polemic. Yet it is nothing newer than the scribes and pharisees before whom Pilate washed his hands! Its inclusion has to be made possible, I think, by a calm and dispassionate treatment. Time will soften the blows which fall nearest home!

(Time: $\frac{3}{4}$ minute.)

13.

CHORUS OF THE SELF-RIGHTEOUS.

We cannot have them here in our just Empires. They shall not work, nor draw a dole.

Let them starve between the frontiers.[25]

---

[25] *We cannot have them in our Empire.*
They shall not work, nor draw a dole.
Let them starve in No-Man's-Land!

14.

Recitative, as in No. 10.
    (Time: $\frac{1}{4}$ minute or less.)
        following straight into:–

14.

BASS SOLO: THE NARRATOR.

And the boy's Mother wrote him a letter, saying:[26]

---

[26] *And the boy's mother wrote a letter, saying:*

15.

This is 'rhythmic translation' as in the scena No. 3. At this point all the soloists take on human form, but the boy and the mother are the two least detached from the consequences of their actions, in the Buddhist sense. The Mother cannot foresee the terrible consequences of her letter, nor detach herself sufficiently from the past which compels her to send it. The boy likewise. The uncle and aunt are wiser as befits their closer association with their transcendental ancestry in Part I and Part III.

(Time: $1\frac{1}{2}$ to 2 minutes or more.)

15.

SCENA: THE BOY'S MOTHER, HIS UNCLE & AUNT, AND THE BOY.

MOTHER: (Soprano)	O my son, I am near to death in the terror of our race. There is no pity, only demented frenzy. Help me!
BOY: (Tenor)	Mother, Mother! What can I do?
AUNT: (Alto)	Be patient. Your young life should not be thrown away in futile sacrifice.
UNCLE: (Bass)	You are one against the world. You must accept the impotence of your humanity.
BOY: (Tenor)	But my mother . . . I must save her.[27]

---

[27]Solo Quartet: The Boy's Mother, his Uncle and Aunt, the Boy

Mother:	*O my son! In the dread terror* *they have brought me near to death.*
Boy:	*Mother! Mother!* *Though men hunt me like an animal,* *I will defy the world to reach you.*
Aunt:	*Have patience.* *Throw not your life away* *in futile sacrifice.*
Uncle:	*You are as one against all* *Accept the impotence* *Of your humanity*
Boy:	*No! I must save her.*

16.

A spiritual, describing the boy's anguish of mind and the general contemporary anguish of soul.

(Time: 2 minutes.)

16.

CHORUS: A Spiritual.[28]

    Nobody knows de trouble I see, Lord,[29]
    Nobody knows de trouble I see,
    Nobody knows de trouble I see, Lord,
    Nobody knows like Jesus.

    O brothers, pray for me,
    O brothers, pray for me,
    O brothers, pray for me, an' help me to drive ole' Satan
       away.[30]

    Nobody knows de trouble I see, Lord,
    Nobody knows de trouble I see,
    Nobody knows de trouble I see, Lord,
    Nobody knows like Jesus.

    O Mothers, pray for me,
    O Mothers, Pray for me,
    O Mothers, pray for me, an' help me to drive ole' Satan
       away.

    Nobody knows de trouble I see, Lord,
    Nobody knows de trouble I see,
    Nobody knows de trouble I see, Lord,
    Nobody knows like Jesus.

---

[28]See note 16 above
[29]*de* becomes *the* throughout the Spiritual
[30]*an'* and *ole'* become *and* and *old* throughout the Spiritual

17.

This is narrative 'recitative' with observations by the anima, e.g. the Alto voice. It is the province of the anima to observe the compulsive movements of the alter ego, which indeed are personified so often in her form.

(Time: 1 minute or a little longer.)

17.

SCENA: DUET — BASS & ALTO

NARRATOR:– The boy becomes desperate
      in his mental agony.

ALTO:–   The fate is drawn.
      The dark forces threaten him.

NARRATOR:– He goes to the Consulate.
      He is met with hostility.

ALTO:–   His other self rises in him,
      demonic and destructive.

NARRATOR:– He shoots the official . . .

ALTO:–   But he shoots only his dark brother . . .
      And lo! he is dead.[31]

---

[31]

Narrator:	*The boy becomes desperate in his agony.*
Alto:	*A curse is born.*
	The dark forces threaten him
Narrator:	*He goes to authority.*
	He is met with hostility.
Alto:	*His other self rises in him,*
	demonic and destructive.
Narrator:	*He shoots the official—*
Alto:	*But he shoots only his dark brother—*
	And see . . . he is dead.

18.

Recitative, as No. 14.

(Time: $\frac{1}{4}$ minute or less.)

18.

BASS SOLO: THE NARRATOR.

And a terrible vengeance was unleashed.[32]

---

[32]*They took a terrible vengeance.*

19.

This is a short constructed chorus like No. 5 in Part I.

(Time: 1 minute or so.)

19.

CHORUS: THE POGROM[33]

---

[33]The text became:
Burn down their houses! Beat in their heads!
Break them in pieces on the wheel!

20.

Recitative as in No. 18.

(Time: $\frac{1}{4}$ minute or less.)

20.

BASS SOLO: THE NARRATOR

THE NARRATOR:
>Men's entrails were wrung
>by what was done.
>
>There was bitterness and horror.[34]

---

[34]*Men were ashamed of what was done.*
There was bitterness and horror.

21.

A spiritual of anger.

(Time: $1\frac{1}{4}$ minutes: followed perhaps by a short musical interlude to mark the height or depth of the drama.)

21.

CHORUS: *A Spiritual*[35]

Go down, Moses,
'Way down in Egypt land;
Tell ole' Pharoah,[36]
To let my people go.

Go down, Moses,
'Way down in Egypt land;
Tell ole' Pharoah,
To let my people go.

When Israel was in Egypt's land,
Let my people go,
Oppressed so hard they could not stand,
Let my people go.
'Thus spoke the Lord', bold Moses said,
'Let my people go',
'If not, I'll smite your first-born dead',
'Let my people go.'

Go down, Moses,
'Way down in Egypt land;
Tell ole' Pharoah,
To let my people go.

---

[35]See note 16 above
[36]*ole'* becomes *old* throughout the Spiritual

22.

This is a solo like No. 6 in Part I.
It describes the boy caught in the outer and inner prisons of
the law. He thinks of his missed life, like Owen's dead soldier:–

> *Whatever hope is yours,*
> *Was my life also; I went hunting wild*
> *After the wildest beauty in the world*
> *Which lies not calm in eyes, or braided hair,*
> *But mocks the steady running of the hour,*
> *And if it grieves, grieves richlier than here.*
> *For by my glee might many men have laughed,*
> *And of my weeping something had been left,*
> *Which must die now.*[37]

It is very quiet in tone, warm and simple, distilling some of the
'pity of war', which Owen wished expressed.

(Time: 1 to 1½ minutes.)

---

[37] *Strange Meeting*

22.

TENOR SOLO: THE BOY

My dreams are all shattered
in a ghastly reality.

The wild beatings of my heart are
being stilled; day by day—minute by minute.

The sky and the earth are for those
beyond these prison walls.

Mother, Mother! Goodbye.[38]

---

[38]*My dreams are all shattered in a ghastly reality.*
The wild beating of my heart is stilled; day by day.
Earth and sky are not for those in prison.
Mother! Mother!

23.

This, and the previous number, correspond to the two homely solos in Part I.

The accent is more poignant, but the metaphor is just as personal and direct.

(Time: 1 to 1½ minutes.)

23.

SOPRANO SOLO: THE MOTHER.

O my son! What have I done to you

What will become of us now?

The springs of hope are dried up, and a
continual pain aches in a mother's heart.[39]

---

[39] *What have I done to you, my son?*
What will become of us now?
The springs of hope are dried up.
My heart aches in unending pain.

24.

This describes the inner and outer state of mankind in general. It sums up the statement in No. 2 of Part I. The irrational elements in ourselves have got to be reckoned with, even integrated into some new synthesis, if a way through is to be found.

'Peace' is the symbol of this new synthesis, as 'armed peace' or 'War' is the symbol for the effort to solve the problem by neurosis and the tension of the opposites.

(Time: $\frac{1}{2}$ minute.)

24.

ALTO SOLO:

> The dark forces rises everywhere;
>   the shadow of universal war.
>
> Men's hearts are heavy
> They cry for peace.[40]

---

[40]*The dark forces rise like a flood.*
Men's hearts are heavy: they cry for peace.

25.

This spiritual describes the common human need for some spiritual certainty, for 'peace'. The way through is only dimly felt, not as yet understood. In fact there is only the awareness of the deep need and sometimes only from the unconscious, while the conscious mind persists along outworn political cliches, etc.

(Time: 1 to $1\frac{1}{2}$ minutes.)

25.

CHORUS:[41] *A Spiritual*[42]

O, by an' by, — by an' by —[43]
I'm gwinter lay down my heavy load,[44]
O, by an' by — by an' by —
I'm gwinter lay down my heavy load.

I know my robe's gwinter fit me well,
I'm gwinter lay down my heavy load,
I tried it on at the gates of hell,
I'm gwinter lay down my heavy load.

O, by an' by, — by an' by —
I'm gwinter lay down my heavy load,
O, by an' by — by an' by —
I'm gwinter lay down my heavy load.

O, hell is deep an' a dark despair,
I'm gwinter lay down my heavy load,
O, stop po' sinner & don't go dere! —[45]
I'm gwinter lay down my heavy load.

O, by an' by, — by an' by —
I'm gwinter lay down my heavy load,
O, by an' by — by an' by —
I'm gwinter lay down my heavy load.

---

[41]Chorus and Soprano Solo
[42]See note 16 above
[43]*an'* becomes *and* throughout the Spiritual
[44]*gwinter* becomes *going to* throughout the Spiritual
[45]*po'* and *dere* become *poor* and *there*

PART III
26.

This short constructed chorus is like the ones at the opening of
Part I and Part II, No.1 & No.9.

It turns again towards the imagery of Part I : — 'But now the
exigent winter and the need Of sowings for new spring — —
etc.' The descent into the water is a universal dream symbol of
the present day.

> Ein protestantischer Theologe traümte öfters denselben
> Traum, er stehe an einen Abhang, unten lag ein tiefes Tal
> und darin ein dunkler See. Er wusste im Traum, dass ihn
> immer etwas abgehalten hatte, sich dem See zu nähern.
> Diesmal beschloss er, zum Wasser zu gehen. Wie er sich dem
> Ufer näherte, wurde es dunkel und unheimlich und plötzlich
> huschte ein Windstoss über die Fläche des Wassers. Da
> packte ihn die Angst und er erwachte.

> Dieser Traum zeigte Ihnen die natürliche symbolik. Der
> Traümer steigt in seine eigene Tiefe hinunter und der Weg
> führt ihn zum geheimnisvollen Wasser. Und hier geschiet
> das Wunder des Teiches von Bethesda: Ein Engel kommt
> herunter und berührt dass Wasser, welches dadurch
> Heilkraft erlangt.

> . . . Den Weg des Wassers der immer nach unten geht, muss
> man wohl gehen, wenn man den Schatz das kostlose Erbe
> des Vaters, wieder heben will.   (*Jung*)[46]

> (Time: 1 minute.)

---

[46]*Uber die Archetypen des kollektiven Unbewussten,* in *Eranos-Jahrbuch 1934* (subtitled
Ostwestlichen Symbolik und Seelenführung), ed. Olga Fröbe-Kapteyn, (A.G. Rhein-
Verlag, Zurich, 1935), pp 195–6. This essay was later revised and published in *Von
den Wurzeln des Bewusstseins* (Zurich, 1954), then was translated by R.F.C. Hull in
the *Collected Works of C.G. Jung* (Vol. 9, Part 1, London, 1959). The passage quoted
by Tippett is translated therein as follows:

> *A Protestant theologian often dreamed the same dream:* He stood on a mountain
> slope with a deep valley below, and in it a dark lake. He knew in the dream that
> something had always prevented him from approaching the lake. This time he
> resolved to go to the water. As he approached the shore, everything grew dark
> and uncanny, and a gust of wind suddenly rushed over the face of the water. He
> was seized by a panic fear, and awoke.
> *This dream shows us the natural symbolism. The dreamer descends into his own depths,
> and the way leads him to the mysterious water. And now there occurs the miracle of the pool
> of Bethesda: an angel comes down and touches the water, endowing it with healing power.
> . . . We must surely go the way of the waters, which always tend downward, if we would
> raise up the treasure, the precious heritage of the father.*
> (pp. 17–18; the italics are the translator's)

PART III
26.

CHORUS:

The cold deepens.

The earth descends into the icy waters, for there lies the jewel of great price.[47]

---

[47] *The cold deepens.*
  The world descends into the icy waters,
  where lies the jewel of great price.

27.

This Alto solo of the anima corresponds to No. 2 in Part I. She propounds the modern paradoxes. When misconceived and suppressed, she is like an impassioned woman, and man is compulsively animated. The problem of coming to terms with her is the problem of a creative impulse beyond good and evil. Yet behind this chaotic face lies another, full of meaning — the *illuminificatio* of the alchemists.

> Es entstehen allmählich Dämme gegen die Flut des Chaos, denn das Sinnvolle scheidet sich von Sinnlosen und dadurch dess Sinn und Unsinn nicht mehr identisch sind, wird die Kraft des Chaos durch die Entnahme von Sinn und Unsinn geschwächt, und der Sinn mit der Kraft des Sinnes und der Unsinn mit der Kraft des Unsinnes ausgerüstet. Damit ensteht ein neuer Kosmos.   *(Jung)*[48]

In Blake's drawings, when Job reaches the point at which he cannot distinguish the action of God from the action of Satan, the Divine Mercy shows him the mystery of re-birth into a new synthesis.[49]

(Time: about 1 minute.)

---

[48] *Uber die Archetypen des kollektiven Unbewussten* (see note 46 above). The passage quoted is translated in the *Collected Works of C. G. Jung* (Vol. 9, Part 1) as follows:
... Gradually breakwaters are built against the surging of chaos, and the meaningful divides itself from the meaningless. When sense and nonsense are no longer identical, the force of chaos is weakened by their subtraction; sense is then endued with the force of meaning and nonsense with the force of meaninglessness. In this way a new cosmos arises ... (p.31)

[49] See *Illustrations of the Book of Job. Invented by William Blake: reproduced in facsimile from the original New Zealand set made about 1823–4. With a note by Philip Hofer.* (London, 1937). See also review of this edition by Evelyn Underhill in *Time & Tide*, 8 January 1938, pp. 46–47; the following passage is relevant:
... The Moral Christian ... must pass from the state of innocence into the anguish of Experience — the only path to full spiritual life. The forces of cosmic violence are unloosed against him; Satan does his worst. Job's world is shattered. He is successively tortured in body, mind and spirit ... till that extreme of interior dereliction is reached in which he can no longer distinguish between the action of Satan and the action of God (Plate XI).
... Then it is, when the terrible night of the soul is fully established and his own nothingness fully revealed, that the Creative Wisdom in its awful majesty and beauty — the real God, whom he had never known before — answers Job 'out of the whirlwind'. There is disclosed to his astonished and purified sight the mystery and splendour of the heavenly and earthly creation; when 'the morning stars sang together, and all the Sons of God shouted for joy'.
... It may well be that the modern world is destined to follow Job's path from 'this life to that which is to come'; and to endure something analogous to that stripping and dereliction, as the preliminary of rebirth ...
(According to some leading Blake scholars these reduced-size colour versions of *The Book of Job* illustrations were not made by Blake, but by a member of his circle of friends.)

27.

ALTO SOLO:
>The soul of man is impassioned
>>like a woman.
>
>She is old as the earth and beyond
>>good and evil, the sensual garments.
>
>Her face will be illumined
>>like the sun. Then is the time of his
>>deliverance.[50]

---

[50]*The soul of man is impassioned like a woman.*
She is old as the earth, beyond good and evil,
the sensual garments.
Her face will be illumined like the sun.
Then is the time of his deliverance.

28.

This scena is like No. 3 in Part I.

The paradoxes are extended in dialogue form. Patience is born in the *voluntary* withdrawal. The 'man of destiny' is conceived as a possible name for the Dictator or his counterpart. The 'man of destiny' reaches out towards the collective powers of God and receives the opposing projections of the Devil. Such perversions of our human origin and fate bring their own self-destruction, which simple people may even rejoice in. The boy reached up likewise to make a judgement in God's name and cannot uphold the contradiction of such judgement with his human flesh. The way out is not along such paths. 'Render unto Caesar the things which are Caesar's, and unto God the things which are God's.'[51]

---

[51] St Matthew, 22:21

28.

SCENA: CHORUS & BASS SOLO.

BASS: The words of wisdom are these;
              Outer cold means inner warmth,
              the secret fermentation of the seed.

CHORUS: How shall we have patience for the
              consummation of the mystery? Who will
              comfort us in the going through?

BASS: Patience is born in the tension of
              loneliness. The garden lies across the desert.

CHORUS: Is the man of destiny then master of us all?
              Shall those cast out be unavenged?

BASS: The man of destiny is apart, cut off from
              fellowship.
              Only time may heal and the simple-hearted
              exult.

CHORUS: What of the young lad, what of him?

BASS: Justice is cold and abstract.
              He is ground to powder in the clash of powers.
              He too is apart like God, though his flesh is
              human.[52]

---

[52]

Bass: *The words of wisdom are these:*
           Winter cold means inner warmth,
           the secret nursery of the seed.

Chorus: *How shall we have patience for the*
           consummation of the mystery?
           Who will comfort us in the going through?

Bass: *Patience is born in the tension of loneliness.*
           The garden lies beyond the desert.

Chorus: *Is the man of destiny master of us all?*
           Shall those cast out be unavenged?

Bass: *The man of destiny is cut off from fellowship.*
           Healing springs from the womb of time.
           The simple-hearted shall exult in the end.

Chorus: *What of the boy, then? What of him?*

Bass: *He, too, is outcast, his manhood broken*
           in the clash of powers.
           God overpowered him, the child of our time.

29.

After the preceding scena there will probably be a short
musical interlude[53] to mark the 'moment of silence' before the
final awareness. The Tenor and Soprano still stand for the
distinctively human figures. When all these texts have been
sung, the Chorus repeats them in a swelling ensemble. We have
reached the point where man must dare to know himself, cost
what it may.

'After such knowledge: what forgiveness? . . .'
.... 'Think
Neither fear nor courage saves us. Unnatural vices
Are fathered by our heroism. Virtues
Are forced upon us by our impudent crimes.
These tears are shaken from the wrath-bearing tree.'[54]

[53]See 55 below
[54] T.S. Eliot, *Gerontion*

29.

GENERAL ENSEMBLE: CHORUS & SOLOISTS.[55]

TENOR: I would know my dark side
               and my light, so shall I at
               last be whole.

BASS: Then courage, brother, and dare the
               difficult passage.

SOPRANO: Here is no final grieving
               but an abiding hope.

ALTO: The moving waters renew the earth.
               It is spring.[56]

CHORUS REPEATS & ENLARGES.[57]

---

[55]Introduced by an instrumental Praeludium

[56]Tenor: *I would know my shadow and my light,*
             so shall I at last be whole.

Bass: *Then courage, brother, dare the grave passage.*

Soprano: *Here is no final grieving,*
             but an abiding hope.

Alto: *The moving waters renew the earth.*
             It is spring.

[57] Chorus and Soloists

30.

This is the generalized expression of the hope of the new spring.

30.

CHORUS & SOLOISTS: A Spiritual.[58]

Deep river, my home is over Jordan,
Deep river, Lord,
I want to cross over into camp-ground, Lord,
I want to cross over into camp-ground, Lord,
I want to cross over into camp-ground, Lord,
I want to cross over into camp-ground.

Oh, chillun, Oh, don't you want to go,
To that gospel feast,
That promised land,
That land where all is peace?
Walk into heaven, and take my seat,
And cast my crown at Jesus' feet, Lord,
I want to cross over into camp-ground, Lord,
I want to cross over into camp-ground, Lord,
I want to cross over into camp-ground.

Deep river, my home is over Jordan,
Deep river, Lord,
I want to cross over into camp-ground, Lord,
I want to cross over into camp-ground, Lord,
I want to cross over into camp-ground, Lord,
I want to cross over into camp-ground.[59]

---

[58] See note 16 above
[59] *Lord* is added to the last line

The Nameless Hero:
Reflections on *A Child of Our Time*

(i)

When any of you hear *A Child of Our Time* for the first time, the most obvious think to strike you will be the five negro spirituals, which come at certain important moments in the story. I might call this the folk-element in the work — folk-music and folk-poetry. The spirituals are only appropriate because the whole oratorio is not so much the record of an individual or personally peculiar experience, but of a common, or folk-experience. What our fore-fathers might have called even, a mythological experience. There are indeed ancient myths very similar to the underlying story of *A Child of Our Time*. Mythological heroes usually had names, though not really personal ones. (Apollo, for instance, probably means the wild apple.) But contemporary myths just have no names. *A Child of Our Time*, from its very title, has the anonymity of 'The Unknown Soldier', on the faceless Cenotaph. There was once a real story behind *A Child of Our Time* just as there was a real soldier, whose body is buried at Westminster Abbey. We can *never* know the Unknown Soldier's *name* — and whoever in fact played out the drama of *A Child of Our Time* to its tragic end, there is no name in the oratorio text.

In my opinion this text is happiest when what it has to say, could be said by folk-idioms. This is so even of the solos:

> *I have no money for my bread.*
> *I have no gift for my love . . .*

is better in every way than the lines which follow:

> *I am caught between my desires and their frustration*
> *as between the hammer and the anvil.*

One feels that the psychological terminology (desires and frustrations) has not yet fused into our common speech. But sometimes the folk-idioms fall pat with an almost terrifying actuality. The self-righteous expressing their eternal refusal to be moved by the anguish of the outcasts, sing these three lapidaric sentences:

> *We cannot have them in our Empire.*
> *They shall not work nor draw a dole.*
> *Let them starve in No-Man's-Land!*

188

Every outcast, be he unemployed or refugee, feels the implacability and the desolation of the 'No-Man's Land' — a folk-idiom born, in fact, from the common experience of both sides on the Flanders battlefields.

There are disadvantages of course too, arising from this use of folk-idiom. For instance, the verbal style becomes so condensed and yet the words so simple and clear, that we note the mechanics of the repetitions in the music, which has so often to meditate, by repetition, upon these sentences, in the traditional manner. We are so used to the repetitions of 'Every Valley', for example, that we do not think about them, and suffer rather the danger of forgetting the text altogether. Very few people now know how, let alone why — that is, dramatically why — the words of *Messiah* were compiled as they were. But the text of *A Child of Our Time* is far too close to us for that. I can believe that if I were to re-compose the work now, in the light of my experience of performances, I might try to disguise these repetitions by artifice. But on the other hand something of the naked simplicity might go. In any case the question is vain.

The pre-eminent advantage of this folk-style wording lay in the means it gave to incorporate the folk-verse of the spirituals into the text, without undue strain. Naturally this was only possible in our own language, in English. (Though the consequent difficulties in translation into French and German have in fact been triumphantly overcome.) For so many English idioms have sprung, at one or more remove, from the Bible, and that is the source of most of the negro poetry; the trumpet that 'sounds within-a my soul', is the same trumpet of *The Pilgrim's Progress,* when Mr Greatheart had safely crossed the river:

> And all the trumpets sounded for him on the other side.[1]

Probably some of the imagery of *Pilgrim's Progress* is older even than the Bible — for instance, the waters into which the hero descends. *A Child of Our Time* makes use also of primeval seasonal imagery. The opening chorus of each part is conceived as observing the drama from some point in interstellar space.

> The world turns on its dark side.
> It is winter.

Only gradually does the camera approach our planet and hover over Europe. Even time undergoes that same condensation, slowly

---

[1]John Bunyan: *The Pilgrim's Progress* (Part II)

moving from the general past to the immediate present and the particular drama. In this telescopic view our period seems restless and violent. Spring seems a long way off.

Although the story of *A Child of Our Time* is indeed tragic, there's no attempt to spotlight the horrors. The artistic method is not a realistic one. It's assumed that we all nowadays know these horrors by heart — they can be read of in the papers. In *A Child of Our Time* the tragic events are brought before us just long enough to reproduce the appropriate emotions in the relative tranquillity of recollection so that we may ask of them their message. But except for the *Chorus of the self-righteous* and one spiritual, which I have deliberately headed *A Spiritual of Anger,* there is no attempt to moralize.

But the desire to moralize is very strong, and to appear to desist from it seems unnatural. So that it was difficult, at least during the war, to believe that *A Child of Our Time* was really intent on other things. One or two English critics thought I had glossed the realities of violence because I am a pacifist; another execrated the oratorio because he considered it an irresponsible plea for political assassination. This latter nonsense was the more stupid, and difficult to imagine on the continent, where even musical critics have all been too close to concentration camps not to know the sort of provocation people may have. But the gravamen of my charge against this criticism (and it's for this reason that I refer to it) is that it misunderstands the method — which brings the events before us in recollection, not to judge, but that by terror and pity we may be moved to stop equating intellect with spirit, and to 'break open the heart'. It's nothing less than the re-birth of the inner imaginative world, that is sought for. To plough the dark ground of our disorders that we may sow new seeds — to 'harrow hell'.

Now Christ 'harrowed hell' as a triumphant God — triumphant indeed because as man he went the way of a barbaric death — but nonetheless victorious.

> *Lift up your heads, O ye gates,*
> *And be ye lifted up ye everlasting doors*
> *And the King of Glory shall come in.*[2]

A child of our time, be he professed Christian or agnostic, has to harrow his hell with less confidence, and humility, armed though he be with every godlike scientific weapon. And maybe there is, no

---

[2]Psalm 24, v. 7

longer, final escape for any of us through a vicarious scapegoat, though the attempt of us all — individuals, races, nations and ideologies — to find one whom we may tear to pieces for our sins, is one of the actualities of this oratorio.

'Behold the man! The Scapegoat! The Child of Our Time!' For surely that is the deepest evil of our day? Every division, every war threatens to become a moral crusade. And the greatest danger point is when our self-righteousness overcomes our fear.

> *Odour of blood when Christ was slain*
> *Made Plato's tolerance in vain*
> *And vain the Doric discipline.*[3]

Because it had to, *A Child of Our Time* receives its peculiar effect from the power of this evil. A Mephistophelean power that pricks us upward, as well as plunging us in catastrophe. The devil is always the wicked other man (our 'dark brother') for *you* and *me*— but it is you and me, of course, for *them*. They will show tenacity and courage and heroism too.

There are two scenes in the oratorio, when the four solo voices have a sort of conversation. These scenes make two of the pivotal points of the work. The first one comes at the moment of decision which precipitates the drama itself. The boy (the nameless hero) is moved to such passion by the agony of his mother under the terror, that he sweeps aside all reason and prudence proferred by his uncle and aunt, and declares his challenge.

> *I will defy the world to reach you.*

For it's the ineluctable fate of mankind to engender tragedy by heroic passion. Nothing in the oratorio suggests that this will ever be different.

But — when the four soloists come together again, at the very end, the plane has been shifted to an examination of the nature of this passion, the nature of our inner life from which the 'dark forces' spring. It may be that the width and intensity of the present continuing catastrophe forces on *all* of us a fresh questioning, a renewed searching, born of our anxiety. But I think there will be a few, whose destiny it will be, to undergo whatever initiation is demanded as the price of the power to decipher the message. Our nameless hero, no longer even the daily outcast who shoots at authority, but one of an even stricter anonymity, will make for us a

---

[3]W. B. Yeats: *Two Songs from a Play*, II

new declaration, reaching out to some re-born humanism within the bitter ideologies.

> *I would know my shadow as my light*
> *So shall I at last be whole*
> *Then courage, brother, dare the grave passage.*
> *Here is no final grieving but an abiding hope.*
> *The moving waters renew the earth.*
> *It is spring.*

First broadcast on BBC radio, 22 April 1950

(ii)

In a programme note to an early performance of *A Child of Our Time* I once wrote:

'Because an oratorio, like an opera, has a story and ideas, these forms are impure musically as compared with symphonies and sonatas. But the impurity can also become the cause that we are moved the more deeply, moved beyond analysis or consciousness of that which moves us.'

This seems to me particularly true of *A Child of Our Time*, for two reasons. First, that the story, the idea, behind the oratorio (man's inhumanity to man) is deeply relevant at this time; and second, because the music is simple, even occasionally naive. But a naivety which is not embarrassing, which is indeed part of the proper means for letting the oratorio speak immediately and to everyone.

It's clear that an idea so permanent and deep as 'man's inhumanity to man' could have been the subject of an opera equally as of an oratorio. Indeed at the very begining I thought it was to be an opera on the Easter rebellion in Dublin in 1916 and the consequent shootings. But that passed — really because the story proved intractable; and because I came to realise that I wanted to present the matter contemplatively rather than dramatically. This is the essence of the difference between oratorio and opera. Both use stories. But opera must present the drama, and the characters, in action. While oratorio only refers to the events of the drama in order, having refreshed our memory of them or brought them to our notice, to consider their moral implications.

In the traditional Christian Passions, the events are described to us by a narrator in recitative, and with the help of interjection by the chorus, while the moral comments are given to soloists in extended arias. The subject matter of these arias is simply: how should the Christian Soul behave in relation to the event just described? The acquiescence and affirmation of the congregation is provided by selected verses of appropriate hymns or chorales.

When I decided to treat the matter of the pre-war Nazi pogroms as an oratorio I turned first of all to this traditional pattern of the Passions. But I also turned to the tripartite division of *Messiah* in which Part 1 deals solely with prophecies and things general, while Part 2 deals with history from the birth of Christ to the last judgment, and Part 3 deals solely with metaphysical comments mostly taken from St Paul. This three-part division works out for *A Child of Our Time* in the following way. Part 1 deals with the general state of oppression in our time; Part 2 presents the particular story of a young man's attempt to seek justice by violence and the catastrophic consequences; while Part 3 considers the moral to be drawn, if any.

But while the traditional forms of oratorio do lie behind *A Child of Our Time,* they are somehow turned and twisted to carry the charge of our contemporary anxiety. I can explain this best by quoting the half-line of verse from Eliot's *Murder in the Cathedral,* which heads the score like a motto. It runs:

The darkness declares the glory of light.[4]

The chief point is that this quotation is itself a kind of quotation — from the Psalms:

The heavens declare the glory of God.[5]

Eliot has twisted the well-worn words and by so doing forced them into our time. I have played this trick, if that is the right word, on both words and music. It appears too even in the Spirituals. For if the five Spirituals, which come at appropriate moments during the work, act as modern chorales, in that we *all* are moved by them beyond the power of the tunes as mere music, yet the Spirituals themselves have turned and twisted Bible language into a modern dialect; the stories they tell of the Bible Jews are used to comfort Negroes in the bitterness of oppression and I use these negro spirituals to symbolize the agony of modern Jews in Hitler's Europe.

---

[4] T.S. Eliot: *Murder in the Cathedral,* final chorus speech
[5] Psalm 19, v.1

It makes a powerful, condensed poetic image. Not only did the Spirituals give me a kind of spirit-level folk poetry to which the rest of the text had to conform, so also did the music.

Just before the fatal act of violence which the young protagonist of the oratorio feels forced to commit in his desperation, he leads the choir in the Spiritual *Nobody knows the trouble I see, Lord.* In the chorus of the Spiritual, the tune is given to all male voices, the counter-tune to the women. In the verse the leader is left on his own and the high voices of the choir thrown up into the air behind him. I partly learnt this method of setting from recordings of negro choirs. Now the syncopations and implied beat of that music are what we find in jazz. This was an added reason why I found the Spirituals so apt to my hand. Because I was convinced at the time I wrote it — twenty-five years ago — that modern oratorio of this direct kind should try to make use of the popular musical vernacular, in the same way as the words made use of general contemporary expressions like: 'They shall not work nor draw a dole. Let them starve in No-Man's-Land'. But the vital consideration must always be, whether this musical (or literary) vernacular can be purified, enhanced, de-sentimentalized enough to carry the charge of deeply serious artistic emotions.

To exemplify how far this was possible in relation to a jazz-derived music, or rather how far I managed to go, it is worth listening to the opening of an alto aria out of the last Part. 'The Soul of man is impassioned like a woman'. It is a dance — as though the Spiritual 'Nobody knows' had produced from within itself a kind of sacred gaiety. There is no question but that this music is jazz-derived (with of course other influences behind it as well), but it is also unquestionably individual music of its author. I did not have to mitigate my serious style one whit. One of the very simple metaphors I used to convey the sense of 'no final grieving' (to quote the soprano) was the age-old one of the Seasons. The opening chorus of all has only the words: 'The world turns on its dark side. It is winter.' When I reached the end of the work I let the alto (then the choir) sing: 'The moving waters renew the earth. It is spring.' I had written the whole text already before the last war. The music began as the war began. Spring (in the poetic sense) was hard to imagine. At all costs I didn't wish to produce mere 'pie-in-the-sky'. But finally the imaginative necessities forced a spring into the music. Before the final spiritual *Deep River,* I let the four solo voices sing together, vocalizing over a pedal bass and accompanied by all the orchestra. It is spring: but spring with an ache in it.

(iii)

In two months it will be twenty-four years since I began the music for *A Child of Our Time*, in September 1939, the day, I remember, after war broke out. I finished it a year and a half later and it was first performed, under Walter Goehr, in war-time London in 1944. Time, therefore, to look back and realise how the war years and after-war years have already obscured the shock of the Hitler pogroms; which were for me the culminating factor that crystallized so many musical and non-musical emotions into oratorio form. At a performance in Germany a few years back, one had to note that at least half of the youthful audience and youthful choir could have no mature recollection of Hitler at all. Their response was therefore to the *eternal* tragedy of man's inhumanity to man, rather than to any historical example. Perhaps the seal on the historical has been set by the 1952 performance in Haifa, when the father of the young man (who became the ostensible hero of the piece and was finally handed over by Vichy France to the Nazis) was brought by the Palestine radio to hear the oratorio inspired by his son.

In England, *A Child of Our Time* has begun to take its place beside greater and more famous works. That is, like all true popular oratorios — oratorios that belong to the mass of ordinary people — it is performed, because it can be, by amateurs as well as professionals. It is simple enough in essence, if occasionally difficult in practice, to be within the scope, as I know from example, of a keen Secondary School and any competent Choral Society.

From a programme note for a performance at the York Festival, 1963

(iv)

I had to attend a performance of *A Child of Our Time* a few years back, in Germany. Someone pointed out to me that two thirds of the young choir, and about half of the audience, would hardly have been born when the events from which the oratorio sprang, took place. It is I, who, when I hear the piece, go back to those terrible events, the rise of Hitler and the concentration camps, but younger people find in the piece, as equally terrible, a relevance to today. When I wrote the work, I was so engulfed in the actions of the period, I never considered its frightening prophetic quality. But it seems that the growing violence springing out of divisions of nation, race, religion, status, colour, or even just rich and poor, is possibly the deepest present threat to the social fabric of all human society.

In the oratorio this violence is presented in archetypal form, a simple murderous shot of protest, followed by retaliatory mass vengeance. It seems possible (within the mood of the piece) to have some understanding of the shot, though there is no condonation. It seems harder to feel understanding for the mass vengeance (and that is why I named *Go Down Moses*, A Spiritual of Anger). But though the oratorio refers to political events, it is not about politics. And though the oratorio is concerned with man's rejection of whole groups of his fellow men, it is not about acts of protest. (I should like to say in parenthesis, that when I wrote the piece there seemed only one kind of shot, aimed at the obvious tyrant. But alas, now, when a shot rings out around the world, its aim can as easily be Gandhi, or Martin Luther King, or John F. Kennedy.)

The oratorio, as is proper, is not dramatically descriptive, but contemplative. The events are presented to us for contemplation only, that we may stand back for the events to induce the deeper emotions which might cross the gulfs of division: compassion, tolerance, acceptance of our 'shadow', as of our 'light', absolute refusal of any stereotype of division that prevents the expression of our total humanity.

Yet, in saying all that, I risk making *A Child of Our Time* sound more didactic than it really is. That is to say, I was committed when I wrote it: to all those rejected, cast out, from the centre of our society onto the fringes; into slums, into concentration camps, into ghettos. But in actual composition of the work, while never denying, I think, this personal commitment, I got drawn by the work itself towards some deeper commitment which needed to embrace both sides: the self-righteous and the rejected. And yet with passion, and not an inert neutrality. This passion, in all the senses of the word, springs from the archetypal nature of the drama as the oratorio presents it. When the chorus ask:

What of the boy then, what of him?

they are answered by —

He too is outcast, his manhood broken in the clash of powers. God overpowered him, the child of our time.

This answer is terrible; but the use of the word *God* is in no way inappropriate. We grope our way towards compassion and understanding, because the shock of the collective tragedy is so great each time any part of the archetypal drama of violence and division is re-enacted.

June 1968

5
Opera

Opera since 1900

Opera is a part of music and a part of the theatre. So that it partakes of the general fashions of music and theatre, as they change from generation to generation.

In a country like Italy, where music and theatre have been always so intimately combined, it could be said that the history of Italy's music is the history of Italy's opera. But in a country like Germany, with a great symphonic tradition, the matter is more complicated. As to England, it can be said that English opera has only here and now become a living force — since the Second World War in fact.

The last Italian world-name in opera is Puccini. We associate Puccini rightly with the theatrical movement called *verismo* — the movement towards bringing every-day life into the theatre. Puccini evolved a style which was able to throw a magical veil of music over the merely common-place. The greatest triumph in this respect being *Madame Butterfly* — an opera made out of an American magazine story. This technique of making music out of the every-day is still with us. For instance it's a big ingredient in the operas of Menotti. Not perhaps so much directly, as via the important turn this technique took in the 1920s, in order to make possible opera of specific social significance — generally left-wing. This was not centred, curiously enough, in Italy, the home of operatic verismo, but in Germany, which in the '20s was in a terrific ferment of experiment and innovation. And because all this fermentation took place in Germany, there were other traditions and other elements mixed into the matter, than Puccini verismo.

The great figure that dominated German opera was Richard Strauss. He had perfected an operatic language which turned the technique of Wagnerian music drama, tempered by some manners of Mozart, to every kind of operatic use. From teutonized Greek tragedy, like *Elektra*, to theatrical discussions of the operatic problem itself, like *Capriccio*. And over all stood his masterpiece, *Der*

199

Rosenkavalier: a glittering product of pre-first-war Vienna.

None of the younger German figures that made their contribution to the violent operatic experiments of the '20s failed to learn from Strauss.

But even while Strauss was writing *Der Rosenkavalier*, other figures like Schoenberg and Stravinsky were at work altering and transfiguring the very language of music itself. So that one can say that while Strauss and Puccini still dominated opera by the force and vitality of their techniques, there was a violent and very self-conscious movement of the younger people away from and against these traditions. And so a masterpiece like Berg's *Wozzeck*, produced in 1925, seemed at first completely revolutionary as if it was unrelated to anything that had gone before. By 1955 we know better. It is seen now to be a transfiguration of the living tradition, not a disrelated accident.

There was another musical element in the '20s that made its contribution to the mixture; the Eastward-moving dance music from America which we call Jazz. It's difficult to recall how this music swept Europe just before the Great War — carrying with it all the old dance music of Waltzes and Ländlers. It was so obviously popular music that it could not escape the attention of those operatic composers who were bent on turning the sentimental Puccini *verismo* into hard political satire. Kurt Weill's *Die Dreigroschen Oper* is one product of this experiment. But it's to be found also in Stravinsky's *L'Histoire du Soldat*; a little masterpiece of the Great War years.

Finally one might say that the element of the theatre in opera (at any rate in Germany of the '20s) was almost entirely under the sign of Expressionism. The movement to drive theatrical plots and situations and characters always towards the impersonally typical or symbolical. The early Hindemith operas are a product of this kind of experimentation. They still have a great vitality. And embedded in all this experimental mud is the strange symbolical jewel of Busoni's *Doktor Faust*, which had to wait till 1954 to have its first really successful presentation, by Ebert in West Berlin.

Summing up so far, we can enumerate some important operatic landmarks thus:

Puccini's *Madame Butterfly* — first produced in 1904;
Strauss's *Der Rosenkavalier* — 1911; Then moving over towards experiment, come
Pfitzner's *Palestrina* in 1917; with Busoni's *Doktor Faust* and Berg's *Wozzeck* both in 1925.

All periods of violent experiment give way in time to periods of reconsideration. Revolutionary figures like Schoenberg and Stravinsky, each in his own way moved towards a new order. Schoenberg arrived at the twelve-tone technique, which is a method of producing an extremely strict order within a composition; while Stravinsky went towards the movement which we call neo-classicism. Both masters have reached out to opera. Schoenberg's *Moses und Aaron* was performed posthumously in Hamburg and elsewhere, and Stravinsky's *The Rake's Progress* has been performed all over the world. Now the twelve-tone technique on which *Moses und Aaron* is based, is still too esoteric a matter for many people, so that a person as old as myself may never know whether this opera will (like Berg's *Wozzeck*) seem eventually within the tradition. In any case I imagine that *Moses und Aaron* remains very much rooted in the period of experimentation. I mean that we shall always tend to set it back in time towards the period of *Wozzeck* — while Stravinsky's *The Rake's Progress* seems so un-revolutionary that it's difficult to believe it is from the same composer as the choral ballet *Les Noces* or the opera-oratorio *Oedipus Rex*.

Not unless, in fact, one has watched the process of neoclassicizing that is the vital thread.

However, another stabilizing opera — if I may use that term — had appeared before *The Rake's Progress*. This was Hindemith's *Mathis der Maler*. And in some ways Hindemith is much more the conscious protagonist of the movement to bring order once more out of innovatory chaos, than Stravinsky. For the story of *Mathis der Maler*, the history of the troubles of a painter during the German Peasants' War is in subject and style akin to the much earlier plot of Goethe's play, *Götz von Berlichingen*. Now Hindemith wrote his own libretto and knew, I'm sure, quite well that he was modelling himself on Goethe. But there are also other theatrical procedures in it, like Mathis's visions which are not at all from the Goethe period, but distinctly modern and expressionistic. So it's both old and new. And the music is also a mixture of the traditional and the new; entirely, of course, within the tradition of German not Italian opera.

Stravinsky's *Rake's Progress* is another mixture of the traditional and the new, but in the tradition of Italian opera, for the music leaps back over Verdi to take its models rather from Rossini and Bellini. Yet the sound is peculiarly Stravinsky. Less easily situated is the Auden libretto to this opera, for while following out the story of Tom Rakewell's progress to ruin and the madhouse, it is full of recondite imagination: card games with the devil in a graveyard and many strange things besides. I might put it to you rather drastically by saying that though contemporary with, it's absolutely at the other end of the world from anything by Menotti. In Menotti the Italian tradition is brought up to date; and is sentimental, satirical, amusing, journalistically serious — but, despite the dream scenes in *The Consul*, fundamentally just exactly what it says. In *The Rake's Progress* there are undertones and overtones of all kinds. It is not at all just what it says.

So let me add to my list of operatic landmarks two further works: Hindemith's *Mathis der Maler* produced in 1938, and Stravinsky's *The Rake's Progress* in 1953.

The first and golden date for present-day English opera was the production of Britten's *Peter Grimes* in 1945. The story of the opera has elements of English *verismo* (what life was really like in a Suffolk fishing village) and elements of expressionism (for the village, called The Borough, is presented as typical of all small communities, and Grimes as typical of all unhappy misfits) — and there is a third, more immediately contemporary element — the interest in pathology (for Grimes is presented almost as a psychological case).

The music to the opera is equally a mixture of the traditional and the new. There is English tradition, through Purcell, as well as Italian and German.

Britten has written many other operas since *Grimes* but none better, I think, than the last, *The Turn of the Screw*. Here (as in the earlier *Billy Budd*) there is the same fascination in the pathology of innocence and its corruption. And there are as many undertones and overtones as in *The Rake's Progress*, if quite different ones. It is an opera of depth.

Its production in September last year was followed by that of Walton's *Troilus and Cressida* in December. This is a much more traditional piece of work, as its author intended. It was splendidly successful and it might be said: it never put a foot wrong. It showed that an Englishman can emulate the acknowledged masters of opera and get away with it. This is said in no derogatory tone. It's an extraordinary thing to have done.

Finally, in this probably remarkable season of English opera, my own *The Midsummer Marriage* was produced in January 1955. It set the critics in a turmoil. According to some, this opera — or at least the libretto, which is my own — has put every foot wrong; and according to others it is of considerable originality and may lead to new ways in opera (a high claim indeed!). When the dust finally settles I think it will be seen to be quite traditionally English in its use of fantasy, while being in the same kind of category as probably Busoni's *Doktor Faust*. An opera where the imaginative and symbolical element is of more consequence than the strictly dramatic, throwing, as that always does, great accent on the magic of the music.

If we are now to hazard a glance at the future of opera in general, it seems clear to me that at the present time absolutely anything is possible. The journalistic, the pathological, the social-realist, the neo-classical, the neo-grand (if I may coin a horrible expression), the magical-symbolic, the simple love story — I could quote examples of the lot. This should indeed give us confidence. I mean confidence in the extraordinary possibilities of this theatrical form and in the great fertility of contemporary opera composers taken as a whole. My motto will tend also always to be the simple one of Ezra Pound's: 'Make it new.' Adventure will in the end take us further than repetition.

Janacek and *Jenufa*[1]

'Bursting out of the Underground station', said Bertolt Brecht, 'eager to become as wax in the magician's hands, grown-up men, their resolution proved in the struggle for existence, rush to the box office. They hand in their hat at the cloakroom, and with it they hand their normal behaviour: the attitudes of "everyday life". Once out of the cloakroom, they take their seats with the bearing of kings.'[2]

Brecht wrote that of bourgeois society going to the opera in about 1930. Perhaps I should have said the 'old' opera — 'culinary' opera, as Brecht calls it.[3] When I saw *Jenufa* at Covent Garden I did have Brecht's description in mind, just because I expected *Jenufa* to be culinary opera, in the Brechtian sense; although this was its English premiere. But was my expectation justified? I think it worthwhile for a moment to consider. The first question I ask myself is: why did I expect *Jenufa* to be 'old' opera?

Before I went to *Jenufa* I knew that Janacek was a Czech genius of the turn of the century, whose music has taken a long time to travel from his homeland to us. I knew that *Jenufa* was written when he was about fifty. That it was first produced in Brno, the Capital of Moravia, in 1904. That it was twelve years before it reached Prague. So that maybe those twelve years taken to travel so little distance are a foreshadowing of the slow way appreciation of his music grows. But grow it does.

About *Jenufa* itself, I knew the story but not the music. It is a story, set in a peasant community, of passion driving people to do things outrageous to all normal codes of behaviour: in other words, a drama of Renaissance cut, though the manners are not Shakespeare's.

Now such dramas of personal passion at odds with the conventions of society, were certainly possible material for Brecht — especially if they were presented with the accent on the social issue, rather than on the incidents between the impassioned characters. And Janacek was certainly not, any more than Brecht, indifferent to the sufferings of certain classes of people (such as the Silesian

[1]First broadcast on BBC Third Programme, 13 December 1956, as a review of the Covent Garden production
[2]Bertolt Brecht: *Versuche 2* (Berlin, 1930); translated by John Willett in 'Brecht on Theatre' (London and USA, 1964), p.39
[3]Ibid., p.35

miners) within an inequitable society. Janacek seems to have felt (at least at the period of *Jenufa*) that his artistic and his humanitarian purposes were fulfilled by the faithful observation of the peasant society around him; and by presenting this less usual operatic material (through his art) to his more lettered countrymen of the town. But Brecht was certain that the power of the theatrical machine was such, that it would eat up any unusual material however initially shocking, and theatricalize it into just another new production of the current opera season. Which is of course how it was at Covent Garden with us on Monday.

'For the attitude that these people adopt in the opera', Brecht went on, 'is unworthy of them. Is there any possibility that they may change it? Can we persuade them to get out their cigars?'[4] What he meant is: If the opera public could once be persuaded to sit back and smoke cigars, in an attitude of dispassionate examination rather than of enthusiasm (because as 'wax in the hands of the magician'), then that would be 'new' opera. Because to induce such an attitude in the public means to stop being theatrical and operatic magicians once for all. Only thus can the audience be prevented from being caught up into the emotion of the drama. Acting and music must henceforward never be used to induce sympathy with, or participation in the emotions of the characters, but used solely to offer something to our heads, rather than our hearts, cooled in cigar smoke.

Brecht's ideas (I realise now) are not at all dependent on his Communist sympathies. I was immeasurably delighted and surprised to find them fully operative in the Jean-Louis Barrault production of *Christophe Colombe* two weeks earlier at the Palace Theatre.[5] Claudel and Milhaud, by extraordinary theatrical tricks, make us 'examine' the story of Columbus — to the expected advantage of Catholicism! In fact the examination is done on our behalf by the chorus of actors, who are, in turn, us ordinary people and the characters of the epic. It was eminently Brechtian — the methods by which the chorus appeared to be smoking our cigars.

The disadvantage of this new-fashioned theatre is precisely in its virtues. We are fascinated by the technique, but at the end of the 'examination' we are little or not at all interested in Columbus.

At Covent Garden such an attitude is out of the question. In *Jenufa* you must assuredly leave your daily-bread life in the

---

[4] Ibid., p. 39
[5] See also pp. 222–223 below

cloakroom, go to your seats like royalty. And then with cigars firmly tucked away, you must submit to the magic of the music and enter absolutely into the emotions of the characters.

You see a story of considerable violence treated with restraint and simple dignity. The music does not crystallize out into many set arias or ensembles. It tries rather to further and enhance the direct action of the story, so that we come away with the drama of Jenufa, her handsome lover gone to the bad, her rougher lover grown into tenderness, and her tremendous moralistic yet murderous foster-mother vividly before our eyes.

The Dimensions of *Die Meistersinger*[1]

We can enjoy Wagner's *Die Meistersinger* for itself alone, as a tremendous lyric comedy, a generous, humane work that deserves its brilliant C major ending. Yet I believe such enjoyment, in isolation from the rest of Wagner's works, and from other contexts in the theatre and in culture generally, to be limiting. I feel every great artist of the theatre reaches out, within his time and temperament, towards the universality of Shakespeare, the only absolute.

We may contrast *Die Meistersinger* with *Tristan*, if only in the simple sense that the latter concerns an overwhelming passionate love that denies the marriage bond, while the former concerns a love which is romantically chaste before marriage and faithful afterwards. If Tristan and Isolde must go to their deaths, we feel that Walther and Eva should live happily ever after.

I think Walther von Stolzing is best compared, though, with Wilhelm Meister. To use more or less eighteenth-century terms, Walter leaves the *Adelstand* (or nobility) for the *Bürgerstand* (or middle classes). The relation is at first commercial —

> Pogner: Half ich euch gern bei des Gut's Verkauf . . .
> *(If gladly I helped in the sale of your estate . . .)*[2]

but finally, after Walther's *Lehrtage* (or apprenticeship) with Sachs, it becomes romantic and spiritual —

> Sachs: Nicht eu'ren Ahnen, noch so werth,
> Nicht eu'ren Wappen, Speer, noch Schwert;
> Dass ihr ein Dichter seid,
> Ein Meister euch gefreit,
> Dem Dankt ihr heut' eu'r höchstes Gluck,
> *(Not to your forbears, however worthy,*
> *Not to your shield, nor spear nor sword —*
> *That you are a poet,*
> *And now a Master,*
> *To that you owe your present bliss.)*[3]

meaning Eva, i.e. marriage into the *Bürgerstand*. But when Sachs

---

[1] This article appeared first in a somewhat different form in the programme for the Bayreuth Festival centenary production of *Die Meistersinger* in 1968
[2] *Die Meistersinger von Nürnberg*, Decca Record Co. translation, p. 19
[3] Ibid., p.110

moves over towards spiritual matters and music *she* is substituted for Eva, then —

> Sachs: Blieb sie nicht ad'lig wie zur Zeit
> Wo Hof' und Fursten sie geweiht
> Im Drang der schlimmen Jahr'
> Blieb sie doch deutsch und wahr.
> (*If not so noble as when*
> *Pledged by courts and princes,*
> *Yet 'mid the stress of evil years*
> *She remained German and true.*)[4]

Wilhelm, on the other hand, leaves the *Bürgerstand,* at first for the theatre people, leaving them in turn for *Adelstand,* Which he leaves for a *Stand* much more nebulous. It's worth mentioning at this point the short final chapter of Goethe's novel (which was published in 1829), where the father rescues the horse-riding son from the river, and the generations, up till then estranged, are reconciled. There is a strange poetic tenderness in the prose, reaching much further than *deutsch und wahr,* which has yet, I think, to be fulfilled. The emotion of the imagined reconciliation-scene draws from Goethe (who never knew reconciliation with his real-life son) a sentence of Hardy-esque 'pessimism'. For Wilhelm, to save the son's life after the fall with the horse into the river, must carry out an operation (he was by then a country-doctor). He takes out the surgical tools from his black bag to bleed the young man (an erroneous medical practice, of course, that was just about to be superseded: it was historically dramatized at George Washington's deathbed!). The operation takes on a symbolic character. Wilhelm looks down at the naked body of the son, who lies asleep and exhausted, to say:

> Wirst du doch immer aufs neue hervorgebracht, herrlich Ebenbild Gottes! Und wirst sogleich wieder aufs neue Beschädigt, verletzt, von innern oder von aussen.
> (*Yet you will always be brought forth again, glorious image of God;* *likewise be maimed, wounded afresh, from within or without.*)[5]

That is not C major.

We may then contrast *Die Meistersinger* with that work of even greater dimensions, *Der Ring des Nibelungen.* This is natural for one who has read Shaw's *The Perfect Wagnerite,* where *Der Ring* is considered as an essential part of the Revolutionary Thinker's

---

[4]Decca Record Co. translation, p. 110
[5]See Michael Tippett: *The Ice Break* (London, 1977), closing scene

Handbook, with Alberich as the *ur-Kapitalist:* a melodramatic view of *Der Ring,* but a portion of the truth. But within the group of mastersingers, though Pogner was quite ready to help sell up Walther's lands, neither he nor even Beckmesser, let alone Sachs, are anything but honest burgers with hearts of gold.

Ultimately, however, it is inevitable that we should measure *Die Meistersinger* by Shakespearean standards: for it has a comparable, all-embracing quality which could not be described any other way. The Shakespearean vision I find explicitly in Verdi, implicit even in Ibsen. Wagner is clearly of this company. Bayreuth is Wagner's Royal Shakespeare Company, re-enacting the whole oeuvre constantly; that is their birthright.

Love in Opera [1]

Russian novels have loomed large in my thoughts in recent years — especially those by Alexander Solzhenitsyn, Vladimir Maximov, and others who have been published in the West, but not in their homeland.

Solzhenitsyn's *The First Circle,* a novel that affected me deeply, contains an account of how certain highly qualified political prisoners fare when employed in a 'special' prison — a technological research establishment, in fact, called Mavrino, based in a converted country-house in the Moscow suburbs. Towards the end of the novel there's a particularly moving episode, where one of the prisoners, a mathematician named Gleb Nerzhin, finds himself alone with a young woman, Simochka. She, actually, is free: she works at the prison, but lives outside. Gleb, however, has been in concentration camps and prisons for at least ten or fifteen years; and he is still married. Now comes the moment that seems so poignant to us — and especially poignant in the context of the whole novel. For now we realise that these two people are about to become lovers. Yet Gleb is stirred not only by love, but by a sudden access of problems which we can call duty or conscience. He suddenly tells Simochka that he is married, that he hadn't until the day before managed to catch even a glimpse of his wife for many years, and then, when they had met, they find that really they are breaking apart.

In order to cover up this extremity of sadness within themselves, when love has seemed so near, Gleb turns on a radio, and they hear the voice of Obukhova a famous Russian popular singer:

But the strange thing was that as Obukhova sang, instead of feeling more and more wretched she somehow felt a little better. Ten minutes ago they had been so estranged that they had no words even to say goodbye, but now it was as though some gentle and calming presence had joined them.

And it so happened that in her present mood, in a special light that fell on her, now at this very moment, Simochka looked particularly attractive.

Nine out of ten men would have laughed at Gleb for giving her up voluntarily after so many years of celibacy. Who could force him to marry her later on? What prevented him from lying to her now?

[1] A newly drafted version of four talks, delivered impromptu, on CBC Radio in 1969

But Gleb was profoundly glad that he had acted as he had. It even seemed as though the decision had not been his own.

Obukova went on singing her heart-rending song:

No joy, no comfort do I find,
I live for him alone. . . !

No, of course, it wasn't coincidence. All songs had been the same for a thousand years, as they would be for centuries to come. Songs are about parting — there are other things to do when people meet.[2]

The situation described here typifies the core ingredient in many novels and dramas. For it comes so close to life as we experience it. Solzhenitsyn's art is at its most powerful in this episode. He not only produces a moment of intense human poignancy by bringing the two characters together in the room. He introduces also the song on the radio, a song that becomes a catalyst, as well as crystallizing the situation itself:

All songs had been the same for a thousand years . . . Songs are about parting.

This statement is true of a lot of popular music which seeks to capture the fleetingness of love. Gleb and Simochka could of course have avoided becoming involved as lovers, and could thus have sung a different song. Or they might have sung later a positive love-song (or duet) which would not appear to be a song of parting at all — although obviously a hint of parting might be in it. There are always these possibilities. We can move towards songs of love, but because we are mortal, and because love is evanescent, we move always to the other side, towards songs of sadness, of parting, or death.

We can observe these two characters in Solzhenitsyn's novel as if they existed against the backcloth of a family: for indeed, it is as if they have come out from a family and at that stage become interesting to us. Now the theatre, according to one view, begins at the point at which a single man emerges from the total mass of humanity. In a Greek drama, for instance, the first chorus singer might step down from the chorus and speak alone upon the stage. Eric Bentley has said that it would be better to think of it as *two* chorus men coming out and conversing with each other, the essence of theatre being dialogue and confrontation. Bentley has further remarks which are worth our attention:

If the raw material of plot is events, particularly violent events, the raw material of character is people, especially what are

---

[2]Alexander Solzhenitsyn: *The First Circle* (London, 1968), p. 521

regarded as their cruder impulses. It is said that babies, being attached to the mother first by the umbilical cord and then by the breast, believe the human world to be all one piece. If so, one concludes, this is paradise, and the dismissal from Eden comes when we decide, as it seems we do in later babyhood, that the world is divided into two parts: oneself and other people. Later still, with our intellects, we make more elaborate divisions: as patriots, we insist on nations, as Marxists on classes, and so on. Even so, the distinction we live with each day remains simply that between oneself and other people. And the primordial group of other people — our family — makes up the original cast of characters in the drama of life, a drama that we keep on reviving later with more and more people cast for the same few parts. As for oneself, one is the invisible man. One cannot see oneself, one can only see with whom one has chosen to be identified.[3]

This pinpoints one aspect of drama which throughout human history has been perennial. We are constantly engaged in rediscovering the family situations, whether they be violent or calm, or whether we have gone in search of the father, the mother, the wife, the siblings or the children. This can cover some extreme manifestations of drama: think of *Oedipus Rex,* the great Sophocles drama that so fascinated Freud. Here it can be said that the drama lies in the fact that Oedipus, the son, murders his father, marries his mother and begets daughters who are his sisters. It's a very curious form of family encounter and it has, of course, a mythological background. But it nevertheless is recognizable as in some strange way part of human life. Freud was fascinated with exactly that situation which he regarded, rightly or wrongly, as fundamental to human existence.

Take another, more modern instance, one which has the very name *The Family Reunion.* In Eliot's play, the son who has or might have murdered his wife by pushing her overboard (whether he has or not is left unclear) returns to the family — to his mother, his aunts and uncles, in order to rediscover his own proper identity. This brings about two great moments in each act of the drama, in which the mythological Furies, called the Eumenides, appear in the English north-country drawing-room and speak a kind of prophecy, which permits the drama in its deepest sense to move forward again. Since only through the medium of words can these two appearances on stage of the Eumenides occur: they're preceded in the drama by a poetic intensification of the text, and as they appear, in the window embrasure in the drawing-room, pure poetry takes over completely:

---

[3]See *The Life of the Drama* (London, 1965), pp. 35–36

That apprehension deeper than all sense,
Deeper than the sense of smell, but like a smell
In that it is undescribable, a sweet and bitter smell
From another world. I know it, I know it![4]

Eliot grew to dislike this later, withdrew from it, and in fact wrote a long account of why he wanted to withdraw from it, stating that these particular moments of pure poetry had become 'operatic arias'.[5] They were disturbing to the sense of drama, going further than the drama intended. Personally, I think Eliot was wrong. I discussed it with him, during his later years, and he very nearly admitted that he had been too extreme in his statements on the matter. It's clear that if we look at Shakespeare, we find him using such poetic emphasis precisely to bring out a particular key-point in a drama: sometimes he used poetry allied with music, sometimes poetry enchained to music in a song.

We reach thus a stage where — as with Solzhenitsyn's treatment of the scene between Gleb and Simochka — song is brought in as that specific and extra something which can clarify and intensify a drama at its most crucial points.

For example, in Shakespeare's *The Tempest,* Prospero sends Ariel to sing to Ferdinand two songs. The first is a song of invitation to dancing and to love:

> *Come unto these yellow sands*
> *And then take hands*

And this is, as it were, the first movement, the movement to love and life, to the dance and to the community. But within one minute of the drama, Ariel is singing Ferdinand another song, a song of death and rebirth, a deeper, stranger song:

> *Full fathom five thy father lies;*
> *Of his bones are coral made;*

When I myself was asked by the London Old Vic Theatre to write incidental music for a performance of *The Tempest,* these songs were the first thing I set.[6] Songs are indeed an outstanding element in Shakespeare's plays. We always know what their function is when they occur, whether they are light or serious. They are also very much of their period. Other Elizabethan and Jacobean songs bear a similar dramatic weight, even though they were conceived indepen-

---

[4]T. S. Eliot: *The Family Reunion,* Part I, scene 2
[5]T. S. Eliot: *Poetry and Drama* (London & Harvard, 1951)
[6]*Songs for Ariel* (1962), originally written for a production of *The Tempest* in April, 1962; first performed separately the following year

dently of any stage situation: cf. Dowland's songs or Campion's. They contain the same verbal conceits, whereby (for instance) 'to die' becomes synonymous with 'to love'. 'To die, to die again' meant not only to die again, but to love again, a curious conjunction of meanings, to my mind, hinting at the evanescence of love expressed by Solzhenitsyn: 'All songs had been the same for a thousand years as they would be for centuries to come.' These songs have always been there, they always will be there. As the music takes over — and if we know its background and can imagine it for ourselves — then the implications of the song become more and more elaborate.

The loss of love, the dying because of love or because of the loss of love, can be thought of artistically as the primal human situation. Monteverdi understood this and realised that his exploration of it could extend from madrigals (cf. *Lasciate mi morire*) to the stage. He and other seventeenth-century composers developed a stylized mixed-media art-form (to use the jargon of today) which could be used, above all, to articulate the primal human situation such as we have encountered it.

Now this sparked off a lot of debate about the aesthetics of opera and drama. From the Camerata in Florence to the time when verse-drama returned in English theatre, through figures like Christopher Fry, W. H. Auden and T. S. Eliot, it has been a major bone of contention. What are the relationships that are possible between the various ingredients in opera and drama? How can they best function? When I myself talked to Eliot about these problems he suggested a *schema* which I have since found valuable. Suppose (he said) we imagine that there are three genres of action upon a stage: the stage-play as such, the ballet and opera. There are three expressive ingredients that belong in each of these three genres: the drama proper — the story, that is, or dramatic action — gesture, and music. In each genre, these three means of expression are in a certain hierarchy. In the stage-play, the dramatic action is on top, gesture is second and music third. In the ballet, gesture is on top, music is second and the story is third. In opera, music is on top, the story is second and gesture third.

Now this for me was a fascinating piece of crystallization. It's quite clear that with Monteverdi and his contemporaries, opera came into existence when music was 'on top' in relation to a story and its presentation upon the stage. Yet the music and the drama never became *disrelated* as a result of this hierarchical pattern. In fact, early on, a distinction was made between the narrative elements and those moments in the drama (such as we have discussed earlier) when songs appear to stem quite spontaneously from particular human situations. Recitative and aria are utilized for quite distinct dramatic purposes: and words and music are brought together in subtly different ways to achieve those ends.

We can find the same principles at work in Purcell. Dido and Aeneas are not so very far removed from Gleb and Simochka. Gleb was too disturbed by duty and conscience to make love with Simochka: they are thus swept away in the sadness of parting. Likewise, in the story of Dido and Aeneas, the latter is called by a godlike sense of duty to leave Carthage and his paradisal existence with the former — the families that re-united Carthage are broken up — and has to go on his masculine and necessary journey to found a new Rome. Gleb tells Simochka he must leave her; Aeneas informs Dido likewise. Dido is left alone and prepares herself for a great ritual death. Purcell prepares us for it with a short piece of recitative ('Thy hand, Belinda') and then moves into the aria that expresses the critical and absolute emotion of the death of love ('When I am laid in earth'). We, in a metaphorical moment, mount the same funeral pyre as Dido. Her anguish is ours, for 'All songs had been the same for a thousand years as they would for centuries to come. Songs are about parting'.

From Goethe to Berlioz and after, one creative figure becomes a powerful and dominant influence: Shakespeare. Shakespeare's richness, exhibited within open-ended artistic forms, contrasted sharply with the purity of style and tightly-knit forms favoured by Racine and other French dramatists. Yet when we consider generally how artists, from Schiller to Wagner, present human situations, we find that Shakespeare was a prime model. Schiller, however, not only concerned himself in his plays with the human family in every sense — social, personal, historical: he wanted, also, Nature to play a role, not just as a setting, but as an integral force within the drama.

Schiller's most interesting experiment in this respect is *William Tell*: a play that focusses on human emotions and problems, and on political questions, but which also brings in nature in an important way. Schiller had never, in fact, been in Switzerland, the scene of the action in the play. His knowledge of the Swiss landscape was derived from letters which Goethe wrote back to Weimar during one of his journeys through Switzerland. Schiller's relationship to the Swiss landscape is a vicarious one, seen through Goethe's eyes.[7] In the first

---

[7] See Heinrich von Stein, *Goethe und Schiller* (Zurich, 1944)

scene of Act I, he gives a kind of paradigm of what was about to happen: the eruption of violence within this small country, and then its pacification. While we are waiting for the human drama itself to begin, a violent storm breaks over the lake of Lucerne. When it has calmed down, the human drama can get underway. The same notion occurs, of course, at the start of *The Tempest* where, likewise, the whole of the pre-figuring storm (the tempest) is presented through the actions and words of people on board the sinking boat. In *William Tell,* Schiller went even further. At the end of Act II, when the men of the cantons meet by night and swear an oath to fight only with outside antagonists, Schiller has them leave the stage silently, while solemn music is played, and the stage fills gradually with the rays of the sun as it rises over the glaciers.

Schiller didn't want nature only to reflect the mental states of his characters, as, for instance, the natural storm echoes the tempest in King Lear's mind. He felt it must add an extra dimension to the human beings in his plays, for such characters are, like the rest of us, conditioned by forces that exist beyond the purely personal. Wagner attained such an end more successfully, two generations after Schiller. In *The Ring,* natural elements have an integral role, and they make their impact through music. Goethe, had he seen a Wagner music-drama, would probably have been less disturbed by the fact that for long stretches the audience watches an empty stage, than he was when Schiller asked for sunrise to fill an empty stage. Schiller is prophetic of Wagner in that he could not bring his stage-directions into force without music: indeed his stage-directions are oddly similar to those in Wagner's libretti, e.g. at the start of *Das Rheingold* the libretto simply states 'The Bottom of the Rhine', and many minutes go by while the Rhine is flowing, and no voice sings.

Nature for Wagner was an extra symbolic element from which the human drama on stage was inseparable. Love and death in such a context acquire an extra exalted dimension. The characters thus exist on an archetypal or mythological plane as well as being human. Wotan, punishing Brunnhilde for her disobedience, has to try and retain his sense of being a father, while acting both as a god and a king. In order to modify the absolute morality which would otherwise make life unendurable, he uses Nature as a mediating agent. Earth, Air, Water and Fire are all important in *The Ring.* Here, in *Die Walküre,* Wagner moves from his pre-occupation with archetypal *Water* in *Das Rheingold* to archetypal *Fire.* Having put Brunnhilde to sleep — a sleep of death — Wotan summons Loge the god of Fire to surround Brunnhilde with flames. Her sleep will only last until Siegfried penetrates the fire and awakens her with an act of love.

Thus for many minutes the stage is empty (save for the sleeping form of Brunnhilde) and flames burn all around, but especially in the orchestral pit. This exemplifies well a type of presentation in which human characters belong partly to an ancient mythological past. The action of *The Ring* proceeds in large mythological steps. Just as Oedipus, after murdering his father, breaks the incest taboo by marrying his mother, as reward for reading the riddle of the Sphinx, and thus releases the community of Thebes from the plague, bringing a great renewal of life: so Siegfried has to 'destroy' Wotan, and with a combination of divine and human youthfulness, breaks through the circle of fire to Brunnhilde, so that after their union, *The Ring* can proceed a stage further. It matters not a jot that he too is breaking the incest taboo by mating with his aunt. Their love has a transcendent quality and value that Wagner marks by associating it with Nature. Brunnhilde, when she wakes, first sings a hymn to the sun (*Heil dir, Sonne!*), before her love-duet with Siegfried gets under way. The sun belongs to the drama as a life-giving element, enabling the world to continue in existence. Of course, such transcendentalism has its price. The archetypal forces within the psyche can overwhelm and disturb human equilibrium to a high degree. Lear's madness, the storm within himself, brings about his death, which however is never absolute in this context. Likewise, Siegfried's death is implied by his previous love: and with Wagner it becomes a great ritual death, marked by a *Trauermarsch* in *Götterdämmerung,* of enormous grandeur.

I believe it still to be possible to work within this tradition whereby the human characters in a drama are encountered half-within their mythological archetypes. Mark and Jenifer, Jack and Bella, the two pairs of complementary lovers in my own opera, *The Midsummer Marriage,* are in direct line of descent from Tamino and Pamina, Papageno and Papagena in Mozart's *The Magic Flute.* Mozart's young lovers go through a series of episodes and trials in order to achieve a sense of illumination through their symbolic union which produces spiritual renewal. In *The Midsummer Marriage,* Mark and Jenifer go through a series of trials that are symbolically realized in ballet, the first three Ritual Dances of animals and seasons, of hunters and hunted. Nature here becomes integral to the unfolding of the drama: and not only here — for Mark, in Act I, where he anticipates his own marriage with Jenifer, also sings a hymn to the sun. When they are united, in Act III, and are seen once more in a pose of perpetual copulation, this all occurs in the context of a ritual fire dance: the whole experience is thus divine, metaphysical as well as physical, an illumination, an ultimate affirmation of life's continuity.

All dramatic works need not, of course, rely so heavily on the symbolic background to the action and relationships. Actuality can on its own carry a lot of weight. When I came to write *King Priam,* I found myself forced to concentrate on an actuality, whose richness was evident to me in exactly the way Eric Bentley indicates when, in the latter part of the quotation above,[8] he talks of 'the original cast of characters in the drama of life . . .' — the primordial family group. Although, in writing *King Priam,* I took portions of various stories, it could all be looked at on one level as a single family affair. For it contains father, mother, children, brothers and sisters: and it includes all the troubles and trials that appear normal between families and generations. To take further the line of thought in the Bentley quotation, the whole of the *Iliad* is one enormous division (into nations, patriots, classes etc) between the families of the Greeks and the families of the Trojans. However, the hero, especially if he's a king, has other responsibilities besides the personal responsibility of the family. Hence the tension that develops between his private and his public life: the hero constantly has to choose between personal inclination and public duty. Othello is a typical example. From the point of view of the Venetian community and its elders, what happened to Othello, their excellent General, was that his sense of public duty was swamped by his personal problems, endangering thus the community and himself. The end could only be a murder and a death. In Verdi's *Otello,* Iago is both a mechanism for playing upon the susceptibilites and weaknesses of Otello and also is our means of knowing the tumult of emotions within the personality of the hero: Iago's *credo* — a dramatic monologue of Shakespearean cast (though not in Shakespeare's play) — conveys all this in an oblique way.

In an opera different from my own, the famous love-affair between Paris and Helen would have been celebrated in a love-duet. But that would have been out of place in *King Priam,* which focusses instead on the consequences of the choice which Paris makes when he accepts an adulterous or immoral love, knowing full well that this would bring war to his home and to the city of Troy. When he is left alone by Helen to choose what he wants to do, there is no love aria

[8] See pp. 211–212 above

218

to be sung. That is all past — in the bedroom beforehand. Instead, he has a dramatic monologue expressing the conflicting emotions inside him:

O Helen, you lead me to the moment so desired and feared. Carried on the wind of love, if I carry you away, another's wife, a City's Queen, who will escape the avenging war? O Helen, Helen can we choose that? You will answer, Helen, do we choose at all when our divided bodies rush together, as though halves of one. We love.

As soon as Paris reaches the point—'We love' he has in fact made his choice.

Again, with the love between Achilles and Patroclus, we concentrate on the state of mind of Achilles, the hero who refuses to take part in the fighting, stays in his tent, and indulges his nostalgia. With one side of himself, Achilles would regain his heroic virtue and go out onto the battlefield, but the negative side of him, the nostalgic element holds him back — for the time being at least: his solo song (with guitar accompaniment), taking us away from the external violence and noise of battle into the inner tumult of Achilles's mind.

Love in conflict with duty is the main focus of an immense quantity of dramatic work stemming from the tradition of the *Iliad*, where the family is entangled in a whole set of historical and necessary wars and responsibilities. Perhaps the tradition that goes beyond this is one where personal relations are considered for themselves alone, and are arranged in a kind of pattern or as a kind of dance. Chekhov's *The Cherry Orchard*, Shaw's *Heartbreak House*, Albee's *Who's Afraid of Virginia Woolf?* are typical examples, studies of the games people play. Shakespeare's late comedies are the best models of all, exploring every avenue of possible forgiveness and reconciliation amongst individuals at war with each other. Shakespeare drew partly on medieval dramatic tradition wherein the view prevailed that however extreme your misbehaviour, if you were able at the last moment, before death, to make a single act of contrition to the Christian God, you could be forgiven all. Isabella's forgiveness of Angelo in *Measure for Measure* is of this kind. Shakespeare had to cope, however, with the fact that while the act of contrition is human, the act of forgiveness is divine. In a society where the Christian religion is becoming less and less all-powerful, who does the forgiving? In *Measure for Measure* it is a duke, who at one point in the story has masqueraded as a monk: the duke demands, by virtue of his ducal power, the act of contrition, which implies the act of forgiveness. In *The Tempest,* Prospero stands in for

God: he, possessing complete magical powers, can do everything; and in the end, can demand the act of contrition that results in forgiveness and the possibility of leaving the island to return once more to civilization. Love and forgiveness, set in opposition to power, are able to transcend the absolute nature of power. If the act of forgiveness were possible, Othello could have gone beyond the problems of love and duty, and Wotan even gone beyond love and power.

To find a musical agency for the acceptance of sadness in a context of love — as Dowland did so gloriously in the time of Elizabeth I, and Schubert in a later period — is, in our time, not at all easy. But it does exist. Hence the impact of Obukova's song in *The First Circle:*

> But Gleb was profoundly glad that he had acted as he had. It even seemed as though the decision had not been his own.
> Obukova went on singing her heart-rending song:
>> *No joy, no comfort do I find,*
>> *I live for him alone! . . .*
> No, of course it wasn't coincidence. All songs had been the same for a thousand years, as they would be for centuries to come. Songs are about parting — there are other things to do when people meet.[9]

We don't know exactly what style Obukhova's song had. It might have been a blues. For the Act I ensemble of *The Knot Garden*, I found nothing more apposite. One sings the blues when one's mood is 'blue', to discharge that mood by the song and so get the courage, or at least some renewal of strength, to go on again. In *The Knot Garden* ensemble, seven persons are entangled in a knot or net, of anguished experience and relationships. They cry, they howl bitterly at each other, with personal, confessional words. The pseudo-Prospero, Mangus, quotes Shakespeare:

> *And my ending is despair*
> *Unless I be relieved by prayer;*
> *Which pierces so, that it assaults*
> *Mercy itself, and frees all faults.*[10]

The blues basis gives the whole ensemble a shape, a beat, slow or fast, that encompasses the complex of love-hating personalities in

---

[9]See note 2 above
[10]*The Tempest,* final epilogue

one musical metaphor. A portion of what Mangus-Prospero describes at the end as

> a music
> Compounded of our groans and shrieks
> Bitter-sweet and wry,
> Tender yet tough: ironic
> Celebration for that trickster
> Eros. . .
> . . . In his masks of love.[11]

The Resonance of Troy:
Essays and commentaries on *King Priam*

(i)

One never knows finally what exact 'ingredients' have gone into one's creation of a work of art — whether the work be in literature or painting or music. To begin with, we can only *know* the things of which we have been conscious — provided we remember them. So all the innumerable and possibly decisive ingredients — emotions, sensations, influences — that are subliminal — remain unknown, or only to be guessed at from a later examination of the objective work from the outside.

Obviously, if one has created the work of art oneself, the incidents lying immediately to hand in the memory are the proper things to speak of, *before* the work. In this case, my second opera, *King Priam,* first stands in its own right, independent of its creator, before the public. There are two incidents which come to mind now: one a kind of opera and one a book; possibly more interesting to you than other memories of mine because they are both French.

A few years ago two continental theatrical companies came to London. One was the Berliner Ensemble with plays and productions of Bertolt Brecht. I found this visit exciting. I had read Brecht, and his theories about his epic theatre, but had never seen the results on the stage. So it was a rewarding experience.

The second company was that of Jean-Louis Barrault, and the production I saw was *Christophe Colombe* by Claudel and Milhaud.[1] This production exercised a decisive influence on me at a time when I was still searching for the right material to use for a second opera.

The first thing that struck me was that the methods of the epic theatre, in their widest sense, were really independent of the *political* ideas of dramatists using them. I mean that Brecht and Claudel, one Marxist, one Catholic, both presented the epic material on the stage by scenes and commentaries; selecting or inventing those scenes out of the epic material which alone presented their view (or were appropriate to their work) *and no others.* In a certain sense this is true too of the historical plays of Shakespeare. So it is no alien tradition to us English.

Jean-Louis Barrault also read in London a paper on what he had

---

[1]Palace Theatre, London, 1956

learnt from his collaboration with Claudel, a copy of which came into my hands. From this paper I learned quite a lot on how to extract and create these decisive scenes from the whole epic. And round about that time I began to lay down the form of the libretto of *King Priam* and to decide on the character of some of the music.

The second incident that I like to recall is my obtaining through the interest aroused by a talk on the BBC Third Programme, a copy of the book by the French Marxist critic, Lucien Goldmann, called *Le Dieu caché* — a book mainly about Racine.[2] Goldmann, through his acute analysis of tragedy in Racine's work, determined the tragic nature of my new opera *King Priam;* although Goldmann was of the opinion that tragedy in the Greek sense is not theatrically viable nowadays, in a world which must either be Christian or Marxist. For these are both optimistic philosophies. But being, in Goldmann's strict sense, neither Christian or Marxist, I am unrepentantly certain, from some deep intuitive source, that tragedy is both viable and rewarding. That when audiences will see Priam's death at the altar as Troy burns, they will feel the old pity and terror and be uplifted by it.

Goldmann, you see, brought me to Racine, one of the acutest masters of theatrical tragedy. This sense of tragedy gave me exactly the correct entry into the vast epic story surrounding King Priam. But Claudel and Milhaud, and of course Brecht, taught me how to pare away all the dross of the story, so that only the essentials — those essential scenes to *this* work — are there.

Nor would I wish to leave out Jean-Louis Barrault himself. The white sail of Columbus's ship still hangs in my mind whenever I talk of the production of *King Priam* with my producer Sam Wanamaker.

From a broadcast in French, 24 March, 1962

(ii)

Modern opera is a risk. In no other field of music, perhaps, is the repertoire so consistently of the nineteenth century. Yet it is always, at least to me, a stimulus and a challenge. I feel that my instrumental music, nowadays, is being fed from the operatic music. That the challenge of a new opera forces reconsiderations of musical style,

[2] Lucien Goldmann: *Le Dieu Caché — Étude sur la vision tragique dans les Pensées de Pascal et dans la Théâtre de Racine* (etc) (Paris, 1955); transl. Philip Thody as *The Hidden God* (London & New York, 1964)

which then flows over into music for the concert hall. It *appears* indeed as if the changes of musical style were even the result of extra-musical qualities of opera, I do believe that these formal qualities must be endlessly varied and changed to meet the needs of whatever 'subject' one is dealing with. The 'subject' is perhaps the stimulus. But the invention of the exactly necessary musical forms is certainly the challenge. (I can remember the excitement of this challenge in my first opera *The Midsummer Marriage*. How I was engrossed for so many years with the tremendous outpouring of lyrical music, which alone could express the 'subject' — The Quest for Illumination. I can recall this excitement, but the events, in my life, are entirely past. It was to be expected that a second opera would be quite different. How different I could hardly have guessed ahead.)

I have not found that when a stimulus to an opera begins to work the ready-made 'subject' comes immediately to hand. In fact, the stimulus seems to begin at a point when it isn't even clear whether the eventual work will be for the concert hall (in the form of cantata or oratorio) or for the theatre. *A Child of Our Time*, for example, began as a stimulus to write an opera, but became gradually and finally an oratorio. *The Midsummer Marriage* was always to be an opera.

The stimulus, (to some large work for voices and instruments) that led eventually to *King Priam,* began as a vague set of eight, somewhat unrelated scenes that might have issued in a descriptive cantata for singers in a concert hall, or even in a choral ballet. A conversation with David Webster of Covent Garden settled in my mind for me that the stimulus was really to an opera — indeed a tragic opera. And conversations with the producer, Peter Brook, convinced me that for this new opera I need not invent all the story myself, as I had done in the opera *The Midsummer Marriage;* indeed that this would now be wrong. That appropriate traditional epic material, *handled in a certain way,* would provide the tragic story, to be played out upon the stage in the actual Present of an evening's performance, yet distanced by being in the Past. A theatrical practice which the Greek dramatists used in their time: as Shakespeare did in his; as Brecht and others have done in ours.

When I at last felt certain that the epic material surrounding Priam, King of Troy, would serve my purpose — or more accurately stated, serve the new opera's purpose — then arose the problems involved by the words 'handled in a certain way'. I felt that another producer, this time my admired friend Günther Rennert, could of all people best help me. In Stuttgart, in Edinburgh, in Hamburg he worked patiently with me to clarify the inchoate urges of the initial stimulus, and by ruthless excision of all the unnecessary detail to produce a book that was both stage-worthy and precisely what this opera demanded. For the secret of dealing with epic material is to use only those incidents *and no others* which do the thing needed.

Thus: Paris and Helen were part of my story. Their adulterous love, indeed, part of the mechanism of the total tragic destiny. In some other opera from the same source-book, this love might well need to be expressed in a love duet. A reasonably tempting thing to do! But in *King Priam* the real issues are the moral ones. Paris, in my opera, is quite conscious of the catastrophic public consequences that will follow from his abduction of Helen. His problem of choice issues musically therefore in a monologue of self-questioning, a questioning of fate, and life's meaning. There is no description of the emotions of his love at all.

These monologues, which come every so often in the opera, perform the same formal tasks as do the monologues in *Hamlet*. They demanded for their musical expression something nearer declamatory arioso than lyrical aria. Consequently I have had to depart substantially from the lyrical style of most of my music in the past and find a hard, tough, declamatory style, that would reflect inevitability. It did not seem appropriate to let the voices float on a web of orchestral sound, as in so many operas, but on the contrary to leave the vocal line free to make a kind of declamatory counterpoint to the simplest necessary instrumental accompaniment — if accompaniment is the right term at all.

The result is a sort of mosaic of musical gestures — theatrically large if instrumentally small. These gestures recur and intertwine. Strange to the audience perhaps at the start, they become familiar by the end, when their interaction must become more intense. And when the end of the tragic drama is reached, which is Priam's death at the altar as Troy burns, there is instantly no more music (only silence) because there are no more gestures. Except the gesture of ourselves in the audience — viz. the momentary musical expression of our inward tears.

As I have said already, although the *story* is from the past, the sense of our performing this story in our own present, on a specific theatre, is consciously underlined. Because the opera is not about history, i.e. how the Greeks appeared to themselves, but about eternal problems of the human heart and human destiny, which since they are eternal, involve us now. But because we are involved, enmeshed, submerged in the events of our own present, we need perhaps specially chosen stories of the past, if we are to be moved in the particular way the Tragic theatre demands. I am not suggesting this to be an absolute rule. It is simply a very natural one.

There remains the problem of whether tragedy, in the Greek or Shakespearean sense, is truly possible in our day. The answer, for me as a creative artist, is simply: yes. I know of course that certain theories about modern society, and therefore of the art that is said to reflect it or alter it, hold that tragedy is impossible. That to a convinced Christian or a convinced Marxist, personal tragedy is unreal — at best sentimental. But I remain, for the present at any rate, unconvinced by these theories. I have on the contrary a positive conviction that the pity and the terror, and the exaltation strangely intermixed with these, which we feel in the theatre before the great tragic spectacles of the past, are both possible and appropriate as a spectacle of the present.

Important for *King Priam* is the Racinian conception of tragedy as being absolute. In each of the Racine tragedies there is always some point when the tragic protagonist accepts, willingly or unwillingly, his or her tragic destiny, and with it the absolute necessity of a certain conduct, which because of its uncompromising *absolute* quality, must finally end in death. And, following from this, since the *absolute* qualities of the tragic destiny and ensuing conduct are refused by the rest of us, who make up the ordinary matter-of-fact world, the tragic protagonist acting out his destiny from this absolute source, is incomprehensible to those around him. No real understanding or communication is possible because *a fortiori* the sense of the tragic destiny is by its nature inexpressible. That is to say, the protagonist cannot express it, in communicative terms to his ambience. But it is expressed to *us,* in the theatre, by his or her actions. The pity and the terror and the exaltation are *ours*, not the hero's.

In *King Priam*, before the final scene of death, I allow a somewhat ironic character, Hermes, the divine messenger or go-between between Gods and man — that is between the inner world and the world of fact — to act as interpreter to us in the audience of what the final scene is to do. And this interpretation is made to us in the form of a hymn to music.[3]

From a broadcast in German, March 1962

[3] Quoted on p. 29 above

(iii)

Priam was the King of Troy. But for the purposes of enjoying, receiving, experiencing the opera *King Priam*, you need know nothing exactly about the story of Troy. Because the resonances that sound in all of us when we speak of Troy arise, I think, from generations, centuries of European concern with that immortal story. (I ask for nothing more than the accepted residue of that concern.)

Priam married Hecuba. ('What's he to Hecuba, or Hecuba to him?' as Hamlet says of the First Player.) I repeat: there are all sorts of resonances that sound in us as the role of Homeric names is quoted. In the opera Hecuba is given more flesh and blood than her verbal appearance in *Hamlet*, or her non-appearance in *Troilus and Cressida*. She is the Hecuba, rather, of Euripides' *Hecuba* and *The Trojan Women,* (written two or three hundred years after Homer's *Iliad*) the proud, violent, heroic, political queen.

This royal couple, Priam and Hecuba, had two sons famous in the story — Hector and Paris. Hector has always been considered the type par excellence of the noble warrior; husband and hero; 'guardian of chaste wives and of little children' as Homer has it. But his name has also given rise to a less noble epithet — hectoring. In dealing with his brother Paris he certainly ranted. Both sides of his character appear in *King Priam*.

If Hector was Priam's beloved son, Paris was surely his rejected son. We are all rejected in some way or other; perhaps nowadays more than ever. I mean, that nowadays, lying behind the eternal rejections of persons, are the rejections of whole races. So that the collective anguish reinforces the personal. Paris was rejected by Priam and Hecuba in the cradle — for the worthiest of reasons; rejected to a death that he escaped through the deliberate, culpable compassion of a young guard. This is the crucial first scene of the opera; the choice which Priam and Hecuba have to make as to whether this second son should live or die. And already in this first scene their characters move apart. Hecuba's decision is single; 'Then I am mother no longer to this child'. Priam's attitude is double; 'A father and a king'. He remains father to this son born to destroy him as king. Though in this first moment he can echo Hecuba and say: 'The Queen is right. Let the child be killed', some element in himself is unsatisfied. It is hardly possible to name Paris without coupling that name with Helen's. Helen became Helen of Troy through abduction. She was wife, and Queen, to Menelaus of

Sparta. Here, at Sparta, Paris ran off with her. This abduction appears in *The Iliad* as the prime cause of the Trojan War, and the acute disrelation between the ten years war, with all its slaughter and eventual sack of Troy, and the cause, abduction of the Queen of Sparta, has endowed Helen with magical, supernatural qualities. She was, in fact, the daughter of Zeus the Swan; 'conceived when the great wings beat above Leda'.

The opera is not concerned with the causes, real or legendary, of the Trojan War, nor with the military fortunes of the Greeks and Trojans. Much other material of the great legend has also to be rejected, however operatically tempting. In creating a fresh work of art out of traditional epic material it is essential, in my opinion, to select exactly and precisely those incidents alone which serve, and indeed which *are,* the new work in question, and to reject absolutely all else. Thus it was tempting to include an operatic description of Paris's and Helen's inescapable, passionate, adulterous love in *King Priam.* But it did not belong to this opera. What did belong was the moral choice set before Paris, if choice there was. Knowing quite well what the consequences of the abduction would be, why did he choose to do it? Nor could he appeal for guidance to Helen. I relieve Helen of all problems of choice, in this sense. She alone perhaps of all the characters in the opera has a true acceptance of herself. As she says, in answer to questions, with ultimate simplicity, 'I am Helen'.

The war therefore appears in the opera as inevitable; as inescapable as Helen's and Paris's love. That is to say, it belongs to the way of life of fighting men; perhaps finally, in some altered form of all men always. There is no description of the war. There are just the necessary formal musical gestures. It is persons within the war that matter. Priam's efforts to unite his bickering, quarrelling sons, Hector and Paris, who, as my text says, 'once they knew they were brothers never got on'. Or, if it is the Greek camp, under the shadow of the ships, staring out across the plain at the walls of Troy, then it is the tent of Achilles, where he sits brooding, sulking with his friend Patroclus, refusing to fight. We watch how Patroclus, 'in the nick of time' restores some manhood to Achilles. And how this virile act ensures his own death.

If the men are so bound into the war that there seems no possible end to the eternal vengeance 'death for death' — have the women any answers to the moral questions? Or are they only reflections of their men? Hecuba, after all, is more single, more fanatic in her pride for Troy, than even Priam. She has never doubted that the fatal Paris should have been killed in the cradle. Helen, as we know, is not a character that ever questions. She accepts herself, she accepts the war, she accepts that Paris is involved in the fighting, in fact she thinks he should fight more than he does, but their love has an absolute quality that transcends for her all problems.

There remains Andromache, Hector's wife. Andromache echoes down the centuries as the proud, passionate, grieving widow. She indeed questions the war, and bitterly. But the solutions she offers are, as always, politically impossible.

After the men have possessed the stage for the war, I give the three women a scene to themselves. Many questions; no answers; vital and eternal differences. For the women so quickly take on the characteristics of ever recurring types. Hecuba bound up solely with all public life and the fate of the city; Andromache bound up in her home, husband and children; Helen fatal to both the city and the home, bound up in the truth of some inescapable passion of love. They are at once persons in their own right, women of a certain type, wives to men whom they as exactly match.

These six characters, Priam, Hector, and Paris and their wives, Hecuba, Andromache and Helen, are with Achilles, the protagonists of the opera. Everything develops from their relations with each other.

The turning point of the tragedy is Hector's death. If this did not unhinge Priam's mind, as Cordelia's death unhinged Lear's, it certainly faced him with a final confrontation of himself. This confrontation appears in the opera as a single huge monologue. It is a scene very characteristic of modern opera, indeed of the modern theatre altogether, because so much of modern drama is an exploration of the inner worlds of the mind. From this confrontation Priam has only one issue — his own death as the tragic hero. Priam's death is the inevitable destined end to which the whole opera inevitably drives from the first moment of action on the stage: the parents' rejection of their second son.

Although it is clear that in an opera like *King Priam* the story has a compelling power of its own, opera is always primarily a musical experience. And because music has always a relation to itself, making a pattern of contrasted or repeated sounds, then it is commonplace enough to realise that this musical pattern must be, at some deeper level, consonant with the ethos of the story. Thus Verdi's *Otello* is not the same as Shakespeare's *Othello*. Not merely in structure, but in ethos; the emphases are differently placed. Verdi's music expresses *his* conception as exactly as Shakespeare's verse does his. Wagner's *Tristan and Isolde* is utterly different in ethos from the divagatory romances where he found the story. His *music* produces what he, Wagner, imagines. All this, as I say, is commonplace. So that it was both natural and exciting as the music for *King Priam* seemed to possess from the first notes this fundamental consonance with the purpose and ethos of the story.

If we return to the matter of Paris's and Helen's adulterous love, an important point will become immediately clear. In some other opera this love might have needed expression in a vocal duet. In *King Priam* what needs expression is Paris's problem of choice. Should he or should he not give rein to his love and abduct the queen. And behind that a more mysterious question: 'Why give us bodies with such power of love, if love's a crime? Is there a choice at all? Answer, Zeus, divine lover. Answer.' This musically, you see, is no lyric love aria but a probing monologue, in the temper of Hamlet's monologues in the play. There are many such monologues in *King Priam*, chiefly for Priam himself, and all are probing, questioning, struggling with the insoluble mystery of human fate. They imply a declamatory rather than a lyrical style, and I can give you one possible, not too dissimilar example from accepted opera: Boris's monologue, 'I have attained to power' from *Boris Godunov*.

Next, in order to produce sharp edges to the scenes and incidents, and even to the characters, I have abandoned the practice of letting the voice ride on a roughly homogeneous flow of orchestral sound, and in place accompanied the voice with only the minimum of orchestral gesture, if I may use that word, the barest minimum necessary to that moment in the drama. If emotions typical to a character return, then the same instrumental gesture returns, for the exact length, however short, that is demanded. And on the few occasions when conflicting emotions are given formal musical expression together, then the instrumental gestures are still, as far as is possible, retained as separable entities.

This method, perfectly proper I am sure to *King Priam, may* be disconcerting at the very start, but progressively it becomes acceptable and exciting. Because the dramatic gestures of the opera end with the death of Priam, before the altar as Troy burns, the music ends with the same sharp edge as the edge of the sword that runs through Priam's body. There is a sudden silence. Then a few curious sounds that might represent *our* inward tears.

From a BBC broadcast talk, 28 May 1962

(iv)

Last year I stood for the first time on the site of historical Troy. It is amazingly like what one imagines from Homer's story of the *Iliad*. I stood on a little rock hill, with Schliemann's excavations everywhere, looking out over the plain towards the sea. Only in one particular is it unlike Homer's Troy, it isn't a raised mound all round, but is a rounded spur of an escarpment.

Homer describes how dazzling Achilles sulked in his tent by the Greek ships, refusing to fight, and forcing his friend Patroclus, the man he passionately loved, to stay away from the battle. Until at a crisis in the war Patroclus persuades Achilles to send him out to the battle in Achilles' armour. Patroclus was killed by the great Trojan hero Hector. Then, and then only, Achilles returns to the war, revenges Patroclus by killing Hector, whose body he drags round and round the walls of Troy. Achilles takes the dead body to his tent, in place of the living Patroclus, and mutilates it. Each night a goddess restores Hector's shattered body, which Achilles mutilates again. It is a horrible story; part of a rich amalgam of heroism, bodily beauty and brutality of the Greek epics. This amalgam partly returns again in the first Elizabethan England, and there are traces of it, I think, in filmed Westerns.

I cannot remember when I first moved over from the Greek ships and tents, where I had always seemed to belong, through the walls of Troy and into the city. Once I had done so I found there, something missing from the other side, the family, viz, the royal family of Priam. (There is no family in this sense within the Greek camp.) Priam had an eldest and favourite son Hector, and a younger and despised son, Paris (the most beautiful man of his time) whom Priam ordered to be killed at birth. All three men were married; Priam to Hecuba (who lived for the city and bore only sons); Hector to Andromache (who lived for her home and whose little son was frightened of his father's huge plumed helmet); Paris to Helen ('the face that launched a thousand ships' and was a Greek King's wife). So that by going into the city I went towards the abiding problems of personal human relationships within the family. This is the true seed-bed for all drama, viz, our efforts to re-find parents, children, siblings. Even the tragic hero who enters a world of absolutes and is somewhere mad still, like Lear, must re-find Cordelia. (Priam had this kind of relationship to Helen.)

These three women, Hecuba, Andromache, Helen are each true to their identity: Hecuba to love of fatherland; Andromache to love of husband; Helen to desire that has no obligations. The Greek goddesses, Athene, Hera and Aphrodite (whom Paris had to choose between) are their proto-types. It was a real trouvaille when I first realised that Paris's goddesses were also the three women in his family. His 'choice' of Helen therefore was integral to him. Even at the price of war!

At the first night of *King Priam* in Covent Garden[3] a present was brought to me, from a nurse, Sister Warren. Inside a coloured case was a conch shell from the sea-shore of Greece. When most of the guests had left the reception after the performance, we persuaded one of the orchestra's horn players to blow notes on the conch: the exact sounds that Achilles might have made as a boy! Answering a letter of thanks for the present Sister Warren sent me a book on Schliemann's discovery of Troy. The author of the book says: 'When Schliemann went in search of Troy, he was searching for the fountainhead of Western Civilization.'[4] But it is not Troy itself but the poet Homer who is a fountain-head. In writing *King Priam*, I certainly drank water from this fountain. Yet *King Priam* does not imitate Homer. There is nothing in Homer which makes Priam the central figure of the story as the opera does. One does not go to a past work of art for the past, but for the present. It becomes one's own work, to live or die on its own merits.

One of the critics of *King Priam* realised this to the full when he quoted some lines from *The Midsummer Marriage*. At the climax of that opera, in the Fire Dance in Act III, the moment of illumination, the He-Ancient sings

> *Fate and Freedom are a paradox,*
> *Choose the fate but yet the God*
> *Speaks through whatever fate we choose.*

This really is the essence of *King Priam*, and the critic was extraordinarily percipient, for I had these lines always at the back of my mind while composing the second opera.

The signal difference between the performances of the first opera *The Midsummer Marriage* and those of *King Priam* has been the excellence of the stage presentation of the latter. This has been conceded and commended by everybody. I cannot say a big enough 'thank you' to all who worked at Covent Garden to bring this about. The proceedings on the stage matched the proceedings of the music at every turn. There was never a moment where they were at variance. John Pritchard, Sam Wanamaker, Sean Kenny proved a remarkable trio producing a splendid cast.

---

[3] 5 June, 1962
[4] Robert Payne: *The Gold of Troy* (London & New York, 1959), p. 151

It is interesting to me to look back and see how the Greek element which is in both operas has flowered so divergently. *The Midsummer Marriage* refers back to Greek comedy not tragedy. And this Greek element was never pure and unmixed. But in *King Priam* it has flowered, as if out of Greek soil, yet in England, and though I have never been to Greece. Because the great legend which has haunted European imagination for 2,500 years is as alive in English minds as anywhere else.

After the dress-rehearsal in Covent Garden, David Webster told me that he had watched the stage with such intensity, drawn by its immediacy and impact, that he had been mostly unaware of the music. This was the experience of many; even in a way of myself, though I knew the music well enough as its composer! But it was the effect I had intended for *King Priam* and it is an essential of the opera. How was it obtained?

I do not want to discuss here the effect of the music itself, or even the story, except to point out that the operatic action is very fast. Even this is a bit deceptive if looked into, but by and large it is correct. The more interesting point to me at the moment is the obvious fact that a misconceived production could easily have impaired the immediacy and impact proper to this fast moving opera, to the same degree that the actual production at Covent Garden enhanced it. Sam Wanamaker and I had long conferences together over the exact intentions of the libretto. We also came to a rough decision as to the style of production which could best suit these intentions. We both agreed to the self-evident but often forgotten proposition, that the *music* dictates once and for all the speed, not only of stage action, but of the characters' emotions. At Wanamaker's request therefore Covent Garden produced last year a tape of the piano-reduction of all the music, and dubbed onto this tape the words in their correct rhythm, if not their actual pitch. Thus the producer had an absolute framework within which his theatrical imagination and skill were to operate.

When Wanamaker came to deal directly with the singers he sometimes asked them to speak, or declaim the words of their roles, especially in those places where audibility of the words was vital. He then asked them if the natural intonations they had given to these words in speech were changed by what they had to sing. The answer was practically never. This is one of the opera's sources of immediacy.

The first big aria, or monologue, of the opera is that of Priam in the second scene of the first act. Wanamaker was quite ready to freeze everyone else on the stage into immobility allowing Priam to sing from within the stage grouping, and then by stage lighting to extract Priam's *mind* as it were, out of the group in order to allow him a special relation to the audience. Once this special relation had been established by the stage convention used, Wanamaker then had to deal with the appearances *within Priam's mind* of the Old Man, the Nurse, and the Young Guard; appearances that we in the audience have to see (and hear) as the audience sees Banquo's Ghost in *Macbeth*. It was fascinating to see how natural this convention appears in modern opera which deals so much with the inner world of man's mind.

Of the stage effects which enhanced the music, which were deliberate though generally unnoticed, were the underlining of musical correspondences of stage placing. Thus the men's trio and prayer at the end of Act II is balanced in the score by a women's trio and prayer at the beginning of Act III. Sam Wanamaker placed the three men and the three women in very much the same positions, so that the women almost seem to step into, temporarily, the men's shoes. I found this sort of thing very exciting.

The climax of the *Iliad* is perhaps the scene where the old man Priam comes secretly to beg Hector's body from Achilles, who, in an unique moment of compassion, gives it him. The point is that nearly all the figures of Homer's epic are still half or a quarter divine. Thus Achilles had a goddess mother, and Helen was born from the egg that resulted from the copulation of Leda with Zeus as a swan. So their whole humanity is still to find. *Achilles is totally human for this one moment*. It is what makes this scene so moving. Clearly, to make a viable opera out of such rich material, I had to pare everything away but the scenes which mattered to my point of view. Priam's attempt to have baby Paris murdered; his subsequent repenting and finding the boy; Paris as a grown man abducting Helen; and thus to the war and the senseless revenge that continues till the city is in flames and Priam himself dies at the altar. Quite as clearly, the music had to be spare, taut, heroic, and unsentimental. So that I had to set aside the earlier lyricism of *The Midsummer Marriage* where the voices ride on a river of glowing sound, for a much more hard-hitting rhetoric, where the voices are often accompanied by a single, but essentially characteristic instrument. I found this style change immensely stimulating and exciting.

Originally written for *Music & Musicians*, June 1967

6
A Private Mayflower

(i) *Roots*

I didn't go to America until 1965. I don't think I had wanted to, before then, or perhaps the opportunity had just not arisen. Certainly, I should have refused actively to go in the late thirties, when Auden and Britten first went there. After the war, I was lazy about travelling anywhere very far from home. But by 1965 something had changed inside myself, and when I was invited to be a visiting composer for ten days at the Summer Music Festival in Aspen, Colorado, I went with alacrity. For even as I flew over the Atlantic, I felt I was voyaging in my private Mayflower, as it were, although I was destined for Colorado, far west of the Mississippi, not for Massachusetts or Virginia.

From the start, America was to me history: history, not just of my forbears from England, but of folk from all Europe. Two almost contradictory but continuing experiences began at the first visit. On one side was an enduring delight at the candour, vitality and friendliness of this polyglot mix of people, with whom I really felt myself to be at home. (I have not experienced the violence of their social and political turbulence at first hand.) On the other side was the stupendous effect of the American landscape. I don't mean the over-large Alpine scenery of the Rockies at Aspen, but further West still: the canyons and high deserts of the upper Colorado river basin, in Utah and Arizona. This is Indian country and one is hardly 'at home'. It is the immensity and the colouring of the red rock and sandstone, eroded over millions of years, of the multi-coloured mesas — and so on — which draws me back time and time again. Perhaps it's a projection of some expansion of the spirit within.

I have travelled now all over the States: from the Pacific to the Rio Grande to the Hudson River. But not till 1978 did I finally reach New England, at a much smaller river, the Housatonic. I was conducting at the Tanglewood Festival, which takes place on the

borders of Massachusetts and upper New York. In the dining room
of a hotel at Stockbridge (an elegant room in a fine eighteenth-
century building), I attended a family reunion dinner. There were
six vaguely related American Tippetts — from grandparents to
grown-up grandchildren — who had come up from Pennsylvania.
Grandfather Harold, a lively octogenarian and former bank
president, had brought with him a family crest (!), which had been
drawn and coloured for him by his cousin, Bishop Tippett of
California. Eating, drinking, laughing, photographing ourselves in
every grouping, I concluded there must be more Tippetts in
America than in Cornwall.

(ii) *Dov's Journey*

Although I had not been to Greece or Troy before I wrote *King
Priam*, I had certainly been to America before I composed *The Knot
Garden* and *The Ice Break:* and since then I have gone, literally, round
the world — though not quite following in Dov's imagined
footsteps. While a specific locale is not intrinsic to the two later
operas — they could be situated anywhere; *The Ice Break*, for
instance, could just as well be in Belfast or Tokyo as in Chicago —
the imprint of the highly developed city culture, a polyglot culture,
and its relationship with an older pastoral culture, is inescapable. To
some extent, Dov, out of *The Knot Garden,* epitomizes this conflict
and the artist's search for either a solution or a middle ground that
is humanly acceptable. In *Songs for Dov*, I tried to take this character
out of the opera and look at his subsequent experience, as a maker
and singer of songs, as well as a human being.

Hence Dov, as singer, is close to myself as artist or composer.
When he does sing a song, he does so not only for himself but for all
his generation, even potentially for us all. So since he sings always of
an *actual* situation, he has invariably to come out of his personal life
into an impersonal world, a world of creation which is the song, the
music. Now this means, on one side, that if he is going to sing songs
that will have meaning for people beyond himself, he must accept
that there is a price to be paid: and part of that price that he will be
constantly divided in this way — hung-up between personal and
impersonal; a very old story, of course — artists have never been
different. The other side is that in his emotional make-up itself, he is

double — specifically, here, in Dov's case, through sexual ambivalence or bisexuality. In the last scene of Act II of *The Knot Garden*, after Dov has nursed the young Flora back into calm, out of compassion and tenderness, almost love (they both know it isn't physical), he turns his back on her to sing his song to the audience. With the exact number of couples (three) available in this opera, it might have been possible for him to go off finally and try to make a family life with her — but he cannot, because his man-friend Mel (currently drawn towards Denise) would not let him. (Hung-up indeed!). If we are to follow his career further, we can only think of Dov as (on the one hand) the loner, and (on the other) the musician who travels the world, searching for that southern land where we hope never to grow old, but which, proving an illusion, drives us ever on towards another beckoning country; a singer, then, who sings of the *Wanderjahre*, those years of illusion and disillusion, innocence and experience, which we all pass through to reach what maturity we may; and then journeying 'full circle west', back to the 'big town' and the 'home without a garden' across the tundra of Siberia. Dov, as the grown man, the fully-fledged mature creative artist, struggles with the intractable problems of 'poets in a barren age'. So, in the course of his last journey, he looks in on Zhivago: and we, too, can look over Zhivago's shoulder.

Pasternak, through Zhivago, suggests that one of the tasks of, shall we say, lyric poets of our period, might be just to sustain the pastoral metaphor, in its deepest sense, against the ephemera of town fashions. What Zhivago wrote was this:

> Where in such a busy urban life, is pastoral simplicity in art to come from? When it is attempted, its pseudo artlessness is a literary fraud, not inspired by the countryside but taken from academic bookshelves. The living language of our time is urban.[1]

But there are no poems by Zhivago exemplifying this supposed 'living language'. In *The Earth*, Zhivago instead comments (and Dov sings):

> *Then why does the horizon weep in mist*
> *And the dung smell bitter?*
> *Surely it is my calling*
> *To see that the distances should not lose heart*
> *And that beyond the limits of the town*
> *The earth should not feel lonely?*[2]

---

[1]Boris Pasternak: *Dr Zhivago*, transl. by Max Hayward & Manya Harari, (London, 1958), p.436
[2]Ibid. pp.499–500

Yeats wrote somewhere that out of the quarrel with society, poets make rhetoric, while out of the quarrel with themselves they make poetry. Pasternak's trope for Zhivago is all rhetoric. So we know that Dov must turn his back on it and peer into himself to find his poetry. For the moment, he finds just two words and a hollow tap from the claves. 'Sure, baby'.

Index